MW00462989

INSTEAD, WE BECAME EVIL

A TRUE STORY OF SURVIVAL & PERSEVERANCE

SLEIMAN

with DART ADAMS

Translated by JESPER "LIVID" HELLES

Translated by NIKLAS HOLMEN BERTELSEN

 Kingston Imperial

Kingston Imperial

Instead, We Became Evil: A True Story of Survival & Perseverance Copyright © 2022 by Kingston Imperial, LLC

Printed in the USA

Rights Department, 144 North 7th Street, #255 Brooklyn N.Y. 11249

First Edition:

Book and Jacket Design: Damion Scott & PiXiLL Designs

Cataloging in Publication data is on file with the library of Congress

Hardcover: ISBN 9781954220423

EBook: ISBN 9781954220430

1

THE SETUP: ASKERØD, SEPTEMBER 2007

W hat you're about to read is a true story. Unlike in the United States of America, Danish law doesn't have a statute of limitations. For that reason, several names and specific details and stories needed to be changed and/or altered to ensure no one written about could potentially be brought up on any charges in the future and to protect all involved parties legally. This is why you may read a quote or a statement that isn't directly attributed to any one individual. This is done to ensure nothing in these pages can potentially be used to bring anyone mentioned in these pages to justice for old crimes or offenses abroad.

This memoir was first originally co-written by journalist Olav Hergel and Sleiman and translated to English from Danish, then edited for the North American market, which is largely unfamiliar with Sleiman, and his unique story of struggle, survival, and perseverance.

Click-clack.

I knew the sound well. It was the sound of a gun being cocked and loaded.

I turned around and saw the man holding the gun. Behind him stood twenty other members of the gang Black Cobra. They had appeared out of nowhere from the heart of the Askerød housing project and were now standing in a parking lot in Hundige. They stared at one another for what felt like a lifetime.

I never thought I would have the chance to look my killer in the eye. I always figured that when my time was up, they would just shoot me in the back or kill me in my sleep. I took a step back. Everything was silent. Completely and utterly silent.

All I had to do was reach the fence that was only ten feet behind me, climb it, and then I could call my own people for reinforcements. They were chilling at the clubhouse, and they were armed. I recalled something a police officer had once told me: if someone tries to shoot you, run in a serpentine formation, never in a straight line. I opted to not run. Instead, I took another step back.

A shot rang out. It felt like a sudden gut punch, but I didn't fall. Black Cobra had come to Askerød specifically to hunt me down, and even though I desperately needed to reach the fence right behind me, I wasn't about to commit the sin of turning my back on my enemy in my own hometown. I instead took another step back.

A second shot rang out. This time, I felt it hit my face, chin, and throat simultaneously. I next felt the blood gushing out, but I still remained standing. This man clearly wanted to kill me, and it was starting to look like I had zero chance for survival if I couldn't make it to the fence and contact my crew. When I finally turned to make a break for it, a third shot rang out. The bullet went straight through my upper thigh, and I felt it swimming through my body. To my credit, I somehow remained standing, and I was just one more step away from the fence.

As I lunged for the fence and freedom, a fourth bullet hit me in my leg. This time, my knees buckled under me, and I finally fell. It was then that everything went quiet. This was not how I had envisioned my death would go down. Then I suddenly heard a familiar voice break the silence.

"Run!" my childhood friend Samir shouted to the others. I heard the sound of several footsteps running away from the scene.

Barely conscious, I grabbed my phone and called my sister. Just then, my boys Abbas and Nazir came running toward me, and I felt a painful suspicion creep into my mind. They belonged to my crew, but they had come to my aid too fast. Almost as if they had known I was going to be ambushed here all along.

Shortly afterward, my boy Rashid showed up. He was my once trusted friend and protégé, but how could Rashid possibly be here already? Had he and the others known what was about to go down? Had they known and done nothing to try and prevent it?

For years, I had given everything to this gang, including going to jail for them. Even today, I had attacked The Mexican for the sake of my people, but now, I was the one who had almost been assassinated in an ambush and possibly betrayed by my own friends. Was this what I had fought for all of these years? All my life, I had longed to be loved and respected by everyone. After years of fighting and being willing to die for my people, had I suddenly ended up as the guy nobody was willing to fight and die for in return?

I looked directly at Rashid and asked, "Who called you? How'd you even know I was shot? How'd you know where to find me?"

"Well, your family. Everybody knows that you've been shot," Rashid told me.

"How? I only told my sister I was coming here and I know she didn't call you."

Rashid was visibly shocked at my response. We haven't spoken since.

A crowd started to gather around. All eyes were on me at that moment. Although I was suffering from multiple bullet wounds and could barely stand, I couldn't afford to appear weak, considering the circumstances, and give those who had conspired to kill me the satisfaction. I grabbed my cigarettes from the inside pocket of my jacket and tapped one out of the pack. I lit it up, took a drag, and managed to sit up slightly.

An older man from the community leaned over to me and spoke in a voice that contained neither pity nor compassion.

"Are you happy now, Sleiman? Is this what you wanted? Are you satisfied?"

I looked him right in the eye and blew smoke in his face. "I'm really happy now. This is what I always wanted."

"This is what you wanted?"

"Yeah, but they couldn't finish the job, could they? Does that make you sad that I'm not dead?"

He walked away, but I knew that there was truth in his scathing sarcasm and the fact that he felt a sense of justice in his lack of sympathy. I realized this as I lay outside the clubhouse I had helped build for my friends, in the middle of the housing complex I had helped turn into a ghetto. I had just been lured into an ambush, shot multiple times, and likely betrayed by my own crew. Blood streamed down my face, neck, and legs and seeped through my jacket. I knew that somewhere deep down in the depths of my soul that every single drop of blood I lost tonight was well-deserved.

I had gone after my childhood friend Samir, I had gone after The Mexican, I had gone after The Serb. I pushed and pushed and pushed the boundaries and stepped over every line imaginable. Day after day, week after week, month after month, year after year, I waged war, took revenge, and terrorized my adversaries. I was the one who had started the war in Hundige in the first place. In a way, I was relieved. Relieved to have survived. Relieved to have proven my loyalty to my brothers. No one on Earth would be able to question my loyalty now.

My own brothers had accused me of being too close to Black Cobra, but it was Black Cobra who had just shot me four times. I used to think that I had gotten off too easily. During the gang war, which had raged for seven years now, I had never been shot, and I knew a lot of people resented me for it. Now I was finally the one who had taken a bullet for the crew. I no longer needed to prove himself to anyone. Not a single soul in Askerød could say that I hadn't paid the price. No one could possibly suspect me of being a traitor or a snitch.

When the ambulance arrived, the paramedic shouted, "God-dammit, Sleiman! Put that cigarette out. It's dangerous to smoke when you're injured!"

I refused. I wasn't about to show weakness with everyone's eyes on me, so I finished the cigarette to send a message to whoever had set me up.

Eventually, the paramedics managed to remove my sticky, bloody jacket. In my inside pocket was the James Bond DVD I had just borrowed from a neighborhood kid before the attack: *Die Another Day*. There was a dent in the cover from where the bullet had hit and failed to penetrate.

As I lay there watching the paramedics work, I felt wet and warm and cold all at once. I, Sleiman, had just cheated death.

2

THE JOURNEY FROM LEBANON TO
DENMARK, SEPTEMBER 1982

The bombs from the Israeli planes fell quickly and in waves. There was fighting in the streets. My mother sought shelter in the bunker with her family. She was thirty-four years old and about to give birth to her third child in the refugee camp of Ein el-Hilweh, which means *God's beautiful eye*.

It was the middle of the first Lebanese War, where the Israeli army marched into South Lebanon in 1982. The most brutal fighting between the Israeli army and the Palestine Liberation Organization (PLO) forces happened in Ein el-Hilweh. The extensive damage to the city has been compared to the devastating bombings of German cities during World War II.

My mother was born in 1948, the same year the State of Israel was established. She was born on the run and without citizenship. Along with tens of thousands of other refugees, her family fled to Ein el-Hilweh, which looked like a war zone back then and unfortunately still does. When you say Ein el-Hilweh, you also say barbed-wire fence, checkpoints, oil drums, sandbags, soldiers, tanks, armed militia, terrorists, freedom fighters, and organizations like Fatah, PLO, and Hezbollah. All Middle Eastern conflicts have found a home in Ein el-Hilweh. Everyone who lives here dreams of escaping, and throughout her childhood, my mother heard stories about the promised motherland of Palestine.

But the dream died, and instead, she grew up in the dusty slum of Ein el-Hilweh, where eighty thousand people live on two square kilometers (.772 square miles). She became a beautiful woman with light skin and loose hair, a woman who insisted on staying thin and dressing elegantly, even as the family lived in wretched poverty. People considered her a snob because she came from an intellectual family, but she was proud of her heritage, even though it brought her little to no happiness. Her father, who was a wealthy editor, had left her mother for another woman, and he rarely kept in touch. As a little girl, she kept hoping that her father would swoop in and rescue her from the camp, but it remained a dream.

The refugee camp was her reality. It was there that she met her husband, who was handsome, intelligent, and had a steady job. They were never head over heels in love, but they both felt that their marriage was a good arrangement. Her first two children were born in 1979 and 1980, and on September 21st 1982, during an intensive bombardment, her third child—me—had his umbilical cord severed while in the bunker. She didn't dare leave. Instead, some of the boys who had also sought refuge down there ran up and fetched the local midwife to deliver her child. The bombs fell so relentlessly over Ein el-Hilweh that I spent the first three days of my life in that bunker.

My mother told me she was afraid she was going to die at first, but I turned out to be the easiest of all of her deliveries. She thought she had to go to the bathroom, but out I came!

From my early childhood, my older sister, Sarah, and I were inseparable. We also had a multi-handicapped, older brother named Mohammed, and as our mother spent most of her time looking after him, Sarah, who was only three years older than me, was left in charge of taking care of me. I followed Sarah everywhere. We would even run away during bombardments. We didn't care. We always left and went to our grandma's house. It was just the two of us and Grandma. We loved her more than we loved our mom and dad. From her roof, you could pick figs right off the tree.

My father didn't belong to any of the Palestinian resistance groups, but as a man, he was inevitably part of the war against Israel. He was arrested on several occasions when the Israeli soldiers marched into the camp, and at one point, he was sent to prison. The prison was built into a mountain and was known as "He who enters has disappeared, and he who escapes is reborn."

Most people never returned. But when my mother realized where he was, she carried Mohammed to the mountain and told the soldiers, "If you kill my husband, then you must take my son and raise him! Because I cannot do it alone. I cannot afford to raise him."

She told me that two Israeli soldiers got into a fight about what to do. One of them didn't care, but the other one did.

My mother appealed to his humanity. I think he took pity on her. It was quite a brave thing to do because no one dared speak to them. But she had to because if my father didn't return, her financial basis for living would disappear along with him. In the end, she got to take my father home.

My father had once been to Germany, and he and my mother often talked about running away there. But they postponed it several times because he had a steady job. He was good at building sewers. In the refugee camp, the Red Cross hired him to lay pipes and drains that led the water away from the houses and prevented flooding when it rained. The Red Cross paid decent wages, and due to that, our family was doing reasonably well financially.

The war wasn't going anywhere. Even though my dad had a job, I don't think it was enough for him. He couldn't secure a future for us, and we had no status in Lebanon. Even today, Palestinians can't obtain Lebanese citizenship and become part of the society, so my parents decided to flee the country.

Back in 1986, fleeing a country was different. You were not crammed into a truck and driven across Europe. One winter day, the family hopped on a plane from Beirut to Berlin. The plane was filled with Palestinian quota refugees whom Germany had agreed to receive. My parents, Sarah, me, and our two younger sisters, Ayat and the newborn Alaa, all went. We had to leave Mohammed behind with our family and intended to get him once we were settled in the new country.

Once we got to Germany, we checked in at a hotel, and, seeing as our father spoke German, the family expected to build our future there. However, he also had friends and family in Denmark, and he called them up from Berlin. They all told him that they were doing well in the north. My father figured that he knew no one in

7

Germany, and even though he spoke the language, he chose Denmark instead. On the day the decision was made, my mother was completely in the dark and knew nothing about Denmark herself.

Three days after arriving in Berlin, we got on a bus filled with fellow Palestinians and headed for Denmark. My mother is the one who recounts the journey. She lives in a 645-square-foot apartment in Askerød, and several blood clots have reduced her to a frail, nervously fidgeting, headscarf-wearing shadow of the beautiful woman with the uncovered hair whom I remember from my childhood. She actually doesn't want my story to be told. She's afraid that it will cause more damage than good, and she fears revenge from those who believe that words are more powerful than swords.

In the stairwell close to the door, someone has written *Bloodz* next to a drawing of the Grim Reaper. This was meant for me. It's saying, "When you leave the gang you helped found, there's going to be some retribution." Outside the building, a dumpster riddled with dents from bullets indicates that I have a past that is impossible to escape no matter how much I want to. At the time when my mother was interviewed for this book, those shots were fired only eighteen months prior. They were meant for me as punishment for leaving the Bloodz, so my mother was understandably afraid.

She knows that my story will open the wounds of her own life, which has never been a truly happy one. Even so, she tells her story in quiet Arabic because I asked her to. Because she has always done everything, she could for me. However, she declines to have her actual name mentioned, so she will be referred to solely as "my mother." I love and honor her because she has always been there for me, no matter how much pain and anguish I've caused her over the years.

3

A WONDERFUL WELCOME

Denmark doesn't get more beautiful than this. The green fields slope down toward the beach at Juelsminde, the spring sun casts a silver mirror across Kattegat, and farther up, the forest is filled with trees about to bloom. Today, the fields are occupied by luxury condos with staggering ocean views, but in late 1986, when my family arrived, they were owned by the Tvind schools, whose buildings were placed all along the waterline. Some of my family's good memories are from this place.

My parents and Sarah took Danish classes, and I began kindergarten, where warm-hearted and caring Danish teachers gave small children who were born into war an insight into what childhood could look like in one of the world's most peaceful countries. They gave us masks to wear and painted our faces. It was very theater-like, and I think they tried to cure us with laughter so that we wouldn't be traumatized. It was kind of hippieish. In the mornings, they woke us up with music, and when it was time to go to bed, they played music too.

Back in the 1980s, there was a song the staff sang to wake the refugees. Translated from Danish, it reads: "Wake up from your dreams. Life is not to be missed. You are needed, there's so much to do. The bat has flown away. Now get up and seize the day. The whistle has blown. The night is over, and daylight breaks through."

Today, Tvind has sold the waterside plots, but the school is still beautifully situated behind the luxury condos. The school is now home to ill-adjusted Danish youths who have been placed there by the municipalities. In recent times, the Tvind empire has been the subject of fierce criticism, but once, Tvind was charged with the task of caring for refugees.

Just as the Tvind schools' innocence was still intact, so was Denmark's immigrant virginity. The Danish Parliament had recently passed perhaps the most liberal immigration legislation in the world, and the rhetoric was different than today. A foreigner was a friend you had yet to meet, immigrants were called "guest workers," and to be a humanist was a mark of honor. Nobody feared Islam, ghettos were something other countries had, and Søren Krarup, the refugee-skeptical politician who would later become an influential voice in the Parliament, was just a cranky priest whom everybody loved to hate.

Several peaceful years would pass before a group of rejected Palestinian asylum seekers occupied Blågård Church in 1991 to protest their deportation. The protest led to the so-called "Palestinian Law," under which 321 Lebanese Palestinians were granted collective asylum. This law contributed to the sharpened rhetoric and partly gave rise to the national fight over immigrants, which took over the media from the mid-1990s and has played a significant part in the first three general elections of the new millennium.

Meanwhile, back in 1986, Denmark was still innocent, and I was a blameless child of four years old who sensed that my mother was legitimately happy during the four months we lived in Juelsminde. In the refugee camp in Lebanon, my parents were optimistic about life, in spite of the fact that they hadn't married out of love. My father was a handsome man who had a job. The problem was when he went on trips, his family wasn't kind to my mother. She was kind of a queen of the refugee camp. She was prettier than the rest. She had bright eyes, bright skin, and hair down to her shoulders. She refused to fall into decay in the slum. Instead, she wore jewelry and silk dresses, and she was thin even though she was a mother. My father's family was jealous of her, and they stole from her when he went on trips. They accused her of pretending to be better than they were, and they gave her a hard time. Coming to Denmark was liberating for her.

When the family went to Europe, my father was certain he would get a job. He knew how to lay pipes and build sewer systems, plus he was a good crane operator. When the family moved to Vejle in the south of Jutland in 1987, he started attending a crane operator course and felt optimistic. He dreamed of returning to Lebanon, but until there was peace, Denmark was supposed to fulfill the dreams that most people have. We could get our own apartment, we could work, and the kids could go to school.

That was a turning point in our lives. We were kids who had grown up in the refugee camp without really thinking about it. But when we got to Denmark, we saw that there were nice buildings here and that the world was pretty, filled with green areas, grass, and fields. We were used to rocks and rubble and ruined houses, so Denmark was a dream by comparison. We didn't know what Denmark was or what "Danishness" meant. We just knew that it was a beautiful place to start a new life.

Moldevej is in the neighborhood called Nørremarken in the northern part of Vejle, close to the industrial district. Today, the neighborhood is made up almost entirely of foreigners and Danes descended from other places in the world. It is a tired neighborhood with run-down houses, a shabby school, trash strewn about the narrow spaces between housing blocks, sparse vegetation, and a few red brick houses that look like they were designed by the same architect who also hastily designed the neighborhood's convenience store.

But that's not how I remember it being as a small child. Nørremarken is the sunlit stage of my childhood, and Moldevej is memory lane. That was where I first got my ass kicked by a group of Danes. Where the bus driver whom I loved, kicked a man off the bus because the man didn't want me to sit next to a Danish girl. And where on a small stage of the after-school center, my friend Aiman and I danced in a hip-hop contest and won every single hip-hop contest there was. We even got to perform on the main shopping street in Vejle while the pretty girls smiled at us.. Little did I know that I would pursue music as a career in the future, at the time it wasn't even a possibility.

That was also where I first danced with Samira and Louisa. They were the most beautiful Arab girls I had ever seen at the time. Louisa had olive-green eyes and long, blonde Arab hair and the same color skin as a tanned Danish girl. I went to the bakery and stole bread to try and impress her. She was no choir girl either: she did the same thing.

Moldevej number 21 is just a regular apartment building with regular windows in a regular neighborhood, but as a kid, it seemed like a luxury apartment where the light streamed in through the windows. We were happy there. My mother baked bread and made homemade cheese, and we got to decide whether we wanted our cheese with or without salt. We had hats, guns, and belts, and my siblings and I played cowboys and robbers. For the first time ever, we enjoyed life. Some wallpaper was missing here and there in the apartment, but we doodled on the walls in those spots. It was a real home, and I was a happy boy who danced around the apartment. Sometimes, when Mom and Dad were watching TV, I would jump in front of the screen and start dancing and annoying them so much that they actually wanted to hit me because I wouldn't stop.

I remember our home as a playful one filled with laughter, and my dad bought us every kind of toy there was. Sometimes, we went to Vejle Bay. There was a music venue there where our dad would sometimes take us to see concerts. He used to show us tons of things back then. We got to see almost all of Denmark. Sometimes, on the spur of the moment, we would go across the border to Germany to eat grilled chicken. We didn't have a car back then, so we took the bus.

Vejle's innocence was also intact. With a few exceptions, my family's relationship with the Danes was fine. We belonged to the first generation of immigrants in the neighborhood, and people would pinch my cheeks, smile kindly, and rumple my hair when I walked down the street. My mother visited neighbors and got a job. The chewing gum factory DANDY had an arrangement with the Red Cross and hired a lot of refugees. My father attended school and tried to have his crane operator license converted to a Danish one. He took us to tae kwon do lessons and sat and watched while we trained.

He was a real dad, a loving dad, and I think he really cared for me. I remember he bought me my first BMX bike, white and red, the one I had picked out. At home, he put pegs on the wheels of my bike. They flicked against the spokes and made it sound like a moped.

But it was when I got that bike that I experienced racism for the first time. We were all standing on the main street, and I was so excited about my new bike. A couple of Danish guys were sitting on a bench and shouted something like, "Dirty immigrant, go home!"

My dad stopped dead in his tracks but told us to walk on. I saw him fly at them with reckless abandon, even though it was four against one. They fought and fought and fought. I honestly don't remember if my dad won, but I remember that one of the guys, who was leaning against the back of the bench, got a punch that sent him flying. My mom didn't want us to see, so she took us to the bus, and we went home. Things like that made me see my dad as a hero.

He was still my dad back then. He was also a wise man. He knew all there was to know about religion, history, cars, everything. During the month of Ramadan, he took me to the mosque, where the adults would sit all night praying and reading the Koran. I loved just being there with him and falling asleep in the mosque. At home, we also had sack races and egg-and-spoon races, and outside, there was a big, green area where people would barbecue when Ramadan was over. It wasn't just a religious thing. It was also a social event, and I had the other kids to play with.

I was raised in a Muslim home, and there were certain basic rules that had to be followed, but it was also a liberal home that was open to the outside world. More things were allowed than forbidden. More yes than no. More halal than haram. The Fiat Uno had just come out, and Dad bought a brand-new one. He called me and told me to come down, and then we sat there in the new car listening to the radio. Just the two of us.

I wasn't the best student in my class in Vejle, but I was definitely third or fourth, and the teachers regularly praised me. Dad was always watching German television at home, and already at an early age, I could make him understand the language after watching Bud Spencer and Terence Hill beat up people while talking dubbed German.

I was a wild child who was almost always in a good mood, but could also get worked up over nothing. Academically, I had no problems.

In an old photo of my class, 4. A. I'm standing in the back row. In his picture, there is no sign of the future gang leader I would grow up to be one day. I'm just a smiling little boy like the others in the picture. More than likely, I was smiling because I was standing next to Nadine. She was my first childhood love. She was the one I wanted to have my first kiss with, the one I wanted to write to. I don't even know if I kissed her or if I dared to. I wasn't bullied, nor did I bully anyone in our classroom. That being said, our class bully was definitely Samilla. She was from Sri Lanka, and she always smelled like Tamil food.

In Vejle, the whole family was reunited when my brother Mohammed was finally brought to Denmark. He lived with us for a while, but unfortunately, his disabilities were so severe that my family was unable to afford to give him the proper care and constant attention he needed. He was ultimately placed with a good foster family in the south of Jutland, with whom we developed a close relationship.

4

THE GLOW OF A CIGARETTE

I absolutely hated my paternal grandmother. I hated her mostly because she appeared like a solar eclipse and stole the light from my entire childhood. She was a mean, wrinkly, old woman filled with Arab gossip and a warped code of honor that crept in and wrapped a knot of poison around my father's soul.

In 1991, my grandmother traveled from Lebanon to Vejle to stay with us for three months. During that time, dusk descended on Moldevej. When she arrived, it was no longer about the European dream and the dream of a better life. Suddenly, it was about my mother being a bad person. My mother carried our home on her shoulders. She was the pillar on which our home was built. She baked, she made cheese, she did everything. All my dad had to do was show up.

My grandmother started by saying that my mother didn't show her the proper amount of hospitality or respect. My mom had made a huge casserole filled with chicken and potatoes and onions, and she had made it as well as she could. We didn't have *that* much money, but my grandmother considered the dish an insult to her. She turned her nose up at it and denigrated my mother's efforts and her cooking. There was complete silence when we sat down for dinner.

To us kids, she was the wicked grandmother from Lebanon. She was never nice to us, and during the three months she stayed, she did nothing but whisper to our dad, "Your wife is a bad woman. She's corrupting your children." My dad didn't think so before my grandmother came to visit. But after she left, our home turned into a battlefield. Maybe it was the poison my grandmother had planted. Maybe it was the job my dad never got or his yearning for the homeland. I'm still unsure exactly why, but his entire attitude and demeanor changed.

One day, Sarah was no longer allowed to take taekwondo lessons. She had been the only girl on the team, and my dad used to be proud of her. He had watched her practice, taken her to tournaments. All of a sudden, she had become too Danish. Too much of a tomboy and not Muslim enough. Proper Muslim girls don't do the splits, so Sarah was forced to quit taekwondo.

Then one day, it came. I got a real beating. Before then, it had just been the occasional slap. But slaps turned into punches, which turned into kicks, and shortly afterward, it was my mother's turn. They had always been equals up until that point, but now my father beat her when she talked back. Whenever his children cried and tried to intervene, he beat us too. I often got the worst of it. The picture my grandmother had painted became reality in that moment. We became the bad children, corrupted by our useless mother who went against our father, and he started hating us because of it.

I loved *lupia*, which is a dish that consists of dried grape leaves that are crushed into a type of soup and served with rice and roasted, minced meat. Unfortunately, one day, my mother bought the wrong ingredients. The soup turned out bitter, my father got angry, and everyone at the table started crying. It was me, who had already dished up a giant serving of *lupia*, who was forced to remain at the table and not only finish my own bowl, but the entire pot. If I refused, my father would beat me. I should've asked first before taking so much instead of being greedy.

We also had to learn more about Islam, and my father initiated an intensive Koran study program. Every day, when we came home from school, we had to read the holy scripture, and he started obsessing more and more about what other people thought of us. We had to be proper Muslims, and he had great plans for us. I had difficulties concentrating on my studies, and I was deathly afraid to make mistakes because if they were grave enough, I would get a beating. The same thing happened when I was sent to Koranic studies at school in the afternoons. I was too hard-headed. The teacher told my father of my poor scholastic performance, which resulted in a beating.

At age ten, I developed childhood asthma and was examined several times at the hospital. The doctors finally concluded I would probably outgrow it in time, which I did. But when I was ten, the asthma made my life even more difficult. I had trouble keeping up with soccer, swimming, and tae kwon do, and the harder it got, the more my father pushed me. He pushed me mostly out of fear that he if he didn't, I would turn into a weakling.

One night, when I had difficulty breathing, I got so scared that I ran into my parents' bedroom to sleep with them. My father was in the bathroom, but when he came out and saw me lying in his bed, he yelled, "What are you doing, you fag? Faggot!" Then he grabbed a pillow and pressed it down over my face so I couldn't breathe, and I had to flee the room to avoid being suffocated to death.

I never had my hair cut at the barbershop as a kid. My parents took care of that for me as opposed to spending the money. One night, when my father cropped my hair very short, I was getting my hair rinsed but got scared because the water was running into my nose.

"I can't breathe!" I screamed.

"You little sissy. You little faggot. What are you scared of? It's just water."

My father got more and more aggressive, and I thought I was going to die because the water kept running into my nose and I couldn't get any air into my lungs. He picked me up and aimed the spray head from the sink directly at my face.

"You little faggot!"

"Stop, Dad. Stop it!" I cried.

"What are you doing?" my mother yelled as she came running into the bathroom.

"This one is gonna be a faggot. You're a sissy, a coward. Are you afraid of water?" my father screamed at me.

———

THE NEXT TIME was brutal too. I bought cigarettes for my father once and regrettably tried to smoke one with a friend. Unfortunately, an acquaintance of my father saw us and immediately ratted us out. When I came home, the apartment was completely dark, and all the doors were closed. Only the living room door was open, so I went inside. There he was, sitting with his glasses on. The glow of his cigarette gleamed in the glass. First came the punches. They kept on coming and coming and coming, and no one else was home but us.

The beatings were unpredictable and frequent. My father slapped me, banged my head into the radiator, and kicked me while I lay on the floor. Once the beating was so bad that fluid started trickling out of my ear, and what once was unconditional love for my father transformed into chronic fear. Fear of coming home from school just to be greeted by a clenched fist. Fear of doing something either in school or at home that would trigger more violence.

He had impressed on me at an early age that it was strictly forbidden to use the bathroom in another person's house without asking permission first. I was told it was better to wet your own pants than going to the bathroom without asking permission. Otherwise, you were just a rude child with no home training.

Once, we went on a weekend trip to visit some family in Aalborg, and all the children were put to sleep in the same room. During the night, I had to pee, but there were no adults around to ask to use the bathroom, and I was afraid to wake anybody up to ask for permission first. I was only nine years old and I was afraid of disobeying my father's instructions, so I panicked. I held out and held out until I finally peed right in the middle of the room as all the children slept. Luckily, my mother came in like the angel of the night and helped me wipe the floor clean of urine with my own clothes, which she then put in the washer before anyone was the wiser.

I was usually far less fortunate, and I ended up in the hospital on several occasions due to my father. The family had a large, marble table in the living room, and one day, he hit me so hard that I fell and banged my head right into the tabletop. My head was cut open and blood flowed out, so I needed immediate medical attention. On the way to the hospital, my father told me to keep quiet about the incident. Out of fear, I did. I never said a word about it. Not even when people asked me directly and alone. I wouldn't even dream of speaking about the abuse I received at my father's hands. Never at school, nor in the hospital.

Underneath the bridge that crosses Vejle Bay is a narrow strip of forest and beach that runs between the water and the main road. The main road leads to Bredballe, which is where the rich live with their terrific views of the bay. One day, my father took me there. I was ten years old, and it was time for me to learn how to swim, in his estimation. A cousin went with us, and when they got to the water's edge, I grabbed my father's hand.

We walked out until the water reached my father's chest. He held me, but I couldn't reach the bottom.

"Swim," he said. "You have to paddle with your hands first, and then you have to paddle with your feet."

I tried to paddle, paddle, paddle, and at first, I thought it went pretty well. My father held me, so I felt reasonably safe. But suddenly, he turned to me and said, "Now it's time to try on your own."

"I can't! Don't let go of me!"

But he let go. "You're on your own now," he said and walked back to shore.

I fought with every fiber of my being, and we were somewhere around thirty, maybe fifty feet out. I legitimately thought he didn't care if I died. Then my cousin ran out, grabbed me, and carried me to shore. I loved that cousin because he always protected me. He was a very understanding man. But he couldn't really do anything because my dad was his uncle. I liked it when he was around because then my dad didn't hit me. He carried me to the car and handed me a towel.

"Stay here," he said. "Don't say anything. Don't do anything to make your dad angry. You'll only get another beating. Just stay here."

The most important thing for my father was that I didn't turn into a sissy who could not take care of himself. In his world, there was no turning the other cheek, no losing face. Hitting back was the only option. One day, a couple of Somali boys harassed Sarah in a parking lot, and I told them to stop. They were a couple of years older than I, and they both knew taekwondo like I did, so we had to fight right then and there.

One of them got into a fighting stance like I did and attempted a roundhouse kick. He hit me in the head, but I didn't hit him, so then the two brothers and their family walked away.

My dad was in the apartment and had seen the whole thing from the window. He shouted at me, "You're not coming home until you get your revenge! You need to learn how to defend yourself!"

I didn't know what else to do. They were both bigger and stronger than me. So I found a rock and ran after them and threw the rock at the guy I had fought.

A man who was parking his car just then grabbed me and asked, "What the hell are you doing?" He shook me, but that was all. The boys didn't retaliate when they saw him.

My dad didn't say anything, but I got the weird sense that what I had done was right. He wanted me to conquer my fear. It didn't matter if they were stronger than you or outnumbered you. You were always supposed to stand up for yourself, regardless of the odds.

5

THE ABDUCTION TO LEBANON

It was a boiling hot summer night in 1993. The tiny alley in the Lebanese city of Tripoli was narrow, and the night sky was pitch black. I was ten years old, and my father told me to wait by the gate. Why I had to sit there, I didn't know. All I was told was that my clothes weren't nice enough for the party that was going on upstairs on the terrace above the alley. There was light and music up there. Guests were barbecuing and dancing on a podium. I could barely make out my father sitting at a table.

At the time, I had no idea what it was all about. I was on vacation with my father and Sarah in Lebanon. We had come to visit our family after my dad had bought a small house as an investment for the future. He had taken out all the money he, my mother, and even my siblings had saved up, which amounted to about $9,000 USD in kroner..

There wasn't a single light in the alley I was sitting in. All the neighbors had been invited to the party. At some point during the night, a man came down and told me that he was supposed to sleep at our house.

The next day, my father came to the house to pick him up, along with a woman I didn't know. They were going to have a barbecue by a waterfall in the mountains.

"Sleiman," my father said. "I want you to meet my new wife. We got married last night."

"But how is that possible? What about Mom? Where is she going to live?" I asked him.

"Well, this is my wife now. I'm not going to be with your mother anymore. Your mother doesn't do as I say."

I was devastated. I couldn't comprehend what was happening. I still loved him, but this scenario wasn't real to me. I didn't want to hear it. I wanted my mom and dad to be together forever. Sarah didn't know what had happened yet because she was staying at our maternal grandma's.

A couple of days later, Sarah was running down a dusty, dirt road in the Ein el-Hilweh refugee camp. She was hoping to reach the safety of our aunt's house. A forty-year-old man from my father's family was chasing after her and yelling.

This wasn't a vacation after all. My sister and I had been taken back to the refugee camp because our father wished to realize his own dream of returning home. First, he had married another woman behind our mother's back. Now it was time to execute the second step of the plan. Sarah was being married off to a twenty-three-year-old cousin of ours. The man running behind her was furious because she had just refused the proposal when our father's family had come specifically to introduce her to our cousin, who was the son of our father's sister.

The cousin liked the arrangement, and the whole family was pressuring Sarah to comply. In their eyes, it was time for her to get married. She had become too European. They thought her behavior was promiscuous, and that's why she needed a husband. Promiscuous? She was only thirteen!

Sarah went crazy. She just stood there, all alone in the family's house, yelling at everyone in defiance. If this was how they wanted things to be, then they were right: she *was* European! She didn't want to marry a twenty-three-year-old cousin whom she had never met before that day!

They commanded her to shut up. She was just a girl, and she had no right to say those things. That only infuriated her more and made her yell even louder, "*You* shut up!"

That was when the forty-year-old man, who was also our cousin, started chasing her. He said, "You have no say in this."

"Who are you? Why are you talking to me? Shut up!"

The punches started raining down on her, and she ran out of the house with the older man at her heels until she reached safety at our aunt's. She stayed there the next couple of days. We called our mother from one of the camp's payphones and told her everything that had transpired. She was blindsided.

Maybe we would never go home again. There was nothing our mother could do, and while Sarah stayed with our aunt, our father frequently came by to threaten her. Every so often, she was also in contact with the cousin who wanted to marry her, and she did everything she possibly could to scare him away.

"Do you really want to marry someone who doesn't like you? Who hates you?" Sarah asked. He told Sarah that it was his sincere hope that she had a bad life, and she told him she hoped the same for him when he would try to force her to marry him at her young age. She told him she hated him, and he should tell his mother that she refused. When that didn't seem to be enough of a deterrent, Sarah told him she'd kill herself and him if they forced her to marry him.

She was a brave and clever girl who had to endure a lot. Sometimes, she felt the pressure lifting. They decided to play reverse psychology and not pressure her or beat her in hopes she'd come around. Sarah stood her ground. In her mind, nothing was worse than the fear of being condemned to a life with him.

We didn't understand why our father wanted to hurt our mother by taking us away from her. What had we done to deserve this?. This harrowing ordeal at a young age forever changed Sarah's personality. Who are you supposed to trust in life when the ones closest to you would do something like that?

Later on, Sarah and I went to visit our father's family again. Present were a bunch of uncles, aunts, cousins, and our father. Once again, they tried to pressure Sarah. One well-educated uncle was on Sarah's side, but he had no real say in the matter. At the time, I didn't know what a forced marriage was, but I had seen my big sister's despair, and I was on her side as they gathered in the living room for the final showdown. I was young, but this was pretty much what transpired, per my recollection.

"I don't want to. He's old. I don't want to. He's old. I don't want to!" Sarah said.

"You'll do as I say," our father said.

"I don't care. Kill me, then. I'd rather die."

"You'd rather die?"

Our father ran to a cupboard and took out an AK-47. I didn't think he would shoot, but he did. I don't remember if it was because his own sister suddenly stepped in front of Sarah as soon as she saw him pull out a gun, but by mistake, he shot his sister in the arm. When that happened, my father panicked.

There was a mildly development-challenged cousin in the house who was abnormally strong. He immediately lunged at my father from behind, held him in a stranglehold with one hand, and used the other to pivot the gun barrel toward the ceiling. In the meantime, Sarah and I ran out into the refugee camp. Our cousin ran out after us.

"I've got it! I've got it!" he yelled euphorically as he ran around with the AK-47.

We ignored him and continued running. We felt nothing but the fear and anger fueling our young bodies and the gravel pounding against our feet as we ran through the camp.

Later, we again called our mother, and together, we came up with a plan. We were going home. The problem was, our father had our passports and refused to hand them over. Sarah feared that we would never return home and decided to embrace our father with false sweetness in hopes of tricking him to let us return to Denmark. My sister is one of the bravest and most industrious people I know.

She said to our father, "'It's true what you say. Mom is evil. She's not right, and she's constantly on your back. When we get home, I'm moving in with you.' Sarah said whatever our father needed to hear at the time to get out of Lebanon, and get us back home. In the end, he was convinced that we were going to live with him and his new wife. Then our two youngest sisters could stay with our mom. That was his plan, and he was so easy to manipulate because of his tunnel vision.

Eventually, we succeeded. Later that summer, Sarah, our father, and I flew to Copenhagen, and when we arrived at the airport, our mother was waiting with our two younger sisters. On the surface, she seemed happy to see us all, but in reality she lied to our father and told him that she was taking the children to Sweden to visit the family. The truth, though, was that she had given notice to vacate our apartment in Vejle, sold all the furniture, and found a room at a women's shelter in Helsingør, north of Copenhagen. She refused to live in Vejle, close to where her now ex-husband would start a life with his new wife, have new children, and maybe also force Sarah and I to come live with them.

So while our father went to Vejle, my mother, my siblings, and I went to Helsingør. Like the refugee center in Juelsminde, Røntofte Women's Shelter is seated high atop a hill and has a magnificent view across the Sound to Sweden. However, at the women's shelter, there was no dancing and singing in the morning. Everything was ripped away from me at once. Only two months ago, my silent friend Camilla from Jehovah's Witnesses; the beautiful Arab girl Louisa with the blonde hair, the olive-green eyes, and the light-brown skin; and my friend Aiman with whom I won hip-hop contests were all a part of my life. Now Vejle was suddenly in my past, and I had never even gotten a chance to say goodbye to my class, my neighbors, or my friends.

When my family first arrived in Denmark, we were given a helping hand, and the world collectively rumpled our hair. Six years later, they were fresh out of helping hands. Perhaps the spirit of the times had changed. Maybe it was just the circumstances. It feels like a fog has settled on my memories of that time because it felt like the world and my own family members had all conspired to do me harm at a young age.

A stronger mother would have cried for help until the world around her listened, but our mother was an Arab woman in a strange country, without a husband and without a firm grasp of the language. Our family's strongest member was now Sarah, who at thirteen sat in a women's shelter browsing the classifieds, looking for an apartment.

"I'm afraid of Copenhagen. Isn't it dangerous to live in Copenhagen?" she asked the social worker.

"No, of course not," the social worker said.

"Should I give that landlord in Ishøj a call? Is that a dangerous place?"

"Sarah, you need to do this yourself. *You* need to find an apartment. We can't help you."

"But it's not me you're helping. You're helping my mom."

"No. I can sit down with you, and I can show you how to do it. But you have to do it on your own," the social worker said.

To this day, I can't wrap my mind around what Sarah had been told that day. They left a thirteen-year-old girl in charge of her entire family!

We ended up in Lyngby, ten miles north of Copenhagen. Sarah found us an apartment in Lundtofteparken, which was a pretty decent place as far as subsidized housing goes. I was enrolled at a local school, but I didn't like it. That was where I started getting into fights, started smoking, and became friends with the twin trouble-makers, Michael and Martin. They accepted me as I was. Only in the beginning did they refer to me as a *perker*, which is a common ethnic slur directed at people from the Middle East, and they respected me for fighting back whenever they tested me. I don't know why, but they weren't happy, so we agreed to be unhappy together. I was a lost kid who didn't know where else to turn to. None of us—not my mom, not my dad, and certainly not us kids—ever got over leaving Vejle. We were like the living dead.

One day, our father called. He started ingratiating himself with my mother, saying he regretted what he had done, that his new wife wasn't right for him either. He wanted to come back. Alaa and Ayat, who were only five and seven years old, at the time, missed our father because they hadn't been to Lebanon and he had never beaten either of them. At the time, even I held out hope that every-thing would go back to the way it once had been. I just wanted my father to be nice again and for us to be a family.

Sarah didn't feel the same way. I said, "'Don't, Mom. Don't.' I knew it was dangerous. But the little ones missed him. 'We want to talk to Dad. We want to talk to Dad. Why can't we talk to our dad?'

It was hard for our mom. She was a young mother with very small children, and she was alone. She had no family and no friends in Denmark. She had no money of her own and no support system of any kind. At the time, our mother didn't know how to do anything but pay the bills and buy groceries. Our father exercised control over her that way.

Our father returned with flowers. A giant bouquet. Sarah thought they were phony and an empty gesture. He had never bought our mother flowers before. "Be careful," she said to Mom.

"Let's give him a chance," our mother said.

She was weak, and he moved right back in. For a while, the living room was quiet. Our father had grown apathetic. He just sat there day after day, drinking coffee. He didn't fight, didn't yell. He never even left the apartment. He just seemed sad, lost, and silent on the surface—or so we all thought. It turns out he was merely biding his time.

6

ONLY THE SEAGULLS CRIED BACK

In her dreams, Sarah was begging our mother to take the kids and run away because our father wanted to kill them. Our mother refused to believe her. Then Sarah woke up.

Sarah was home from school with mono. Our father grumbled about it. The term *kissing disease* did not sit well with him. "Maybe she caught it kissing someone?" he asked. That made Sarah angry. She was only thirteen years old, and she wasn't kissing anyone.

I had left for school already with Ayat and Alaa. Our father wanted a cup of coffee. Mom offered to make him one, but he objected to her brewing it. "It's not proper coffee," he said. She again offered to make him another cup, and he asked her to drink it with him. She refused, and supposedly, that was what ticked him off.

Sarah's memories of that day have faded, but nowhere as much as she would like. At the time I'm writing this, nineteen years have passed, and still not a day goes by when she doesn't pray for the grace of repression.

It was just past 11:00 a.m. when she heard our mother's muffled screams from the living room.

Sarah ran through the apartment. This wasn't the sound of our parents playing around. It was the sound of sheer panic.

Sarah entered the living room and saw our mother lying face

down on the couch. Our father was straddling her back while clutching a knife. He raised it and stabbed her. Then he raised it and stabbed her again, then again.

Sarah had once witnessed the slaughter of a sheep. To her, this looked terrifyingly similar. Blood was gushing out of a wound in our mother's throat.

Sarah was a sick child, but she had never felt stronger than she did in her life at that very moment. She hurled herself at our father with the single-minded focus of saving our mother's life. Thanks to her previous taekwondo training, she knew how to fight, and she managed to throw him off balance.

However, my father hadn't lost possession of the knife when she had attempted to tackle him. Once he got a hold of Sarah, he started stabbing her as well. He stabbed her in the neck, arms, and hand, infuriated that his child had dared intervene.

Now the fight was between Sarah and our father. A sick, teenaged girl was facing off against a grown man armed with a knife. She fought him tooth and nail for between ten and fifteen minutes, but to her, it felt like a lifetime. She knew where to kick a man and inflict maximum damage. Here, her memories start to become blurry, but she does remember banging our father's head into an iron electricity meter, which probably gave her the window she needed to open the safety lock he had installed on the front door.

Sarah doesn't remember how she managed to open the door. These days, she wonders if maybe someone was watching over her and our mother. Dad had hidden large knives all over the apartment. Filleting knives, carving knives, kitchen knives. It was as if he had planned the whole thing all along, stashing the knives away solely in anticipation of this day. Our mother had been stabbed in the stomach, hand, and back, but the wound to her throat was the most critical one. It was a deep slash that ran from her neck down across her chest. Sarah desperately needed to get her to safety, so once our father went down, she mustered the might to gather her up, then made for the stairwell. Sarah carefully cradled our mother's head on the way down the stairs in an attempt to simultaneously hold her neck and torso in place and prevent the major wound from bleeding out before finding any medical help. Later on, the doctors told Sarah that our mother would not have survived without her having the presence of mind to do this.

While stumbling down the stairs, Sarah feared that she was about to lose the only caring adult left in her life. They were barefoot, and their torn-up clothes were drenched in blood. Sarah screamed and screamed and screamed while holding our mother together. At the moment, she was oblivious to her own pain. When they walked out into the street, she screamed even louder, but only the seagulls cried back.

An elderly man and his wife drove past them. Sarah and our mother ran after the car. They knocked feverishly on the windows, hoping to catch a ride to safety, but the couple got scared and drove on. Eventually, our building's landlord came outside. He had heard Sarah's cries for help and called for emergency services. Once an ambulance arrived on the scene, the stunned paramedics saw both women were covered in blood and visibly shaken.

"Take my mother first!" Sarah cried.

The paramedics helped our mother into the ambulance. Shortly afterward, another ambulance arrived to pick up Sarah, the brave girl who had fought off a grown man while sick at home from school and saved her own mother's life.

The two young police officers entered the classroom at Lindegård School in Lyngby and asked for a boy named Sleiman. I followed them out into the hall, where one of the officers knelt and kindly placed his hands on my shoulders. He said, "Your mother has had an accident."

I didn't even wait around to hear the rest. I ran down the hall and up the stairs to Ayat's first-grade classroom. I said, "Something has happened to Mom."

I grabbed her hand, and together, we ran across the school to where Alaa was being taught. I walked in and grabbed her. By now, the officers had caught up with us, and we all walked down to the patrol car.

"What happened?" I asked the policemen.

The officers were evasive, probably to avoid traumatizing us. We were told we weren't allowed to visit our mother in the hospital or go home and see Sarah, nor our father. Instead, the officers drove us all to Strandriddergården, a children's home in Vedbæk, half an hour away from home. We were given a warm welcome, and the staff showed us to a room with bunk beds. Later, someone went by our apartment to pick up some clothes, but no one there ever told us what had happened.

I was eleven years old at the time, and Alaa and Ayat were eight and nine, respectively. I think we all stayed at Strandriddergården for at least two weeks, but not more than two months. I honestly don't remember exactly how long the three of us were there, but I distinctly remember feeling like a ghost floating through time.

The police came to take our statement. They asked, "Where is your father? Does he have any family aside from you? Where have you lived? If you know something, you have to tell us."

All we knew was we had family in Aalborg and in Flensburg, Germany. We wanted to talk to our father as well, but the police didn't know where he was either. They thought he had gone abroad, they told us.

Each morning, a taxi arrived to drive us to school, and in the afternoon, we were brought right back to Vedbæk. Eventually, we were informed that our mother was at Gentofte Hospital, but we were still not allowed to visit her. We began to suspect that she might be dead. Why weren't we allowed to see her? Why couldn't we see Sarah? My little sisters didn't understand what could've possibly befallen our other family members, but slowly, I came to realize my father had to be at fault. Had he shot our mother? Drowned her in the ocean?

One day, I was chopping wood on a tree stump with a small ax in Strandriddergården's garden. I was wearing a Batman wristwatch, but suddenly, instead of Batman, I saw my father's face beneath the glass. I immediately took it off, placed the watch on the stump, and smashed it to pieces with the ax, my mind racing, coming up with possible scenarios in which he harmed my mother and Sarah, the two people I loved most in the world. I kept on smashing it with the ax even as my little sisters came running toward me, screaming.

One night, we all put together a plan. The next day, when we were dropped off at school, we instead turned around and trudged toward Lyngby Station. When we got to the station, we boarded the first train. All I knew was we were going to Gentofte, but we had no money and no tickets. When we boarded, I told Ayat and Alaa to hide under the seat.

The train passed Gentofte without stopping, and shortly before Hellerup Station, a woman who was a ticket inspector entered the compartment. "What are you doing here?" she asked and then spotted the two girls underneath the seat. "What are you two doing down there? Do you have a ticket?"

"No," I said.

"Then you have to get off. Where are your parents? Do you have their phone number so I can call them?"

"No."

"Well, then I'll have to call the police," she said.

My sisters started crying, and the inspector asked, "But don't you know where your mother is?"

Our answer surprised her. She was a very loving woman, and in the end, she was crying with us. She called the police, and when they arrived, she said to them, "These children can't find their mother. Would you please take them to her?" The officers decided to do as she asked.

Our mother had been placed in the same room as Sarah in the hospital. They were both wearing white clothes, and our mother's head and face were partially covered by a large piece of white cloth wrapped around her head like a turban. During the fight, it seems our father was trying to drag Sarah around by her hair so it was reduced to wisps after her long fight for her life.

Our mother was sad when she saw us. She said, "Your father did this. He hurt me."

"My hair. My hair is gone. But I stopped him. I saved our mom," Sarah cried.

I looked at my mother. She had been cut from the cervical vertebrae around the neck to her throat. She had stab wounds on her arms, elbows, and stomach. Sarah had wounds on her throat and several other places. They were both as white as the sheets that covered them, and they looked like two women who had given up on life. But seeing us there seemed to restore them.

We sat together for a while. Then Sarah and our mother went to take a shower, which they hadn't done since the assault. They undressed and started washing each other. They had the door closed, but I heard them crying. At that moment, Ayat and Alaa ran to join them. Our mother and sister were both naked and crying while they washed each other's wounds, determined to live through this horrific act. Later that day, my little sisters and I were taken back to the children's home. Tears still fill my eyes as I think about it.

On November 10, 1993, our father was brought before the court in Lyngby and charged with attempted homicide. One of the biggest Danish tabloids *Ekstra Bladet*, was present at the trial and the next day the paper published an article detailing the events and all the gory details. This article would provide the fodder for us to be ridiculed and harassed for years to follow. Please keep in mind that we were only children and our mother was ill equipped to deal with the notoriety or to help us cope with the unwanted attention that was to come.

While Sarah is glad that she saved our mother's life, she has never been truly happy since. Something inside her died that day. She's now forty-one years old and the most enchanting woman you will ever meet. She has luscious, dark hair and radiant, brown eyes that sparkle when she smiles. But underneath that smile, there is a grief similar to that of a soldier who has been to war and seen the cruelty of the world. After the assault, nothing was ever really the same, and during the years that followed, she fell out with the entire world because she was left to her own devices.

We had been living in an orgy of violence. Our father had tried to force Sarah to marry against her will, and he nearly killed our mother. We received no help whatsoever, we were left to our own devices. We fought for each other. There were no doctors, no psychologists, no social workers. Maybe they didn't know how to deal with us because we were immigrants. But in that specific situation, we weren't Danes, and we weren't immigrants: We were kids screaming for help, and we never had the chance to properly process what we'd been through or be given the tools to overcome it. Sarah was thirteen and should have been treated like a child with an enormous weight upon her shoulders . Instead, she just stepped up and took care of her entire family.

Sarah is aware of the impression she makes. She is beautiful, intelligent, eloquent, and the mother of three adorable little girls. But appearances can be deceiving. Occasionally, when she goes to work, she must come back home because she feels overwhelmed and suffers from anxiety. When she is around too many people, she must leave to avoid having a panic attack. She feels sick inside.

Because of the people I'm involved with now, people have openly hated and despised her, thrown bricks through her window simply because she's my big sister. And regardless of all of this, she is still always there for me

7

THE BUTCHERED WOMAN'S SON

A mother and her four children arrived in Askerød, about fifteen miles outside of Copenhagen. Not even they can explain exactly why they ended up there. Sort of like how they ended up in Denmark in the first place. A man had told them that there were lots of Arabs in Askerød, and my mother wanted to live somewhere with a lot of people like herself. We were told Askerød was that kind of place.

Askerød was a social housing complex built in Hundige in the mid-1970s. The grounds were equipped with green areas, soccer courts, small hills where the kids could go tobogganing, and a well-developed system of roads and paths. Here, the children could play in a car-free area without being disturbed on bright, summer evenings, and if they wanted to go to the library, the youth club, or the mall, they could ride their bikes or walk without ever having to cross an actual street.

In the beginning, Askerød was modern. School teachers, lawyers, medical students, architects, and other members of the well-educated Danish middle class saw an opportunity to live both separately and as part of a larger community. In the mid-1980s, however, the composition of residents changed. Whenever the municipality was unable to find housing for social security recipients, the unemployed, alcoholics, drug addicts, single mothers, refugees, and large immigrant families, they were sent to Askerød. And as the lower-class residents moved in, the middle class moved out. Soon Askerød was no longer a place for people who got up at seven, went to work, paid their taxes, came home at five, ate, read a bedtime story to their kids, and fell asleep in front of the TV.

During the 1990s, things further deteriorated. The story is similar to that of the other large ghettos in Århus, Odense, and Copenhagen. Askerød is the story of a restless, rootless generation of culturally confused, angry, young men who—armed with knives, Nike shoes, cheap gold chains, and pimped-out BMWs—sought revenge on everything and everyone, including themselves. Out here on the outskirts of the big cities is where the anti-immigration Danish People's Party was born. This was where Denmark lost its innocence as an immigrant nation and one general election after another was decided. They helped create the parallel society that Lars Løkke Rasmussen would talk about sixteen years later, when he gave his inaugural speech as prime minister in 2010 he identified Askerød was one of Denmark's twenty-nine ghettos.

In 1994, my family found itself without a male head of the household, without money, and without friends. We were assigned an apartment but never a psychologist or a counselor to help us deal with the trauma we had recently experienced. Perhaps one would have advised Sarah against visiting our father in prison. But she did.

The information provided by the medical report earned him a two-year stretch in prison for aggravated assault, but he avoided a conviction for attempted murder. Our mother took the witness stand but had difficulty describing exactly what had happened. Sarah chose not to testify. She couldn't bring herself to testify against her own father.

I never understood what Sarah was doing when she went to visit him in Vestre Prison. It was very hard seeing him the first time. 'Why did you do it?' I asked him. Our father never gave us a satisfactory response, often insisting he had no recollection of what happened that day.

In most places in Denmark, children and women in similar situations would be met with sympathy and understanding, but in Askerød's Arab village, things were different. Instead of compassion and tenderness, my family received condemnation and disdain. No man would do something like that to a woman without good reason. Our mother must have committed adultery. The daughter must have been promiscuous. So, their honor turned into dishonor, and every aspect of their womanhood was slandered. They became known as "the butchered ones."

To begin with, my mother related her story to other women in the Arab community even though Sarah asked her not to. Sarah maintained that she thought our mother needed someone to talk to. She soon found some Arab women she considered friends. Not too long afterwards all hell broke loose: They would point fingers at my mother and gossip openly about us. Sometimes they'd flat out yell that our father butchered her and Sarah.

Sarah became a teenage girl who walked through life burdened by her nickname, and she never really went back to school. To this day, she hates the name given to her by those in the community.Sarah is a hero. Our neighbors should have rallied around her and protected her rather then make her an object of derision, scorn and ridicule.

At this time, I was eleven years old, and when I stepped out the front door of my house, I stepped into a jungle filled with Greencoats, a subcultural group associated with skinheads; racist biker gang members; young alcoholics; potheads; and angry, young immigrant boys who had been raised the same way I had. If they did poorly in school or got in trouble with the police, their fathers would beat them with leather straps, hangers, canes, and fists, and the boys ended up resenting their fathers, who were on welfare support and spoke less Danish than their children did. They had come to Denmark in search of a better life only to end up in Askerød, where there was never any doubt of their failure as men and as heads of their families.

I was the only one who wasn't beaten at home, but that was because my father was already in prison. Violence was the language in these homes and the currency of the streets, and violence became the means by which I, as the male of the family, defended my mother, my sisters, and myself against the stories of the butchered women. One time at the local mall, a man called Sarah "the butchered woman's daughter," and I reacted by beating him up. At a peaceful church party, a boy called me "the butchered woman's son," and I kicked his ass too. The older boys knew how to provoke me, and whenever they got the chance, they took it.

We had no one to protect us against the slander, and we became outcasts. The messed-up thing about Arab culture is that the man is always right. A lot of women are battered at home, but the women of that generation kept their mouths shut and learned to live with it. My mom was strong. She rebelled against my dad. She went against the system. That's not how the Arab system works, and my mom became the villain of the story.

One day, I was riding my bike through Askerød but was stopped by three boys I didn't know. I was twelve, and they were about fifteen.

"We want your bike."

"You're not getting my bike."

"Yeah, you're that butchered woman's son. Give us your bike, you little shit."

"No. It's my bike."

One of the boys started punching me, but to his surprise, I hit him right back. The boy grabbed my bike, but I hauled off and punched him full force in the face.

"Next time I see you, I'm gonna beat you up, and I'll bring chains," he said to me.

"Fine, see you then," I defiantly responded.

Another time, a guy who was around eighteen was picking on me. He said, "Look who it is. It's the butchered woman's son."

"Fuck you. Shut up and eat shit."

"What did you just say, you little shit?"

I remember it clearly. He lifted me up and hurled me to the ground. I felt like crying, but I suppressed the tears because I didn't want to appear weak. A man doesn't cry. My dad had taught me that. And I didn't care how big he was or how hard he punched. My dad had beaten me worse. The scrapes I got from this kid meant nothing at all.

The nickname they gave us in Askerød also helped harden me. I was now a boy with nothing to lose, and I gained respect because I talked and fought better than others and I always sought revenge. One of the rules of Askerød was that every offense had to be avenged, and it had to be avenged tenfold. For every punch you received, your enemy got ten. If you got your head bashed into the asphalt, your enemy's head had to be bashed into the asphalt until he was lying unconscious in a pool of his own blood. This was where knife fights turned into gunfights. I became Sleiman—the boy who time and again beat and stomped on my adversaries, I was also doing it to the entire world that had done us harm. Avenging every single infraction soon became my trademark, and Askerød was full of angry boys with tragic fates who saw the world as I did.

Over the years, I have acquired many friends and just as many enemies. What the majority of them have in common is that I earned them through fistfights.

8

MY FIRST FRIEND

On a bleak, gray day, I was walking down a path when two Turkish kids and a Danish boy walked straight toward me. The boys in Askerød had a habit of bumping into one another in order to provoke a fight, and one of them deliberately bumped into me.

"What the fuck are doing? Watch where you're going," one of them said.

"What are you talking about? He bumped into me!"

Then one of them punched me in the face, and I immediately felt my eye swell up. I fought back, but it was three against one and one of them held me as the other two beat me up. When they finally let up, I was staring at the pavement with my hands on my knees. I felt the growing knot above my eye and looked up at them, fighting off tears.

"I'm gonna fuck you up!" I shouted as they walked away, and I swore to myself I would take revenge.

I waited two months until I found out where the boy who had thrown the first punch lived. I waited for him in the stairway of his home and attacked him, but the boy managed to flee into another building but I chased him down and confronted him.

"Why did the three of you jump me?"

"Stop. I don't want to fight. Can't we be friends?"

An elder man who lived in the building appealed to me. "Stop it now. Can't you see the boy just wants to be friends? He doesn't want to fight."

"But I do!" I blurted out in anger.

"Forget about it. It doesn't matter now. Shake on it, and move on" the man said.

In order to appease the man, the boy and I did as we were told. The boy's name was Hamza, and he became my first friend in Askerød. That was the beginning of a violent friendship.

The two other boys who had attacked me eventually befriended me as well, and shortly thereafter, I found my first real sense of community. Meanwhile, it became one of those communities that no society wants, and we became the kind of children who our parents just couldn't reach.

I started to resent my mother's goodness because I didn't feel that the world was consistent with what she told me. I didn't feel like we had anything to be thankful for, and I hate that part of my life because that's when I started being mean to her for not properly preparing me for the environment I was presently living in.

Hamza was fifteen. At home, he was beaten, and when he left the house, he loved to destroy things. He destroyed things when he was angry, when he was sad, when he was bored, and if you refused to join him on his destruction sprees, you were a wuss. I wasn't going to accept being called a wuss after enduring years of being berated by my father, so together, we wrecked and destroyed things. We smashed the store windows at the mall, we broke lampposts, and we trashed the youth clubs that denied us access.

We went on robbery sprees around the western suburbs of Copenhagen and used knives to cut up train seats. This was a daily operation. Ballerup, Rødovre, Glostrup, Hellerup, Lyngby—no town in the vicinity was spared. We simply went into a store, and while one of us distracted the shop assistant, our friends emptied the shelves and dumped the loot into their backpacks. We stole Mini-Discs, radios, LEVI's jeans, cameras. My boys learned how to use the pull tab of a can to break into most stores. At night, we broke into electronics stores and stole even more.

Even as teenagers, we were stone cold and devoid of mercy. Conscience was something other people had, and we convinced ourselves that because the world had dealt us all such an unfair hand, we had the right to do whatever the hell we wanted. The other kids in my class had nice clothes and cool stuff. They had MiniDiscs and listened to music when we went on field trips. I didn't have any of those things because we were poor, so I stole the things I wanted. We also just wanted to ruin things for the rest of the world. We wanted the system to pay. We felt that everybody was racist and that no one took care of us.

Sometimes, we got caught, and the shop assistants tried to chase us. But my boys and I were fast, willing and able to fight, below the age of criminal liability, and quite frankly, we didn't even care if we got caught. The first time it ever happened was at a mall in a neighboring town.

We were riding the trains and robbing shops. That day, we had been to Ballerup and all sorts of other places, and I thought to myself, *Why not go to Rødovre and steal some jeans?* Back then, these 501 jeans had just come out. I wanted a Champion jersey too because a guy named Peter had just stolen a green one. We thought it was dope, and we wanted a gray one. The police arrested us and took us to the station. But we were young boys, so they just drove us back home again.

I also went to visit my father at my mother's request. She wanted her children to remain in contact with him. In prison, my father had grown a big, bushy beard like a Taliban soldier, and he was bald. The first time I went to see him, I didn't utter a word. My hatred for the man was simply too intense. I thought about killing him like he had killed my family. We would never be able to celebrate Eid together, and I would never have his protection. I had already had my first beatings, but who was going to protect me when the person whose protection I desired the most was my own oppressor and abuser?

The second time, I finally spoke my piece. I asked: "How could you do it? *Why* did you do it?" I never got an answer. My father has never apologized or shown remorse for his actions on that day, and I have never forgiven him.

9

THE DANISH BASTARD

I n the mid-1990s, the bikers, the Greencoats, and the tough soccer hooligans on social welfare still ran Hundige. So, when my teenage gang wanted to resell their stolen merchandise, we had to go through them. This transaction happened at the Mall Pub, the neighborhood's main trade hub for stolen goods. My boys were small, and they were immigrants, so sometimes, we just got mugged and beaten.

The people who hung out at the pub were bikers and wannabe bikers, plus your standard drunks and local bodega boys. There were hardcore supporters of the soccer team Brøndby, too, and kids from a local gang called Red and White. Strong guys who liked to fight. They had an apartment where they sold weed, and back then, the cops used to call one of the streets in Askerød Pusher Street. It was a rough environment, and if you wanted to be left alone, you had to be strong. I didn't care about getting beat up, so I decided to be the one who talked back. That became my role: the guy who walked in front and the guy who took revenge.

When I was only fourteen, my worst enemy was a man named Tonny. He was in his early twenties, and everybody was afraid of him. Tonny was a member of Red and White. He was a big, ripped, strong guy who always walked around bare-chested and in shorts to show off his muscles. He knew karate and constantly kicked things to exhibit his strength. He kicked lampposts, signs, anything he could put a visible dent or a hole in. A lot of the time, he walked around with a hunting rifle in his hands. He was this white, wannabe Rambo. Tonny didn't care about anything. He just wandered around with his hunting rifle, threatening everyone who looked even remotely foreign. He was a very scary person.

Tonny would routinely kick my friends too and kicking me became a sort of sick ritual he performed every time he saw me. He would call me "Little *perker*," kick me in the back, then spit at me. He hated me because I talked back. At that time, I hated my life so much I didn't care. I wanted to die, and he was welcome to kill me. He didn't understand why this little shit didn't just shut up. He beat me up several times. A punch in the gut, a kick in the back, and a gob of spit in my face. Then I would run away, yelling, "Fuck you!"

One time, Tonny brought his hunting rifle. He said, "Tell all your *perker* friends that if I see so much as one *perker* in the street, he's getting a bullet." Then he fired a shot right above my head.

I got the point then: This wasn't a game. These people were dangerous. I ran and ran, and when I stopped and looked back after a while, he was still standing there, looking at me. "Didn't you hear what I just said?" he shouted.

But I shouted back, "Fuck you, you Danish bastard! You White motherfucker! Fuck you!"

A group of guys who were sitting at a laundromat heard me talking back to a grown man with a gun, and after that, I had earned my stripes in the immigrant community.

Tonny was the leader of the biker community in Askerød, and he had soldiers. Three of them were called Karate Karl, Jimmy, and Tiny. They were all in their twenties, and now they were after me. I took detours to avoid them, and one day, I walked above the train station to get around the pub where they hung out. But they had my route figured out and caught up with me at the parking lot.

They had been beating me regularly for years, but that day, they jumped and stomped on me. They didn't care that I was only four-teen. I was a punk who needed to be taught a lesson: no more talking back. They gave me a serious beating, and that episode turned me into a real thug.

I decided to get back at them, so I was going to wait for them to come out of the pub, good and wasted. Then I was going to beat them so hard they would never touch me again. I decided to go after Tiny in a way that everybody would hear about, and no one would ever forget.

A couple of nights later, one of my friends and I were ready. We had arranged for two younger boys to be on the lookout, and I was armed with a couple of thin but sturdy crowbars. My friend (whose name is being withheld) and I hid behind a couple of shopping trolleys and waited for Tiny. He was around twenty-five, a supporter of the local Nazi branch, and looked up to Red and White in Askerød. He was also a regular bar fighter and a soccer hooligan. I hated his guts.

I knew that at some point during the night, Tiny would leave the pub to buy weed from a big local dealer named Holger. Tiny would walk past the gas station, cross a lawn, and end up where I planned to attack.

Things went according to plan. I jumped Tiny and started beating him with the crowbars. The two younger boys and my friend were initially not supposed to take part in the assault, but in the end, they were all stomping on Tiny while I repeatedly hit him in an absolute rage. I kept hitting him in his head, and I didn't stop to think whether he would die or not. I didn't give a fuck. I *wanted* him to die. That would have served me better. I welcomed the idea because then it would all stop, once and for all. But I also kept hitting him because I wanted to be a hero. The neighborhood protector. The guy who was against everyone who attacked us in Askerød. The guy who beat down those who walked around shooting and calling us "fucking *perkere*" and "black scum." The guy who wasn't afraid to stand up to the bikers, the Greencoats, and the racists. I wanted to be that guy, and when I beat up Tiny, I was. They deserved it.

It added to my reputation as the fearless boy, the one who took revenge with a ferocity that bordered on outright insanity. Tiny survived without permanent injuries, and the police never knew about the incident. The rules of the street were obeyed. I had achieved my goal. My enemies saw me as a monster, and Tonny, Jimmy, Tiny, and Karate Karl never touched me again. I also learned a lesson: Violence works. Might is right. What is wrong to others seems right for me.

After beating up Tiny, I made a decision to be on the giving instead of the receiving end of the beatings. I only knew violence from my father, but in Askerød, beatings were everyday events. People would punch you, and if you didn't fight back, that made you an easy target for everyday ass whoopings. I didn't want to be that guy because nobody liked that guy. So, in order to be accepted, to gain recognition, I allowed myself to become evil.

In a world swarming with social outcasts, drunks, and junkies, there was enough easy prey to go around. The last Thursday of every month, the welfare recipients got their unemployment checks, and a lot of them went straight from the social security office to the Mall Pub. Here, I bided my time until they were adequately wasted, and then I struck.

None of those welfare recipients let their money stay in the bank. They took out every dime—1,000 or 1,200 kroner. So, when they staggered home, we mugged them. When they got drunk out of their minds, it was also easy to enter the pub and pick their pockets. We even stole from them when they were in the public toilets taking a dump. We waited till we knew they were sitting down, then we kicked down the door and took their clothes. They couldn't get up because they were afraid, they would shit on the floor.

But we didn't just go after the weak. We also mugged the strong biker types. When they were drunk and we had the numbers, they didn't stand a chance. We were assholes.

We made good money committing burglaries too. My friends and I would steal a car and prowl about Zealand, the island where Copenhagen sits. The Opel Kadett was the easiest to steal. I had a friend who could open and jump-start an Opel Kadett using only a teaspoon. Fords were easy too, but car makes like BMW and Saab were more difficult. On a regular night, we would roam around the residential neighborhoods until we found a car. It had to be well outside of Askerød so that the police would not automatically assume it was us. Normally, it took about two to three minutes to break in and jump-start a car. Then it was on to some provincial town.

For a while, we mainly went after specific jackets from clothing stores. They cost around 750 USD, and my friends and I could strip a store of all its jackets in only four minutes. Finding a buyer was easy. We knew where we could sell them. At the bars, you could always find buyers, and our friends and cousins wanted to buy too. We normally charged one-third of the original price. Eventually, everyone knew that we always had stolen goods.

The first night I stole some jackets, I filled my black trash bag with so many that I couldn't carry it all the way back to Hundige. Instead, I had to hide the bag in a bush and call up a Turkish guy who had a cousin who was willing to buy the whole lot. There were five jackets. The guy paid the equivalent of $600 total in kroner, which for a teenage boy was a lot of money.

10

YOU'LL BECOME A MURDERER

It was a school day in 1996, and I was in the seventh grade at Tjørnely elementary in Hundige. I was chasing a ninth-grader through the schoolyard. He was called Arab Tommy because he was of both Danish and Arab ancestry. I had a baseball bat in my hands and was trying to hit him with it because he had kept my classmates from playing basketball on the court, and as always, my classmates had turned to me for help.

I was always ready whenever a classmate needed help. I would beat up boys, I would even bully and threaten teachers. I was both the clown and the protector of the class, and I did anything to be popular. When I acted the hero, I felt accepted.

However, Hussein needed my help the most. Hussein was a small, weak, Arab kid who was always getting beat up by the older boys. He had money and could afford to buy food in the school cafeteria. They sold freshly baked buns along with chicken and turkey meatballs. I loved the food from the cafeteria, but I could never afford it, so I made a deal with Hussein and his friend Buster: I got food in exchange for their protection.

There was something cool about being the seventh-grader who protected his peers from the older boys, and on this day, I had just told Arab Tommy to get lost so my classmates could finally play basketball. He had responded by picking up a handful of small, red pomegranates from the ground and throwing them at me full force. That was when I started chasing him with a bat. I had already hit him several times in the back and was trying to land a head blow.

Arab Tommy was terrified. "You're crazy!" he yelled as he ran through the schoolyard and into the principal's office.

The vice principal's name was Harald, and when he saw me running toward his office with a bat, he managed to stop me. A few days earlier, I had thrown a rubber hammer at a teacher, and Harald had sent me to the school psychologist.

I felt condemned and I took it out on the psychologist. It wasn't constructive, if you ask me. She was just there to tell me how lost I was and how everything I did was wrong. She brought me these weird, colored, shrink pictures and asked me to interpret them: "What is this? What do you see here? What does this mean?"

It was like she was trying to make me look dumber than I was. I was furious because I was fully aware of the shitty situation my mom, my siblings, and I were in. I wasn't gonna let this shrink make me feel dumber or even more worthless than the world already did, so in the middle of the consultation, I pounded my fists on the table and shouted, "That's it!"

The psychologist lost her temper. "You'll become a murderer just like your father!" she yelled. I tuned her out immediately because I was determined to be nothing like him. Between Social Services, certain teachers that insisted I was a troublemaker, and a school psychologist who simply didn't like me very much, I was failed at every turn during my time attending that school. The incidents piled up until they finally washed their hands of me.

I got expelled from Tjørnely after three years there and was instead enrolled at Hundige Elementary. There, I had two teachers, Keld and Ulrik, but I didn't receive much education from them. We spent most of our time roller-skating or on Ulrik's boat, where he would drink. After walking him to his boat, he usually just let me go home.

As time went on, I attended fewer and fewer classes, and even though I was banned from the local mall, I would still hang out there, being a general nuisance to shoppers and shop owners. In the fall of 1996, things got seriously out of hand. I was so fucked up that everybody had given up on me, and my friends. Plus, they had made these new police regulations, which made things even worse for us. We were fined every time we went to the mall, so that got quite expensive. In the end, I was 75,000 Krone ($11,400) in debt just for mall violations alone.

I had become too much to handle, and the municipality decided to take action.

11

NORWAY

Two days into the new year of 1997, two officers approached me and told me to come with them. I complied.

I got in the car fully expecting to be taken to a meeting with Social Services. I had been out partying the whole night before and was so indifferent to everything that I actually fell asleep in the patrol car. The officers woke me up at Sank Annæ Square in Copenhagen, where the car was parked right in front of the Oslo ferry.

One officer got out and was greeted by two men. One of them was wearing green pants and a green, fleece jacket and looked like a proper G.I. Joe in camouflage. He was tall and dark-haired. The other one was short, chubby, and looked like a lazy general.

"Sleiman, get over here. There's someone I want you to meet," one of the officers said.

I had no idea what was going on, but I shook hands with the two military-looking men and followed them onto the ferry. Once we were all on board, the officers sat down in a lounge filled with red chairs and started discussing something with the two strangers. After a while, the two officers got up to leave, and I got ready to follow them.

"Where are you going? You're not coming with us. You're staying here," one of the officers said.

"Fuck no, I'm not staying here. I'm coming with you."

I then attempted to get off the ferry, but I was instead detained and got into a fight with the officers and the two strangers. The four of them cuffed me and locked me in a cabin. From the window, I saw the officers leave.

This is a bad joke, I thought to myself.

Soon afterward, the ferry left the dock. I was left with no other options, so I went to sleep. I later discovered the ferry ride took eight hours.

At the breakfast table the next morning, I soon realized that I wasn't the only abducted kid the ferry. There was another boy named Jens. Very few words were spoken when the ferry arrived in Norway, and the two men ordered us into an old Volkswagen Golf. They drove into the center of Oslo, where they bought thick socks, a warm sweater, and a blue jacket for each of us.

We left the city and drove through a dazzling, sunlit, Norwegian winter landscape complete with mountains, rivers, and lakes. No one uttered a word in the car, but I was boiling with rage and quietly contemplated how I would go about smashing the two men's heads in. If they were up to something, I was going to defend myself to the death. I truly had murderous thoughts. I had no idea what was going on and didn't ask.

We took a turn and drove up a mountain and into the forest, where we continued down a winding road. Eventually, the car stopped in front of a Norwegian cottage in the middle of a vast, white landscape called Feforkampen in the county of Jotunheimen. We all entered the cottage, where we were finally given a brief explanation as to what we were doing there. As I was stuck in a strange country by myself, there was little I could do except talk to the other abducted kids and get their stories so we could compare notes.

Jens had stabbed his mother. Later, he told me that she had always invited men over, who would get drunk, have sex with her, and beat them both up. One day, he decided that enough was enough and stabbed her with a knife. I honestly can't recall whether or not he killed her or merely injured her. His case was even worse than mine, and he didn't have anyone, no family, nothing. We never really bonded, but unlike me, he seemed happy to be there.

After Jens, it was my turn to talk to the two strangers who brought me there. One told me that I was suspected of being an errand boy for a group of drug dealers in Copenhagen and that the purpose of the abduction was to mentally cleanse me. They wanted to erase my past. In a calm voice, I was also informed that it meant I would never see my family again.

"What are you talking about? Of course, I'm gonna see my family again."

"You will never see them again in Denmark. Maybe they can visit you abroad once we're done with you. But you won't see your family again until you turn eighteen."

I absolutely refused to cry in front of them, but I couldn't hold it in forever. I just wanted to go to my assigned room. In there, I wept without making a sound because I didn't want Jens to hear me. *Is this the end of my life?* I thought to myself. How were my mom and my siblings supposed to live without me? I had a girlfriend. We were so young, there was no way she was going to wait for me.

I began to weigh my options. Should I run away? If I killed the two men, I would go to prison in Denmark, but then my family would be allowed to visit me. This was my actual thought process at that moment.

When I woke up the next morning, the two men finally introduced themselves. Their names were Hasse and Jørgen. They told me they were former special operations soldiers and that their job was to teach me how to survive in the mountains. I will never forget Hasse. He told me he had once been in a fight with Jean-Claude Van Damme. Apparently, when Van Damme was in the military, a fight had been arranged between Danish and Belgian soldiers.

Van Damme was my hero at the time. "Get outta here. You're full of shit. He would kick your ass any day," I told Hasse.

I also said that I wanted to see my family, but they made it clear that that was not going to happen. I wouldn't be given any money either. They would supply all of my food and clothing. They would also make sure I survived. I immediately wondered if it was possible to escape without killing them. "Watch out. I ain't scared of you," I said.

"That might be true. But we're in charge here," they said.

I attacked them in anger, but they ended up throwing me out into the snow. They told me "You can leave if you want to."

I sat in the snow. I refused to give in. I was determined to prove that I didn't need them. It was freezing cold, but my rage and stubbornness kept me warm. At one point, they tossed out some warm clothes for me. I put them on and went to the outdoor bathroom. I sat there for four or five hours until they came out and told me to come inside. Even the smallest concession was a sign of weakness in my world, so in my young mind, I had just won a battle of wills against these two tyrants. Of course, this pyrrhic victory left me sick for several days afterward.

There was a mountain in front of the cottage. I recall it being about three thousand feet high. One morning, Jørgen ordered me to run to the top of it. I ran halfway up the mountain, but then Hasse came out of the cottage.

"What the hell are you doing up there? Get down here. Who told you to run up there?"

"Jørgen did."

"Jørgen isn't in charge. I am. Did I tell you to do that? Why are you wearing so many clothes? Take them off. And you stay here till I tell you otherwise."

Hasse left and soon Jørgen returned.

"Why are you down here? Didn't I tell you to run up that hill! And who told you to take your clothes off? Put them back on and start running again."

I began to run back up the mountain. A little later, Hasse came out and ordered me to come back down. They pushed me around like that all day long until sunset. They kept at it for four months until they felt like they controlled me mentally. I started to forget my friends and family.

One day, when Hasse and Jørgen told me to sleep outside all night, I jumped them while armed with a knife. Since I was a child and they were two highly trained and experienced soldiers, the attack was unsuccessful. They forced me to dig a hole in the snow and handed me a sleeping bag as punishment. I learned that it was possible to sleep outside in minus thirty degrees Celsius weather while fearing for wolves and bears. It was a damn good sleeping bag. It covered everything except my face so I could breathe. It was completely sealed apart from that. And comfortable too. That might have been the best sleep I ever had. The night sky was completely clear, and I woke up fresh in the morning.

I also learned that you could climb a frozen waterfall with an ax and spiked shoes and cover twenty miles on cross-country skis in a single day. I got very fit. At fourteen years old, I weighed 163 pounds, and there was not a single ounce of fat on my body. I started feeling better and better.

One day, Hasse and Jørgen gave me a pat on the shoulder. "You have done well," they said. But I was still not allowed to go home. When I was done in Norway, they would send me to Eilat in Israel, where I would be taught how to dive.

They only allowed me one fifteen-minute phone call per week, but the one stipulation was I couldn't use it to call family. The only phone number I remembered was that of a girl named Ayse, a girl from Ishøj who had a crush on me. She was friends with a girl named Fatima, whom I had a crush on. I was allowed to give them my address, and they sent me back cigarettes and letters.

With the cottage came four huskies. They were called Anabol, Blixen, Bokser, and Lisa. In the beginning, I despised them all because they smelled like shit and barked like crazy and also because I had been afraid of dogs ever since bikers from Red and White had gotten a large German shepherd to chase me around Askerød when I was twelve.

As part of the mental and physical training program, I had to take the dogsled and go fill different food depots set out for cross-country skiers. I rode alongside Hasse and Jørgen, but once, I lost control of the sled and fell off while the dogs kept running. I thought Hasse and Jørgen would stop and come to my aid, but they kept going.

When I fell off the sled, I thought, *That's it. I'm fucked.* I wasn't sure whether or not they were keeping an eye on me, but it was minus four degrees Fahrenheit, or minus twenty degrees Celsius, so I hurried back to the cottage before the snow erased my tracks. I walked eight miles, and when I got back, the others were there, warm and cozy. Things get dangerous once we need to start measuring temperatures with Celsius instead of Fahrenheit.

I asked, "Why didn't you come get me? Why didn't you come back for me?"

"Why would we do that? You know how to take care of yourself. We taught you."

It was ski season, and there was a hotel nearby that was owned by a Danish family. I would help them in the restaurant and in the kitchen, where sometimes I had to peel ninety pounds of potatoes before dinner. The family was kind to me. They took me skiing, and I actually became quite skilled at both cross-country and slalom. Norway became my home, and I liked it there.

Come spring, the tourists left, and there was no more work for me at the hotel. Instead, I was supposed to go to Israel and learn how to drive. I had originally planned to contact my mother once my time in Norway was up, but three weeks before my departure to Israel, I was suddenly allowed to call her. "You've got fifteen minutes for your friends, and then you'll get another fifteen minutes for your mom," my caretakers told me.

When I called home, my mother was upset. "I'm leaving Askerød. Social Services said that I can have you back as long as I leave the municipality," she said.

"Don't do that."

"But I have to. I want you back. I miss you. I agreed to let them take you away so that they wouldn't kick me out. But I can't wait till you're eighteen." We both started crying.

After that, things were set in motion. My mother had reached out to one of the local shot-callers in Askerød, who had contacted a Norwegian attorney. The attorney put pressure on Greve Municipality to send me home. My mother might have agreed to let them take her son away, but surely not to a foreign country.

It is difficult to determine exactly what happened next. Several people from Greve Municipality remember my case, but the details surrounding my abduction have since become obscured. I'm fully convinced that Social Services officials feared that the project was in fact illegal and that they rushed me back before it came to public attention. René Milo—the mayor-elect at the time who later would become the most prominent political figure in Greve Municipality—remembers the case. He is unsure if what they did was legal.

The rumor was people were afraid to go to the mall because of me. They claimed that Christmas trade had come to a standstill, and the shop owners' union demanded action. Story goes it was a situation where a lot of citizens were uneasy, then the Social Services Board presented Milo with a solution which he accepted. I was to be removed. Can you believe that one person without superpowers could possibly deter people from holiday shopping? .

Greve Municipality has shredded the official documents from that time, in addition, they've attempted to reconstruct the course of events in an effort to cover their own asses.

So I was brought back to Denmark just as abruptly as I had been shipped off to Norway. I was informed that I had to be in Denmark within seventy-two hours, and I left with Hasse and Jørgen. When we arrived at Copenhagen Central Station, they said goodbye. No hugs or any other signs of affection were given when I departed.

Today, I have conflicting feelings about them. Sure, I grew to care about them in the mountains, but they were always rather cold. They had been hired to do a job, and the moment they said goodbye to me, it was as if all the time we had spent together meant next to nothing.

I also had mixed feelings about coming home. I was thrilled to see my family again, but my hatred toward Social Services was now full blown. These people hated me so much that they had sent me abroad and forced my own mother to abandon me so she wouldn't get evicted from her home with her three young daughters. My mom wasn't going to get me back if she didn't move away from the municipality. So, when I got home, my family was forced to move to a women's shelter.

Unfortunately, I wasn't allowed to stay at the shelter with them. Instead, I lived on the streets of Askerød. It was the only place where I knew anyone, and Social Services couldn't forbid me to roam the streets of the ghetto. I slept in basements, in friends' apartments, and, occasionally, out on the streets. Almost daily, I would meet up with my mother, who took the train from the shelter to Askerød with a packed lunch for me. We would meet at the train station, where she gave me my lunch, and then she went right back to Copenhagen. Her love knew no bounds, but in my stubbornness and anger, I never thanked her.

One of the things I feel most guilty about is how ungrateful I was to my mom when she lived at the shelter. One time, when she and one of my younger sisters came all the way from the city to see me and bring me a homemade sandwich, I just took the sandwich and told them to leave because I was eager to hit the streets with my boys. I didn't really think about all the things she did for me, and I completely ignored what she was going through because of me. Her only concern was to keep my belly full, and I was just being destructive and self-centered. It pains me to think about how she must have felt on the way back to be rejected by a son whom she did everything for. She is one of the greatest victims of my actions.

Nothing was gained for Greve Municipality. They had sent an angry, young, charismatic, love-hungry, fatherless, self-destructive teenager off to Norway, and in exchange, they had gotten the same teenager, only now he was burning with resentment too. At only fourteen years old, I was strong as an ox after four months of hard, physical military training, and I was now ready to wage war against everyone, René included.

12

THE FIGHT

Back in the mid-1990s, there was a youth club in the small town of Tune, which was supposedly filled with attractive girls. At least, that was what my friends and I had heard. We begged Bjørn Nielsen, who was head of their own local youth club, to let us go to a party there.

Apart from girls, Tune was full of tough guys who favored bikers over immigrant gangs. My friends and I knew this, but we insisted that we only wanted to have a good time and look at girls. Bjørn was persuaded. He talked to a colleague from Tune and vouched for his boys whom he really liked, especially me. He was convinced I was a charming boy whose reputation might have been a bit worse than he deserved solely due to name recognition. I was always the easiest to identify for one. I was the only Sleiman anyone knew so if anything went down, I was subject to an inquiry.

The night of the party was a bright, summer night, and the weather was beautiful. Bjørn bought pizza and soft drinks for the eight boys who showed up. Before we set off for Tune, he told us, "Listen up. I'm putting my reputation on the line here."

"Relax, Bjørn. Chill. We made a deal, and we're gonna stick to it. Tonight, we're just having fun."

But as soon we arrived, I sent the eternally provocative Arab Tommy over to the group of tough Danish boys. Tommy asked for a light in a way that was going to inevitably lead to a fight, and five minutes later, the party exploded.

The Danish guys were pretty hardcore, but they were up against more than they could handle, so they fled the party. So did the youth club employees. Besides Bjørn, there was only one adult who dared to interfere, so had to run around and grab guys up and get us out of there.

He managed to get us all onto the bus, and he was furious. He told us he'd be ridiculed everywhere for allowing the brawl to happen. We felt genuinely guilty and apologized profusely, but when we all got dropped off, Bjørn got the sense that we'd forgotten all about it and would do exactly the same thing if he gave us another chance.

Nothing unites people better than a common enemy, and when my crew was banned from all the local youth clubs after the Tune incident, the whole world became our enemy. It was us against the school, against the teachers, against the racists, the guards at the mall, the police, the municipality, the system, the youth club teachers. It was also us against the tabloids, the politicians, and Denmark as a whole. We firmly believed that anyone who was not with us was against us. When we could no longer hang out at the youth clubs, we just started attacking them. At the time, I felt that I was fighting for a just cause. I saw myself as a freedom fighter, fighting for myself and my friends. Individually, we were weak. But together, we were a force to be reckoned with.

There was a seventeen-year-old boy named Dennis who hung out at a youth club in one of the neighboring towns. He was half immigrant, half Danish. Braver than most, had a big mouth, and knew how to throw a punch. He told everyone that he was not afraid of the guys from Hundige, so they went to his club and beat him up. It was the same every time someone challenged us. My crew had grown from a core of about five guys to a real goon squad of about twenty, and the youth club teachers did not dare touch us. Most Danes were disgusted by the cowardliness when ten immigrant boys beat up a single victim. But to the Askerød boys, what the Danes considered dishonor was to us an expression of honor and unity.

When we first moved to these ghetto blocks, we were met by a lot of hatred. There were racists, Nazis, and nationalist Red and White gangs, so we had to stick together. If you got my back, I got yours, and suddenly, there are many of us helping one another out. And if someone refuses to help, he lets down the group. So, when he's suddenly the one who needs help, he can't ask for it. Without the group, you have zero status 'cause everyone else is against you. I can't give my brothers riches, but I can give them my word, and if that's worthless, then I'm nothing.

For my friends and I, "One for all and all for one" sounded grand and noble, but to the world around us, it resulted in raw, unscrupulous brutality. Perhaps the victim was alone, but from my peers' point of view, it was justified because in the bigger picture, *we* were the ones who were all alone.

Even in our early teens, this code became the foundation of my boys' lives. The same code the Mafia, blood-frenzied soldiers, some police officers, Hells Angels, Bandidos, and all criminal networks have always shared and in all layers of society. A code that states that you are the one who lets down the group if you refuse to participate in the thrashing of an enemy. The code that states that everyone must get their hands dirty. If you say no to a robbery, you can no longer be a part of the group because you can't share in the spoils. If the cops are after you, you can't snitch on your people. If you do, you've betrayed your own. The same rule applies if you testify in court. If your brothers need you to, you are expected to give false witness. If a witness needs to be threatened into silence, you must step up. I grew to have contempt for those who just stood back and watched while we got our hands bloody or those who always showed up three minutes late when a brother needed defending.

On one hand, I've gained the utmost respect for some of the criminals that the rest of society regards as the worst of their kind because they have stood shoulder to shoulder with me in the past in critical situations. In an amoral world, this code of brotherhood made me a very moral man.

We all know how thin the line between love and hate can be, and if you break the bond and try to leave the gang, then there's only hate left. "I love you" becomes "I hate you" because you betrayed me. You're no longer part of the family. You're the new enemy. If a mother suddenly tells her son that she doesn't love him anymore, then that son will never love his mother again. The same went for our brotherhood. The love we shared was stronger than the love we had for our own families. We had all seen how our families had failed to protect us. But we knew the streets, and we knew how to protect one another.

In that sense, the Askerød Boys, as we were called when we were younger, were just like any other immigrant gang in the country. We were teenagers who grew up to be members of the gangs that are now at war with one another. When immigrant groups are called the Askerød Boys, the Pladsen Boys, or the Tingbjerg Boys, it sounds more innocent than it is, but the names derive from fact that they grew up together. Often, they are also blood related. Unlike Hells Angels and Bandidos, who operate with ranks, spokesmen, and secretaries of arms, the immigrant groups have no formal hierarchy, nor do they have initiation rituals. They are just a bunch of young guys with roots in the same neighborhood who band together in loose structures.

Like myself, some grow up to be hardcore felons, while others are just part-time criminals. Some buy stolen goods and marijuana; others are just friends who hang out without committing crimes. The latter is not part of the brotherhood. They merely circulate in the periphery and do not have to get their hands dirty to smoke weed and hookah with the others. Then there are the younger brothers who look up to the older ones. Some end up choosing a different path, and some become part of the inner circle. These boys are usually between twelve and fifteen years old and can be summoned quickly if needed.

I'm a stateless Palestinian, and we were strongly represented in Askerød. No ethnic group in Denmark has a more violent, traumatic, and criminal track record than the stateless Palestinians. Their parents, with only few exceptions, live in refugee camps before they come to Denmark, and even though Palestine is far away, the never-ending war with Israel plays a significant role in the environment.

Ghetto Outlaws is a gang based in a suburb of Copenhagen and has at times been a close ally of mine and at others a sworn enemy. Today, I don't harbor any hate for Jews or Israel. But the hatred still lives in the heart of many of my acquaintances, and in the bigger picture, Israel is still an enemy to them.

Those of us who were of Palestinian descent probably felt even more alienated than the others. We have no state, you know. We're not accepted anywhere in the world. Who are we? Are we Palestinians? Apparently not. Are we Danes? Nope, not that either. But then, who are we? It may be difficult for Danish people to relate to the idea of being rejected because of their heritage. How it feels to only be partially admitted into a society where you want to be. A society where you belong, but at the same time don't belong. I mean, I'm physically present here, but no one recognizes me and my struggles. No one wants to help me. So, what can I do to make people listen to me and acknowledge my presence?

I can stir shit up and create chaos. If we create enough chaos, then the rest of Denmark will take notice. Then you'll hear us and feel our presence. We may get bad publicity, but you'll be paying attention, and as long as we're hurting, so are you. 'Cause when you see shootings and violence in the streets, it's not just our reality. It's your reality too. As a stateless Palestinian, you must create your own identity, so a lot of us joined a gang.

My personal idol was American rapper Tupac Amaru Shakur. Tupac was incarcerated multiple times, and he rapped about despair in the city, racism, social issues, and conflicts between the East Coast and West Coast rappers. Tupac was fearless. He lived fast and died young when he was gunned down in Las Vegas at the age of twenty-five in 1996.

He said the things I always wanted to say. Like how the politicians had money to fight wars in the Middle East but couldn't afford to help us living in Askerød. I felt like I lived in a war zone. Even if there were no shootings back then, my friends and I were at war.

The older guys in Hundige who had been failures at school, were unemployed, and were headed for a life of crime, also passed on their sense of victimhood to my generation. Everything was somebody else's fault. Our older brothers told us that there was no place for us in society, that the Danes hated us, and that they didn't want to give us an education or a job, so we might as well become criminals. I know that Danes talk about how we just blame everyone but ourselves, but there's a difference. If you're an immigrant from the ghetto who wants to be somebody, the odds are stacked against you. You can try and convince yourself that it ain't like that, but it is.

The Askerød Boys were also at war with the police. Back in the early 1990s, police officers and firefighters who tried to enter Askerød had to dodge a hail of flying rocks. They had never experienced that before. There are few countries in the world where the public has as much confidence in the police force as is the case in Denmark. But for my friends and I, that confidence was long gone. Just like we weren't welcome anywhere, the police weren't welcome in Askerød. They represented a society that we hated and that hated us. Normally, we would talk nice and quietly with the cops, but if they disrespected us, then they didn't deserve our respect either. We weren't scared of them, and the more we showed our contempt for the society that we felt alienated from, the cooler we were in one another's eyes.

We have much less faith in the law than you guys do. We believe the police force is corrupt. We believe they cover up for one another. We believe they lie. When Turkish national Ekrem Sahin was killed in custody in Denmark back in February 2011 because officers sat on top of him and put him in a leg lock, they said it was cardiac arrest. That's bullshit, and it was revealed by a tape recording and by English coroners. That just confirms what we already knew. You can't trust the cops.

Despite the fact that great uncertainty surrounds the circumstances of his death, the Sahin case has been closed, and no officers have been charged. But in my world, this is just more proof that everyone isn't equal in the eyes of the law. I don't despise all police officers, and I know that they aren't responsible for the crimes I've committed in the past. But I've had run-ins with the law where I believe the officers were out of line and provoked me in a way that inspired hatred instead of trust.

Strange as it may sound, one of the officers I respected was one who beat me. I once had a Polish girlfriend named Fransizka. She lived in a neighboring town, and I had stolen a moped so I could drive her back and forth in the name of gallantry. Fransizka loved that I was a bad boy.

One day, as I was driving her home, I realized the police were chasing us. "Get off!" I shouted.

Fransizka jumped off while I continued down a tunnel, trying to escape into Askerød. The patrol car following me sped up and grazed the rear wheel of the moped, causing me to fall off. The officer got out of the car and ran toward me.

"You're not running from the police, are you?" he yelled and hammered his torch into my stomach.

"Ow, for fuck's sake!"

"Get outta here. But if you ever run from me again, I'll kick your ass."

"Okay," I said and went right up the block and stole a bike so I could take Fransizka home. He was a respectable man. Old-school cop. He was in his fifties, and we were only fifteen, but he was all right.

13

THE ASSAULT

On the streets of Hundige, we had an associate known as Baloo. It was a fitting nickname because he was six feet six, two hundred and eighty pounds, black-bearded, strong, and good-natured like the bear from the Disney movie. Baloo wasn't a stickler for the rules and didn't take any shit. His real name was Peter Laurents.

One afternoon in 1997, he was at work as an SSP representative at a local youth club located inside the mall in Hundige. SSP stands for School, Social Services, and Police and comprised a group of outreach street workers who dealt with the toughest kids in their respective areas. They were a buffer between the system and the disenfranchised youth that always answered to and reported back to the authorities.

On that day, Baloo saw a terrified boy running full speed through the front door of the mall and into the club. I was one of the five guys who were right on his heels, but Baloo managed to step in and block the door just before we got in. I was in front, looking up at Baloo. I was no more than fifteen years old and five feet eight, but when I realized that Baloo was going to use his superior size to keep us from entering, I went ballistic.

Baloo hung on to the doorframe and blocked the door while we pushed him. Once I started realizing we weren't getting in, I jumped up and headbutted him. I guess my reputation has been earned.

Throughout the 1990s, Peter was one of the social workers who put his personal safety on the line in a neighborhood where a group of around fifty kids, almost always led by me, stole and vandalized their way through their teenage years. Within Social Services and the school system and among the street workers, the name Sleiman was well-known. Since Baloo also personally worked on my case, he had in-depth knowledge about me back when I was a short-fused, headbutting teenager.

Peter remembers some interesting moments where I showed him a different side of myself. One night, he was walking around the local train station with a police officer. The officer was there to check on a group of boys who were reportedly causing trouble around the station area. The situation escalated. Suddenly, the usual game of cops and robbers was reversed, and the police officer was being chased around the station by a large group of boys.

We really didn't like that particular cop, and the atmosphere was tense. It could have gotten completely out of hand, and they were debating whom they could call for backup or pondering how fast they could run. At the last moment, I stepped in and made the mob stand down. I told them not to touch the cop with Baloo 'cause Baloo was cool with me. The guys were pissed but we all avoided any further issues with the authorities so I saw it as a win-win.

With Baloo on board, the municipality established a workshop, which the young men were supposed to help run daily. After what was once a promising start, the boys eventually began to vandalize the place, and he was forced to ban them from the workshop. He was supposed to be their ally, but instead, he became the subject of their rage. They slashed the tires on his car, and when he got new ones, they slashed those too. This happened four or five times. Once, flammable liquids were thrown into the workshop.

I wasn't involved, but my group was. Someone was supposed to stay in the workshop at night, taking turns guarding the place, but eventually, the politicians thought it was too risky and didn't want to take responsibility for the consequences. They were afraid that someone would get hurt.

The street workers refused to give up and approached my boys' parents to tell them that their sons were headed down a bad path. Unfortunately, they didn't have sufficient knowledge about the culture in these families' households because this only made the boys despise them even more.

Suddenly, these boys had to answer to their bewildered fathers, who didn't know any better than to beat them when they came home. The truth is that many of the fathers in Askerød were ill prepared to parent in the fashion that their sons needed. They didn't speak Danish, they weren't integrated into anything, so they were ashamed to face Social Services. At the same time, they were furious that the authorities dared to criticize their sons as it reflected on their failure to keep them in line. So, the boys got slapped around, and a lot of them even got their heads shaved so the community could see how badly they had behaved.

The gang culture is a brotherhood and we got our opinions from the brotherhood and not from our fathers. The truth is the street workers failed by not familiarizing themselves with our culture our how things worked with us before they acted. As a result, the boys ended up seeing the street workers as traitors as opposed to our allies.

Baloo refused to accept the boys' reign of terror and started touring the local schools, encouraging the other youths not to be afraid of me and my crew. His message was: "Don't let them bully you. That will only empower them more than they deserve. They're really not that dangerous."

From my crew's point of view, our former buddy and confidant was now going around the city belittling them and calling them soft. This made them feel even more alienated, and they focused their hatred on Peter. The police told him to be very careful. According to their information, there was now a bounty on his head. Allegedly, the price was $3,000.

If I had to describe my situation with one word, it would be *desperation*—a desperation that resulted from being caught up in something he really didn't want to be a part of.

Here's the thing: I wasn't the leader of the Askerød crew, but many people thought so because I always appeared to lead the way. Just like any soccer team wants the best players to join them, all the criminals in the suburbs of Copenhagen wanted me on their team. I loved being needed and in demand. I was willing to play ball. I wanted to climb the ladder and I wanted everyone to know who I was. And I succeeded at it. In the process, I earned a reputation as the worst of the rotten apples.

One day, I was sitting in court because of a fight I had been in. I wasn't the only offender, but I tried to take the fall for the others because I was the only one under the age of fifteen, and therefore I couldn't be punished.

"You are of no use to me," the judge said.

Instead, one of the other boys who had already turned fifteen was convicted. After that, his parents forbade him to hang out with me. The other boys' fathers soon followed suit. Even though I was the youngest of the lot, the parents believed that I was the bad influence on everyone else. I was heartbroken, and once again, I felt misunderstood. All I wanted to do was live up to the code of the streets and be a stand-up guy. I wanted to be the hero. That was why I had tried to take the blame in court. However, the immigrant parents in our community didn't consider me to be hero material. Sleiman was a pariah in their eyes.

If my friends and I had to pass through the mall, they would go around it without me 'cause if their parents caught them hanging out with me, they would beat them when they came home. They weren't allowed to hang out with the butchered woman's son. They saw me as the bad guy, but to me, we were all the same. We were all troublemakers. We would pick a fight with whomever we could. We would bust windows, trash clubs, and beat up anyone who got in our face.

I was only fifteen when Hundige started to become too small for me. In the neighboring city of Ishøj, the immigrant community was older than in Hundige, the criminals were more established, and I befriended some of the older guys. They taught me to smoke pot, do drugs, go to nightclubs, and terrorize downtown Copenhagen. I began to carry knives and used broken bottles as weapons.

Like in most other places, the Danes controlled the marijuana trade in Ishøj. In the mid-1990s, it was the influential criminal known as The Fox who called the shots. My crew thought The Fox had too much power, and when some of his soldiers beat up one of my new friends, we decided it was time to take action. At the time, I didn't know exactly how powerful The Fox was, but if my friends were at war, so was I, and in my haste to be the hero, I was ready to confront The Fox on their behalf.

One night, me and three guys from Ishøj went to The Fox's apartment. We rang the doorbell and said we wanted to buy some weed, so The Fox let us in.

He asked, "What do you want?"

"To buy weed."

"Hmm."

"Did you just have this guy beat up?" I asked and pointed at my friend.

The Fox just looked at us with a cold expression in his eyes. We were smaller, but I was not afraid. One of his soldiers was in the apartment, and The Fox probably never imagined that an immigrant boy he had never even seen before would smash him over the head with a full bottle of wine.

"Bring it on," he said.

I took a full step back before I slammed the bottle right in his face at full force. The Fox went down. My crew grabbed bottles as well, and before The Fox's soldier had time to react, he too was on the floor. We threw furniture at them. Next, we emptied the apartment of marijuana, cash, and anything else of value. We left the place covered in blood and wine with two grown men lying on the floor humiliated and beaten beyond recognition.

Later that evening, we rampaged through Copenhagen. There were four or five of us, and we randomly bumped into people on purpose. We went after anyone who looked the slightest bit tough. If anyone so much as told us to watch out, they got a beating. That night, I earned my respect in Ishøj. But I also lost my last shred of innocence. We were like animals.

During the rampage, we of course avoided women and men walking with their families because even hoodlums have a code. And although I continued to spiral out of control and became increasingly violent, I developed a code of decency toward girls, which made them feel comfortable in my company. I couldn't rationalize treating women the same way some in the community treated my sisters. Defending them and my mother's honor is partly what led me down this path in the first place.

One of the girls remembers some of the nice things I would do for her. Her name was Thessa. Today, she is in her forties and works as a kindergarten teacher. She is a petite, attractive woman with red hair. She grew up in a middle-class residential neighborhood, but she was always drawn to the wild life. When she was fifteen, she and her friends dated hardcore criminals from Copenhagen. Some of the leaders belonged to an influential, criminal Pakistani family whose male members were in their late twenties. They were highly regarded in the immigrant community, and even though they were not from Hundige, they hung out at the local nightclub.

Thessa thought hanging out with us was exciting. She got presents and was treated like a princess with free booze and VIP access. She was suddenly around older guys who had money and would buy the entire front row at the premiere of a movie just to show off.

Eventually, Thessa began to seek out local boys her own age. One day, four Audis pulled up in Hundige, and the men from the Pakistani family jumped out. They stared at Thessa and the boys.

"Who's in charge here?" one of them asked.

I stepped up as the junior gang leader because I always took responsibility and initiative. The men took Thessa and I aside and said, "Listen, Thessa used to chill with us. Now she's hanging out here, and if that's her wish, then fine. But you can't let anything happen to her. She has to be treated really nice, and that's your responsibility."

I accepted that responsibility. It was a violent environment, and I never wanted women to feel unsafe when I was around.

She hung out with us for a couple of years and saw a group of boys who were out of control. We would hang out in front of the mall and smash shop windows with rocks, but not to steal. Vandalism was merely a way to kill time.

Jens Frederik Rossen was also a prominent figure in Hundige in the mid-1990s, and he became one of my enemies during the early years. When Jens Frederik was young, he thought his family was rich. His father owned several establishments at an amusement park, and Jens Frederik lived with his parents in a big house in an upper-class neighborhood.

But behind the pretty facade, there was alcohol and violence, and a life-shattering event that occurred when he was eleven years old. One day in 1986, a van pulled into the driveway of the villa, and a group of men started emptying the house

At the same time, Jens' father just disappeared and no one's seen him since. Story goes he owed 6 million kroner in taxes. The police never found him.

While his mother drowned her sorrows in alcohol, she once left Jens Frederik alone for ten straight days without a word. He reacted by banding together with a group of boys who all had similar stories.

They formed a community that always had each other's backs and developed gang-like habits like beating people up and engaging in vandalism.

If we were *perkere*, then Jens Frederik and his friends were white trash. Without being a sworn member, he started hanging out with two different Hundige-based gangs called Psycho Kids and Power Team. He hung out with the leaders of the worst gangs. He had other people do the burglaries, while he had a knack for selling the goods. They had apartments where we sold the loot from, but Hundige Mall was the center of their criminal enterprise.

Jens Frederik and his friends all became kickboxers. They were strong, ruthless, and didn't allow anyone to challenge their dominance in Hundige. A local pub at the mall was considered their spot, and it was there that they traded their stolen goods.

In the mid-1990s, a wave of immigrants started moving to Hundige, settling in Askerød and another housing project called Gersager Park. My friends and I were among them, and we all started hanging out at the pub when we were teenagers.

To Jens, it was simply them against the *perkere*. White versus black. Up until that point, they had been running things, but the immigrants steadily grew in numbers. Jens Frederik saw a bunch of Arabs, and it recognized that we had the potential to become a strong and dangerous group. I was the leader: considered the craziest, the wildest, and the most violent. Every time there was trouble, I was always ready. They would never openly admit that they were scared of us. Even though they were older, I knew they were.

One act of revenge succeeded the other in a conflict that could almost be defined as a race war. One time, my gang caught and severely beat Jens Frederik in a tunnel. Another time, his crew caught me off guard and returned the favor. One night, when Jens Frederik was standing in line outside a nightclub, I stood right behind him. It was a peculiar relationship in many ways. In times of peace, Jens Frederik and I would sit and talk to each other almost as if we were friends. Even though we saw each other as enemies most of the time, he also knew that my crew would always leave him alone if he was with a girl. You gotta have a code. But when he was alone, he could never let his guard down.

There were unwritten rules that were never violated, and in a strange way, we respected one another. But that night, in front of the club, the respect was gone, and we got into an argument. He turned his back on me, so I immediately struck him in the back of the head with a bottle. He was wearing a baseball cap, and the bottle went through, slicing his skull.

Some of Jens Frederick's guys pinned me against the wall and beat me up until I passed out. Sounds crazy to you, but for us that was just a routine night at the club.

Today, Jens Frederick is in his early sixties, and after a life that accumulated three hundred criminal charges, four convictions for assault, and acquittal of murder, he now has a clean criminal record and runs a successful clothing company. Seems for some there is hope after gang life after all?

14

THE FIRST CONVICTION

In Denmark, certain detention centers are called "secure institutions," which means they have a fence around them. They have various names and are located all over the country, meant for young people who are supposed to serve jail time but are too young to be incarcerated with adults. In the mid-1990s, young people with Middle Eastern backgrounds began to dominate the population of these institutions, and I was among the first generation of second-generation immigrants who inhabited them.

After the assaults on Baloo, Greve Municipality sent me to The Pinecone, a secure institution located in Jutland, about two hundred miles from Hundige that was given its name due to it being surrounded by nothing but pine trees as far as the eye could see. There, I befriended Wasim, who was from Denmark's second-largest city, Århus. He was seventeen, and while I only smoked weed, Wasim was addicted to smoking heroin and determined to become a career criminal.

After a week at The Pinecone, we didn't feel like staying there any longer. When the inmates were called to dinner, we jumped the fence and ran through fields, mud, and forests. We had absolutely no idea where we were going. When we finally came to a small town, Wasim said, "Let's steal an Opel Kadett."

Wasim also knew the trick of starting a car with a teaspoon, and luckily, he had brought one with him. Even though neither of us had a driver's license, we drove the Opel to Århus. There, I found myself with Wasim in an apartment. It turned out to be a drug den where five grown men smoked heroin and were high in a way that made me realize off the bat that I couldn't stay there much longer.

The next day, Wasim went to see his father, who had settled in Århus with his new wife after being released from prison. My father had family in the city, and they had all sided with him after the attempted murder of my mother and Sarah. While my father was incarcerated, he and my mother had spoken, and he had asked her if there was any chance she would take him back, but Sarah and I had objected.

He kept insisting that he couldn't remember exactly what had happened, but we refused to believe him. He wasn't willing to own up to his crime, and we weren't going to take him back. I had no contact with him, but it was still a love-hate relationship. I still hate my father for all the times he beat me, for what he did to my mother, my sister, and my life. At the same time, I love my father because I will always long for the good father of my early childhood before my grandmother poisoned his mind against his own family. I was suddenly a fugitive in a strange town with nowhere else to go. After all he had done in the past, my father owed me.

"I thought you were in jail?" my father said, surprised to see me.

"I was, but I ran away."

"What can I do to help you?"

"I need money so I can get home."

"But they'll just arrest you again."

"If you don't wanna help me, I have no choice but to go stay with the junkies," I told him.

He had just been released from prison and didn't want to risk going back for aiding in his son's escape, but he relented and gave me the cash I demanded from him.

I went home to Hundige, lived on the streets, and resumed my war against the youth club by stealing computers and stereos with my people. We just went inside and took the stereo right off the wall. There were so many of us and we were so aggressive and determined that the employees didn't even dare to intervene.

This time, Greve Municipality chose to send me to Jutland with a personal escort to live with Sarah and her husband. A few years earlier, Sarah had found herself a big, strong, good-humored man from Lebanon. His name was Karim, and he was about ten years older than she. He had been part of the countless wars between feuding militias and had come to Denmark in 1990. After a long stay at a Danish refugee camp, he had come to Jutland and met Sarah in a neighboring city where he was attending a family meeting. Sarah fell in love. She was a bright and beautiful girl who wanted to leave the hell she called home behind.

After our father had tried to murder our mother, Sarah isolated herself from other people. She didn't want to stay at the women's shelter with our mother. She was kicked out of foster care, and when the family moved to Askerød, she also wanted to escape. All this time, Karim had been on her mind. One day, his phone rang.

"Hey. It's Sarah. How are you?"

"I'm all right."

One year later, they got married. She was only sixteen and he was twenty-six when they moved in together in Jutland. There was nothing arranged about the marriage. Unlike when our father had attempted to marry her off years before, this was Sarah's choice. Now the young couple were tasked with having to take care of me.

One summer day, Karim and his buddies took me to the beach with them. One of Karim's friends got into an argument with a Danish guy, who had flipped them off and shouted, "Fuckin' *perkere!*" at them. Karim grabbed a baseball bat from his car and gave the guy a couple of whacks across the legs. That was it. But I was in the car trembling with rage. *They call that a beating?* I thought.

I jumped out of the car, ran to the beach, and hopped onto a big rock, which put me in the perfect position to kick the man directly in the face. Once the guy went down, I started stomping on him.

"What the hell are you doing? There's no reason to beat him like that. You're gonna have to go back home," Karim said.

Once again, I had ruined it for everyone else by taking things too far. I had been raised to earn love and friendship by proving my loyalty with violence. I thought the way to show my family that I was willing to do anything for them was by beating that guy up. But when they sent me away, it just confirmed the feeling I had of being unwanted everywhere. Because of my actions, a couple of family members went to jail, so I destroyed a friendship while trying to reinforce it.

The Danish dude got beaten up, but nothing serious. Karim got six months' probation because of it and I was once again in the crosshairs of the Danish prison system.

In the meantime, the real Danish prisons were waiting for me. One day in 1997, when I was fifteen, I was kissing a girl at the mall. If you remember, I had been banned from entering Hundige Mall, so one of the local officers told me to leave the premises immediately. I told the officer to chill and went into a supermarket, hoping the cops would be gone by the time I came back outside. Instead, the officers had put one of my friends, Bilal, in handcuffs. Next, they forced him to the ground, where they beat him with their batons.

"He's in handcuffs. Stop hitting him," I said.

"Stay out of it. It's police business."

"I don't care if it's fuckin' police business. Leave him alone or deal with me!" I responded.

"Get lost."

I attacked the policemen, they turned to deal with me instead, and I punched one of them in the face. This gave Bilal the opportunity to escape. The police instead focused their attention on me, the infamous Sleiman. I ran into the supermarket, where I was eventually caught, arrested, and charged with assaulting an officer on duty. At the same hearing for that offense, I was also charged in another case.

To this day, I don't know exactly why I ended up in prison because I was only fifteen years old at the time. It was more of an adventure than a punishment. I was suddenly surrounded by real, grown-up criminals. I was fed three times a day and had all the time in world to work out. Aside from storing the inmates, the prisons have become training camps for gang members, who go in and build bodies that make them even better equipped to beat people up when they get out. I was no exception. I worked out and did pushups and sit-ups to build my strength so that I would gain respect when I finally got out. The training camp worked. After a month in prison, I was once again fitter and even better suited for combat than I had ever been before.

While I did time, Bilal sued the officers who had handcuffed him. A hearing was held in my case, but now that the officers were being sued in a different case that was connected to mine, they chose not to testify. A possible conviction of the officers could take years, and this meant my original case could not be settled. The judge said he didn't want a fifteen-year-old boy to spend two years in jail with adult offenders. He thought that the month that I had already served was enough, so I was released right away.

15

ANNA

The first time I met the great love of my youth was at Nicoline's apartment, where a bunch of us were meeting up to drink tea and smoke weed. Nicoline was seventeen and had recently given birth to a little girl whom the father refused to acknowledge. When I arrived, Arab Tommy was threatening to beat a girl up and calling her a whore.

"What the fuck are you doing, Tommy? It's a girl. What the hell, man!" I said to him as I shoved him.

The girl's name was Anna. I thought she was hot, but I had no idea who she was. She fled into the apartment, and I managed to put Arab Tommy in his place. He had told his friends that he and Anna were dating, but Anna had denied it, so Arab Tommy had publicly lost face and was angry about it.

Today, Anna is married and lives in a house with a picket fence. She works as a kindergarten teacher and has two children with a good man. She is a slender woman of forty-three with brown hair and a quiet, pretty face. The night we met, she had not been expecting any drama. Nicoline's baby girl was sitting on a friend's lap when a group of immigrant boys suddenly entered, and one of them slapped the girl with the baby on her lap.

Arab Tommy and his crew were standing outside the apartment and wanted Anna to come down, but she felt really, really threatened so she refused to go outside which made them furious. I offered Anna that I could smooth things over for her, went outside and calmed things down with Arab Tommy's crew by explaining how the entire situation made them look. I made him apologize to Anna and after brokering peace, the rest of the night was without incident.

We didn't see each other for the next couple of years. Anna got a boyfriend, and when we met at the mall, we would just say hello, but I was captivated by her

Anna worked as an assistant kindergarten teacher, and when the two of us met at the mall at the close of 1999, we got to talking about our jobs. Anna still had a boyfriend, but a couple of days later, she called me up and asked me if I wanted to go for pizza. I said yes.

When I saw her at the restaurant, we began to catch up. I asked her what her boyfriend thought about us having pizza together. She said that he should mind his own business because she was allowed to have friends. She told me that she was sick of her boyfriend because they weren't evolving together, and then she asked me to walk her home.

Outside her house, I hugged her and gave her a kiss on the cheek. It felt like the right thing to do, and she didn't object. We didn't see each other for a while after that, but then she called me up and told me that she had broken up with her boyfriend.

A couple of days later, she invited me over for dinner. Mid-dinner, she told me that she thought there was love between us. Did I feel it too? I did. I kissed her, and we started dating. I couldn't believe my luck. What the hell did she want with a guy like me? What did I have to offer? I just figured she was in it for the sex and thought, *All right, if that's what she's looking for, I'm happy to oblige.* But I couldn't believe she actually liked me. She was nineteen and I was seventeen, but I pretended to be twenty-one because I figured she wouldn't have anything to do with me if she knew how young I was.

Anna was from the nice residential neighborhood in Greve, and I became a regular visitor at the house. Unlike Sally's stepfather, Eddie, who loathed immigrants and represented my only experience with Danish homes so far, Anna's parents were hospitable and had a different perspective. Her dad was a very open-minded person who had worked around the world as a construction engineer. He wasn't judgmental in any way, and he never said a foul word to me, even though he had heard all sorts of things about me.

Anna had not expected a guy like me to walk into her life, but she thought I was sweet, charming, and good-looking. Who was I to argue?

Anna was completely oblivious to my criminal behavior. She knew I was involved in something, but she thought of it as more along the lines of boyish pranks that my friends and I happened to get into from time to time. I wasn't going to correct her.

16

THE SMASHED-UP HOTEL

Everyone has a story about their favorite teacher. Maybe you've been lucky enough to have one. One who listened and understood, even though you were completely hopeless in school, and recognized there was another space or field you excelled in. One who was like a breath of fresh air and turned what would otherwise be sleep-inducing lessons in the classroom into delightful recesses on long, dark winter days.

World-renowned literature and films have been created about a life-changing teacher. Great teachers abound in world history, inspiring great men and women alike. There are countless stories about those beloved teachers, social workers, or coaches who used their unique social talents to break through to the seemingly unreachable and turn children many considered monsters into men and women.

In the 1967 classic film *To Sir, With Love*, Sidney Poitier delivered one of his most memorable performances as an unemployed engineer who takes a teaching job in a rough neighborhood in London's East End, where the students are dead set on making his life a living hell. Portier faces the challenge head-on by treating the students as young adults as opposed to treating them like animals. In 1995's *Dangerous Minds*, Michelle Pfeiffer also took on the role of the teacher who makes a difference by seeing her young inner-city students of various ethnic backgrounds who grew up in a proverbial war zone as human beings. In 1989's *Dead Poets Society*, Robin Williams plays a teacher who arrives at an American all-boys boarding school and replaces the strict, borderline-military discipline culture with poetry and encourages them all to seize the day.

In Hundige, that person's name was Birger Mosholt. When the municipality of Greve called him up in 1998, he had received almost every accolade a social educator could accumulate. He had started his career as a library attendant at the Library of Freedom in Avedøre back in the 1970s. There, he spent most of his time kicking out the Greencoats and aspiring bikers who ran around with leather jackets and bicycle chains, tearing up everything they could get their hands on. He was a tall, gangly kid who soon realized that if he kept on throwing them out, it was only a matter of time before they would seek retribution. He decided to be proactive and set up a room in the basement where they could all hang out and invited them in. This action marked the beginning of a controversial and remarkable career.

Birger felt that if no one talks to us or wanted to develop a relationship with us, we'd become even more dangerous. Birger disapproved of our criminal behavior and our violence, but he first wanted to get to know more about us as people.

Birger established The Octopus in Avedøre, which became a famed project where troubled youths could come and develop the kind of relationship with adults that they didn't have with their own parents. He became known as the father of all the Danish, halal-hippie social educators, but his efforts paid off. Crime went down in Avedøre, Birger became the leader of SSP in Hvidovre, and he was considered one of the country's trailblazing social educators. In 1996, he was given the Peter Sabroe Award for his work.

At this time in his life, Birger decided to start a career as a private consultant. Even though he had been a successful consultant, he was tired of the time-consuming municipal system and wanted to be his own boss. Shortly after he quit his job in Hvidovre, Greve called up Birger and said they needed him. They had lost control of the young people in Hundige, and Mayor René Milo wanted Birger to help. The municipality was ready to give him anything he wanted if he accepted the post. He would be the leader of the SSP collaboration, he could bring in his own team of educators, and since the local politicians were keenly aware that something extraordinary was needed to save Hundige, he was offered a high salary. Financial resources were also guaranteed for the project. He wasn't sure the system would back his methods, as they ran counter to the ones already in place, but in Greve, they assured him they were sure. For that reason, Birger accepted.

By this time, I had become a household name in social educational circles, and Birger was familiar with the mythical, violent monster who took revenge on his foes by lighting cars on fire and thrashing his way through the mall and youth clubs. I sounded like the tales people told about conquering warlords who marauded and pillaged towns in dusty, old history books. Mind you, I was still a teenager.

One of the first things Birger and his two trusted coworkers, Tom and Kim, did, was talk to the young people. He believes that it paid dividends immediately. Birger trusted them, and they trusted him. Crime rates began a steady decline, and one of Birger's greatest personal triumphs was when he got a boy named Samir an apprenticeship as a mechanic.

It took a while before he got the chance to talk to me, but one day when Birger arrived for work at the youth administration, he was told that I was already waiting in his office. Again, I prefer to be proactive and take initiative.

Birger came into his office, and to the best of his recollection, our conversation went like this:

"Hi."

"Hi."

I was sixteen at the time but had the attitude of a seasoned biker. "You're Birger."

"Yes, and you're Sleiman."

"That's right, and I've heard you've helped some of my friends. You're welcome to do that."

"Why, thank you. It's very nice of you to grant me permission to do my job."

"But there's something you need to know."

"Yeah?"

"You need to stay away from me. Don't try to help me."

"Why not?"

"Because I've met too many guys like you. Teachers and social workers and staff who talk a lot. But I'm not gonna be taken for a ride by a bunch of people who's all talk, so you just stay away from me."

"Let's just talk about this first."

We started talking because even though Birger saw what was a hardened gangster on the outside, he simultaneously saw a boy looking for someone who could take away the responsibility of all his misdeeds and tell him that he was cruel to others because others had been cruel to him. I shared my story with Birger, and out of all the angry, young men Birger had met doing his job, he thought I was possibly the one who was best equipped to reflect on his own life.

We talked for about an hour, and for Birger, it was a great experience. He had sat down with a reputed terror who had done so much shit, and then there he was, the seasoned educator being introduced to social mechanisms that no one had introduced him to before involving the criminal underworld and gang life.

Finally, Birger said to me, "Okay, Sleiman. I know you say I'm not allowed to help you. But what if I pull some strings and find you a place to live?"

"If you do that, you'll be the first person to ever do something for me."

Birger was high on dopamine when he left his office and went in to see his colleagues, who had all been employed by the municipality for years and knew my exploits well. Exalted, he told them about his experience. He said, "What a wonderful kid. A diamond in the rough and intelligent as hell."

They all looked at him and shook their heads in disbelief and insisted he was being seduced by a psychopath.

Birger insisted that they were all wrong and blinded by their own prejudice. They just waited for everything to go wrong so they could tell Birger "I told you so".

The next morning, Birger and I met again. I was standing at the mall by the escalator with a handful of people. Birger walked up to us with the best of intentions and told me how much he had enjoyed our conversation. He said he would like to write some of it down and explain to his colleagues my experiences within the system so that we all might meet somewhere in the middle.

I looked at him sideways. "Did you not understand what I said? Don't you fuckin' dare write my story! You just stay the hell away from me."

Meanwhile, Birger opted not to comply with my instructions, and I went from being an angry, young man who refused to accept help to being an inquiring boy who demanded a great deal of attention. I called Birger constantly to test him. Was this guy worth trusting? Was he more than just hot air?

In time, a degree of confidence was established between the two of us, and when the young people of the community needed permission to do something, I took it upon myself to act as the liaison. Whenever my friends were in trouble, Birger would receive a phone call.

I called Birger up one Saturday night when my friend Farid had been beaten up by his father and cousin at a gas station. Farid had been beaten up really badly and didn't have a place to stay, so Birger let him stay with him so that his father wouldn't know.

I was very keen on helping my friends and took responsibility for a group of young boys who grew up under very rough conditions. All the really hardcore criminals and gang leaders I've met, almost all share the same story. They have been locked up in closets and beaten to a pulp. They have been hung by belts in the living room, where they were thrashed by fathers who were desperate and powerless and thought that that was the medicine they needed.

In the beginning, the Birger Mosholt project was a success. Crime didn't disappear overnight, but the rates did go down. An important element of his philosophy was that it was vital for the kids to have something to lose. The kids caught on to that quickly.

We asked one day, "Birger! We have never been on a real trip together. We've never experienced anything together! Can't we go on a trip to Spain?"

"But how would that work? What are the conditions? Who is going with you? Tom and Kim?"

"No," we said. We decided it should be a self-appointed group of fathers because, in order for us to have something to lose, they should also have a stake in the responsibility in case things went awry. Birger accepted, and the trip was arranged.

It was an early Sunday morning during the summer of 1999 on the vacation island of Gran Canaria. After a wild night of drinking and doing drugs, me and one of my friends (whose name is being withheld) were lying in our beds and had just fallen asleep when we heard a knock on the door. Two of the youngest boys, who were brothers, were standing outside, yelling, "There's a fight outside. Come on!"

Drunk, high, and half-asleep, we both ran out on the hotel lawn and joined the madness. The two brothers' older brother was getting his ass kicked by a couple of Irishmen. We each grabbed a chair and jumped the Irishmen, and suddenly, the brothers' father, whom we had called for backup, came gliding across the lawn as if shot from a gun. In front of him stood a six-feet-five Irishman who was as broad as a bathtub. We started throwing chairs at him. He and his friends had knives, and so did we. When we realized that these Irishmen weren't tipping over so easily, it got wilder and wilder because we actually had to defend ourselves.

The police arrived, and it turned out that the Irishmen were part of a larger tour group who had basically booked the entire hotel. Since our group was the smaller one, we got half an hour to pack up our things and immediately vacate the premises.

Birger was interviewed by the paper and confirmed that the municipality had received an additional charge of approximately $400 USD from the hotel for destroyed furniture. He said, "Obviously, it is extremely annoying and frustrating, but I certainly don't think it detracted from the educational aim of the trip . . . Let's not blow this out of proportion."

The charge was added to the $13,000 USD in kroner that the trip had cost the local taxpayers of Greve.

The paper reported that the above-mentioned father had participated in the brawl against the Irishmen. The newspaper also interviewed René, who said that Birger had never revealed to him that trips to Gran Canaria in high season were part of his educational practice. The mayor continued: "I fully understand that certain alternative methods must be employed, but Mosholt must also understand that some people in this municipality may question the relevance of such a trip." He added that even though Birger had a budget at his disposal, it did not imply that the whole world was his oyster, and he intimated that he never would have signed off on the trip had he been consulted.

In spite of the fight, Birger did not regret the trip. Two educational standpoints had collided. For René , the case was clear: to him personally, to the system, to the police, and to the inhabitants of the municipality, Birger had crossed the line. René has since left Venstre, the main center-right party in Denmark, and formed his own local party.

The articles in *Ekstra Bladet* were published while Birger was on vacation. During his vacation, he received a call from his boss, urging him to keep fighting. But it was too late. When he returned to his office, there was a note on his desk saying that he should report to René immediately.

Birger basically received a letter that said, 'Sign this and get lost.' It was a shame for him personally, for the kids, and also for Hundige.

"You'll get wiser," they had told Birger at town hall when he had had his first conversation with me and called me a diamond in the rough. But did he get wiser?

In that regard, Birger is still the same person. To this day, when I describe something humane, understanding, and perhaps a touch naïve, I refer to it as "a Birger project." I still regret the consequences the whole affair had for him. Like so many times before, we had failed. We had failed to keep our promise, and it had cost Birger his job and a lot of grief. He stood tall, but we had destroyed his life's work, and I contributed to his downfall even though he had put his faith in me. I had let him down.

Birger is now head of department at Kofoed's School, where he teaches socially deprived youths, and he still believes his approach to troubled criminal youths in the Danish ghettoes is the right one. But back in 1999, the project ran aground on the front page of a newspaper, and in Askerød, things ended the same way as they did in *Dead Poets Society*: in tragedy. Once again, I faced charges. There were thirty-three cases in total in which my friends and I were involved. For all of these infractions, I was sentenced to three months in prison.

17

SAMIR AND BEKIR

I was from Askerød, and my boy Samir was from Gersager Park. Both housing developments were on blocks placed on opposite sides of Hundige train station. We were each leading figures of our neighborhoods without possessing an official title. Samir and I had become close, dating back to even before I was shipped off to Norway, and while I was there, our bond grew stronger. Samir is two years older than me, and during the months I was gone, Samir and his family helped my family. They provided my mother with occasional financial support and friendship. When I returned, Samir picked me up at Copenhagen Central Station.

However, our friendship was sealed one night when I was standing at Hundige Station with about ten of my boys. Three of the Ishøj Boys were after me. At the time I was being hunted, I was only fifteen. One of them, a man who was about twenty years old, was enamored with a Pakistani girl who instead had a thing for me. In order to get some backup for his attack, he told his friends that I was going around calling his father a drug dealer. Now the Ishøj Boys were after me, and they found me hanging out at the station.

"You've been telling people that my dad is a drug dealer," the twenty-year-old said and walked right up to me.

I was used to headbutting people who got in my face, so that's what I did. After that, I told him to fuck off 'cause I hadn't said shit about his dad. He continued harassing me, so I headbutted him again, this time directly in the nose. He fell and passed out. At that moment, one of his buddies punched me in the back of the head. I turned around and started advancing on him, but then suddenly, there were two of them, and they both had knives, so I couldn't really do anything.

Mind you, of all the guys with me at the station, not one of them lifted a finger to help as I was single-handedly fighting off three attackers. I was seething with rage and thought they were a bunch of cowards.

At the time, it was the trend to wear these heavy iron belts. One of the younger boys threw me his belt to defend myself with. I tried, but one of the guys stabbed me near the mouth. The tip of the blade cut through my lip and broke off, so it was stuck in my gums. Meanwhile, I was so furious I hardly noticed that I was stabbed until the police arrived and the boys from Ishøj took off.

"What happened, Sleiman?" the police asked.

"Nothing. Not a fuckin' thing," I answered. Again, snitching is against the code of the streets. A couple of girls arrived and cleaned my wound, and the police called an ambulance. The doctors removed the knife tip stuck in my gums, and I was sent on my way home.

Per usual, I wanted revenge. I was still furious with my boys for not helping out during the attack, and Samir agreed with me. They had betrayed me because when you grow up in the same neighborhood, you're supposed to have one another's backs, no matter what. That night, a boy from Hundige was attacked by a group of boys from Ishøj. According to Samir's code of honor, the reasons behind the specific incident were completely irrelevant.

Not a single one of my boys at the station was willing to go to Ishøj with me. But Samir was. We went together and walked straight into the mall. There were about thirty to forty Ishøj Boys there. We were fearless, and that commanded respect because that wasn't how you normally did things back then. The guards and cops prevented a fight, but Samir was the only one standing by my side. It was a huge deal for me back then, and I won't ever forget it.

Samir was also a Palestinian refugee kid. Born in Dubai, he and his family had come to Denmark in 1987 when he was seven years old. Aside from that, he was everything I wasn't. He was pensive and intelligent, with a calm father and a strong family. On top of that, he had a good reputation, whereas I was considered the scourge of Hundige. Samir's house was strict, and the punishments were physical, but they weren't a broken family. They commanded respect in the community.

I was still friends with the other boys from my gang, but I truly admired and loved Samir like the big brother I never had. Samir is a smart person, smarter than I am. I was more heart than brains, and I reacted on every impulse. It wasn't that he didn't have heart, but whenever we were about to do something, he was always the one to say, "Let's just think this through." He was an intelligent person, and he wanted to make something of himself. He got an apprenticeship, and the people at town hall saw potential in him.

After Norway, I never went back to school. The only thing I brought home with me from that trip was an irrepressible hatred for the system. Also, another important thing happened in Askerød: I started getting close to Bekir, a man who would have a decisive influence on my life and still does to this very day.

Bekir was a strong, intelligent, and charismatic man gifted with the powers of persuasion. He was a disciplined ascetic who never smoked, drank, or took drugs, even though he has been a major player in the Danish drug market for years. He was born in 1965 and used to be a militiaman in Lebanon. According to several sources, he often spoke of the battles he fought, and he didn't let an opportunity slip by to remind us all of how brutal he could be. He came from a powerful family. In Askerød, where he had a wife and children, brothers, and nephews, he was widely regarded as a dominating figure. Bekir was used to war; he was used to controlling grown men in battle. Askerød was like a playground to him.

When my poor mother felt that she was losing her boy to the lure of the streets, she turned to Bekir. In him, she saw a man who wanted what was best for me and possessed some of the fatherly qualities her son was missing. I was out of control and could be gone for days in a row without letting her know. One day, I had been out partying for three days with some older friends in Slagelse, a city about an hour from Askerød. I met Bekir at the local gas station.

He grabbed me by the ear and asked, "What do you think you're doing, you little shit? You can't just disappear from home for three days at a time. That's no way to treat your mother."

I left the gas station unnerved. I was sort of surprised that my mother had finally found someone who could get me to listen. In a way, I was happy that someone was trying to steer me away from the path I was walking.

Bekir was also the one who had reached out to the lawyer who brought me back from Norway. While I was stuck there, Bekir also helped out my mother. I started calling him uncle, and Bekir also introduced himself as my uncle in town. Many people in Hundige actually thought he *was* my biological uncle. However, Bekir wasn't your garden-variety uncle. He was more like the godfather of Askerød. Bekir was a convicted drug dealer with close ties to the biker community. He operated as a collector of debts, and rumor had it he had made a small fortune providing people with protection against assaults. He was already running the young boys of Askerød. His plan was to build a small army of child soldiers who would do his bidding in return for small rewards.

I was the one closest to him, and I learned a lot from Bekir. I learned that knowledge is power, and if anyone was disloyal to the group or tried to run a little side business, it was my responsibility to keep an eye on them and report back to Bekir. I enjoyed being his eyes and ears. I felt like I had been promoted to prince of the streets, right hand to the king of Askerød.

Supposedly, that was also how Bekir saw me. I was fearless, borderline crazy, and my sense of loyalty to the brotherhood knew no limits. I never backed down if someone from the group needed defending, and I attacked my adversaries with terrifying determination. If a member of the group was disloyal, I learned how to be ruthless. Bekir had a new name for the gang. He named it the Iron Fist, and while he ran the operation in Askerød, his close friend Serge from the biker community took care of business in Odense.

We were supposed to be a kind of tool for him. A shield unit that provided protection for the grown-ups and took care of their business transactions. He kind of started taking us under his wing. I liked it. I thought it was cool that the group had a name. We only did petty crimes—burglaries, that kind of stuff. We were willing to do anything for cash, and we wanted a shot at the big money: blackmail, collection of debts, protection. I mean, if you had a store in Copenhagen, we wanted to be able to go in and say, "If you pay us a fee every month, we'll make sure no one messes with your store."

The day Bekir truly became aware of my potential, it had to do with a girl. I went up to her and kissed her at a club right in front of her Pakistani boyfriend. At first, the boyfriend made no move to protest, but I took it a step further and ended up sleeping with her that night. A couple of days later, a caravan of cars drove into Hundige, filled with about forty angry Pakistani guys who wanted to get their hands on me. The cuckolded man had lied to them all. He had led his friends to believe that I was going around town spreading false rumors about him. He didn't dare tell them that the infamous Sleiman was sleeping with his Danish girlfriend.

I managed to flee to Askerød, where I quickly assembled five or six of my own guys. I quickly got hold of an iron club, and we ran to the mall, where half of my pursuers were waiting. I didn't care about anything, and as always, that was my strength. On a wall next to my Pakistani pursuers was a glass bottle. I crept up, aimed for the bottle, and swung the iron club at full force. The bottle broke into a million pieces that flew toward the group.

I demanded, "What do you want? What are you doing here? Are you gonna fight me over a girl?"

"What are you talking about? We're not here about some girl. We're here because of what you said about his family."

"I didn't say nothing about nobody's family. I just fucked his girl," I told them.

When the others realized why they really were there, they got mad. "Are we here because of some girl? Fuck him and his problem! Fuck her, man, we don't give a shit. We're not gonna fight a Muslim because he fucked your girl. That's your business."

I had gambled big and won. I think that's when Bekir realized that I could be useful to him.

Samir and his brother Zaki didn't like Bekir. Their father warned them about him. In his opinion, just the fact that an older man was hanging around with so many young boys was unnatural. "Sleiman, let's bounce," they said whenever they saw Bekir approach the other boys, who were all between fifteen and twenty years old.

Samir and Zaki weren't exactly paragons of virtue, but they

weren't serious criminals, and neither of them had any intentions of being useful idiots to a man they considered a full-blown gangster. The two brothers were well respected, and a lot of the young boys in the neighborhood looked up to them. Consequently, they posed an obstacle to Bekir's plan of forming a united gang under his leadership.

At night, Bekir would often visit me at home. He told my mother that he just wanted to impart some words of wisdom to her son, so she would leave us two men to talk. Looking back, I realize that I was brainwashed. He was in his thirties, and I was a teenager. He wanted Samir and me to hate each other. "Samir is a rat," he said.

I tried to stay in touch with Samir, but something between us broke. He felt that I had betrayed him. When I had gone to Ishøj to get revenge, Samir was the only one who had backed this play. Later, Samir fell out with a couple of Turkish guys during a time when there was tension between the Turks and the Arabs in Hundige. Samir got into a serious fight with one of them who happened to be my friend. Samir wanted me to intervene and take his side because he had always been there for me. But I just wanted us all to be friends. After that, he was kind of pissed at me. We were still part of the same group, but our relationship changed.

Besides, Samir was slowly turning his back on life in the streets. He was full of ideas and initiatives, and many people expected him to be the role model who would break free from the chains of the ghetto and create a better future for himself and others. He was earning legitimate money hosting children's discos for the young people of the community, which was a great success among immigrant teenagers. He got an apprenticeship as a mechanic, and he had a close relationship with a female social worker named Jette Sørensen. Together, the two of them established a soccer team called the Banana Boys.

For a while, it looked like the yellow-jerseyed team was exactly what the community needed to draw the young boys of Hundige away from crime. Everybody wanted to be on the team. They played well and developed a strong sense of solidarity, and Samir became the captain and unofficial leader. When TV2, the country's second-largest television network, did a show about the Banana Boys in 1996, Samir was the face of the team.

I, of course, declined appearing on the program. The way I saw it, the show merely wanted to tell the world that everything was fine in Askerød. To me, Askerød was a war zone, and I had no interest in washing the neighborhood clean in the eyes of the public when it was festering with problems.

I played midfielder for the Banana Boys, but ultimately, I was unable to leave the street activities in the locker room. I would head-butt opponents and kick them in the back. It got so bad that they couldn't justify having me on the team. We were supposed to be the immigrant team that *didn't* do those things. Finally, Samir kicked me off the team, and yet another piece of gossip spread around the Arab village. In protest against the Banana Boys, I founded my own team called No Name.

"Samir is too powerful. Why does he get to decide? He thinks it's his team. Is he putting aside some of the jersey money for himself?"

I even began to believe the rumors spreading about Samir.

Bekir was also whispering in my ear. A member of my family overheard him telling me to shoot Samir—not to kill him, just a shot in the leg. Afterward, my relative pulled me aside and said, "Can't you see that Bekir is your enemy? He wants you to shoot a boy who's older than you because he is on bad terms with his father. It's not because he loves you, Sleiman. If he has a problem, why doesn't he deal with it himself? He wants to use you. You are not his weapon, and you must never be."

I was young and dumb, so I didn't heed the warning and conflicts kept arising. At one point, I robbed an apartment in Askerød with some associates. We were caught, and rumor had it that Samir was the rat. I was unsure if the rumor was true, but it lodged inside my head along with the rest of the rumors floating around town.

Samir fixed cars. He hosted discos. He made a bit of money. Bekir didn't like him, and people started envying Samir because he made money. Bekir spread the rumor that Samir was the one who ratted me out.

18

GAME OVER

One day in April 2000, both my life and Samir's changed forever.

I spent the night at Anna's house. Her brother was there, and he dreamed of becoming a police officer. The fact that his sister was dating the most notorious young man in Hundige didn't exactly sit right with him. Because he objected to me being in his home, he kicked me out. Anna wouldn't stand for it, so we left together.

I had a soccer game the next morning. Before the game, Anna and I ate breakfast and made a deal that we would take a trip to the zoo when I got back. I wasn't a domesticated boyfriend, but I was good at arranging excursions, Tivoli, surprises, gifts. Even when I brought home roses that Anna knew were stolen, she just went along with it for my sake.

My team was playing away that weekend and we won 8–2, so I was in a great mood after the game. A teammate dropped me off at Hundige Station, where I ran into Hamza, my first and oldest friend in Askerød. Hamza was pissed off. He said, "Sleiman! They're waiting for you in Askerød. They want to fuck you up."

Meanwhile, Hamza neglected to mention *why* they wanted to fuck me up and that he was partly to blame. While my team were away, the Banana Boys had been practicing on the lawn in Askerød. One of the players had left his bike by the field, and Hamza had taken it without asking permission. Hamza had a date with a girl and seeing as he didn't have his own bike to pick her up, he figured he might as well borrow this one.

When he returned with his date an hour and a half later, Samir, Zaki, and the bike's owner barked at him, "Who the fuck do you think you are? You can't just take another guy's bike without asking permission."

"I do whatever I want," Hamza answered to avoid losing face in front of his date. A minor but loud fight ensued, and Hamza lost the fight to the owner of the bike.

"When Sleiman comes back, we're gonna fuck you up!" Hamza shouted.

"Let him come. We'll fuck him up too," they countered.

Hamza left all these crucial details out of his story. Instead, he just told me that a gang of people back in Askerød that included Samir wanted to fuck me up.

In my heart, I still loved Samir and Zaki. Why were they waiting for me now? I was furious. I drove toward Askerød. At the end of one of the paths, I saw Samir, Zaki, and a bunch of other players from the Banana Boys. So, it was true. They *were* waiting for me. But why?

I walked toward them, but in the middle of the path was Anna, crying. From her balcony, she had watched Hamza fight with the others, and she had sensed that I was somehow involved. When she saw me walking down the path, she urged me to turn around. I pushed past her, went into my apartment, and got my butterfly knife. When I came back out, a group of my own friends had joined the commotion.

"If you're a man, then come down here!" one of the Banana Boys shouted.

He was standing next to Samir and took a couple of steps toward me, so we were now standing face-to-face. Before I knew it, I had stabbed someone for the first time in my life. I had been accused of being involved with stabbings in previous years, but it never had been me.

"He's got a knife!" Samir's friend screamed.

Samir ran to his friend and lifted his shirt. He was bleeding. Samir walked up to me and grabbed my collar. He demanded, "Sleiman! Drop the knife!"

Panic began to spread. Bekir had arrived with some of my friends, but Samir refused to let go of me.

"Samir, I don't want to fight you. Let go of me. You're my friend!"

Samir maintained his grip. The noise was growing louder around us, and the tension built until I attempted to stab Samir in his upper arm or shoulder area in hopes he would let go. Instead, I missed and the blade went deep into the middle of his chest. It also penetrated the soul of Askerød and changed everything forever. Blood began to spurt out, and a shocked Samir took a step back.

"Sleiman, what are you doing?" he asked incredulously and lashed out at me. I hit him back.

"Sleiman! Drop the knife!" a man yelled.

A Danish woman started taking photos, and my associates jumped her and broke the camera. Samir was carried away by some of his friends. Someone else called him an ambulance. I dropped the knife, and one of Samir's friends shouted, "I'm gonna fuck you up!"

"Who is going to take revenge on me?" I asked the crowd.

Suddenly, Bekir had a machine gun in his hands and let everybody know that he was on my side in this dispute. Another man immediately came over and took the gun away from him, and the police arrived. But just as the police started to question people, I fled the scene. I ran down the path and into Sarah's apartment. I disguised myself in a scarf in female, Islamic-looking clothes, and I snuck out of Askerød with her. Shortly afterward, we were picked up by some friends who drove us to a nearby train station.

Most Danish people would probably have encouraged their brother to go to the police, but Sarah saw things differently. She knew I had to turn myself in, but I had to get out of there because my life was in danger. Sarah was afraid Samir, and his brothers would go after me and kill me so she aided my escape.

During the flight, the police had my phone number and called me. They ordered, "Turn yourself in, Sleiman!"

"No!" I yelled into the phone before I ripped the SIM card out of it and threw it out the window. I had no idea what condition Samir was in, and I prayed to Allah that I hadn't just killed my own friend for reasons that were still unclear to me.

My prayers were answered, but Hundige was forever changed. Two childhood friends had now become mortal enemies. Two soccer teams born out of a hope of drawing the boys away from the streets had lost their leaders and were never revived. Two housing developments were suddenly at war and still are to this very day. Two boys who had more potential than most and had the chance to become good, instead became the leaders of opposing gangs. Blood would be repaid with blood, bullets with bullets, vengeance with vengeance. And I had drawn first blood in a war that began simply because a boy had borrowed a bicycle without asking permission.

19

THE RACE ACROSS DENMARK

Anna was standing in the middle of Askerød. I had fled, the police had arrived, and in the midst of all the confusion, one of my people told her, "There are three guns in the apartment. You need to get rid of them."

In that instant, Anna realized that there was a more dangerous side to the man she loved than she had been willing to see before. She rushed back into the apartment, found the guns, and put them in her bag. Then she hopped on a bus and switched to the train to her family's house, where she hid them under her bed. She was on the verge of a nervous breakdown, but she did it anyway out of love for me. When I finally called her to let her know I was safe, I was in Jutland with my father, and I wanted her to join us there.

The next day, she took the train to Fredericia, where I was waiting to pick her up. I was a fugitive from the law. The story of the seventeen-year-old suspected of two counts of attempted murder had hit the national media. She still came regardless

During the escape, I learned that Samir and his friend had both survived, but Samir had nearly died. His lung collapsed, and the doctors spent the entire night trying to save his life. I hadn't stabbed him with intent to kill. I had just desperately wanted to get him to let go. I still considered Samir my friend. Bekir was the puppet master behind that whole incident, and we were all being manipulated.

Nevertheless, it will always be a fact that I was the one who stabbed Samir and his friend, and only fate and a few millimeters prevented me from becoming a murderer.

I both loved and hated my father and Bekir, but during my time as a fugitive, I had nobody else to turn to besides my two deeply flawed father figures. First, I visited Århus to find my biological father. Where else was I supposed to go? I wasn't going to turn myself in because I was still hoping to deal with the matter internally between the families. My plan was to return to Hundige and hand Samir's family a knife. I would tell them that they could do as they saw fit, and then blood would be repaid with blood.

My father couldn't find me a place to stay, but Bekir did. He called and said that I could stay with some of his connections in Vollsmose. I understood I was eventually going to jail, but I had a plan I wanted to carry out first.

Anna and I met at the train station in Fredericia, and the two of us drove to Odense with my father. Anna asked what had happened, and I told her that the unfortunate stabbing was done in self-defense. She didn't doubt my story. She knew that I was going to jail, and she decided to grant my big wish: for a long time, I had wanted us to have an Islamic wedding, and now she was ready.

To me, it meant everything. She wanted to prove to me that she was not going to desert me. That was the only reason to do it. When I met her in Fredericia, she was wearing this light shirt and black jeans and a long, black jacket. She wasn't dolled up or anything, but she was as beautiful as she had always been to me, and the situation made me love her in an entirely new way because she was by my side when everybody else had turned their back on me.

In Odense, some of Bekir's criminal connections helped us out, and we sat down in the apartment in Vollsmose and waited for an imam to come marry us. Anna was asked if she acknowledged God and his scriptures, and she said yes. He asked me if I believed in Allah and his messengers, and then he asked if she would have me, and I her. We were married in front of three witnesses, and then she was my wife and I her husband. I gave her a ring and a dowry of $150. But those things were mostly symbolic because they're mandatory elements of an Islamic marriage settlement.

After the ceremony, my father went to bed. The plan was for me to turn myself in after we were married, but first, I tried to call a friend who knew both me and Samir. I still harbored hope that Samir and his family would punish me for my actions.

His friend shot down the idea of reconciliation. "What you have done to Samir will never be forgiven," I was told.

Everyone I reached out to said the same thing. No one in Hundige had ever attempted to kill anyone. They belonged to different groups and sects, but they were all from Hundige, and they were all immigrants. I had crossed a line I never should've crossed that day.

Anna and I walked down to the local McDonald's to have our private wedding reception, donning our wedding rings. After that, we took a walk to a nearby forest, where we carved a big heart in a tree and wrote our initials *A* and *S* inside. On the way back to the apartment, Anna sensed that something was wrong.

"These creepy guys are watching us," she told me, but I brushed it off.

When we got to the house, something was wrong with the elevator. We kept pushing the button, but the elevator never came. When it finally did, a Somali family was standing in there and rode up with us. When we got to the second floor and opened the door, twelve men in combat uniforms armed with machine guns rushed all of us. The officers pulled the Somali family out of the elevator and grabbed Anna by the hair.

"You're under arrest!" one of them shouted.

"What the hell am I under arrest for?" Anna yelled back.

I pushed the officers away from Anna. "What the fuck are you doing?" I asked. I had changed my clothes so no authorities would recognize me at first glance. Or so I thought.

"It's him!" one of the officers shouted.

"Don't hurt Anna!" I yelled at them.

In the end, Anna wasn't arrested, but she was shocked by the episode. Was her new husband really this dangerous?

There were twelve cops with machine guns and gas masks as if they were trying to catch The Punisher or something. Anna screamed and panicked as they took off with me.

The newly married, infamous fugitive Sleiman was transferred to Odense Detention Center, where Anna got to see me one last time before I was incarcerated. I met her in this long, white hall, where we kissed and held each other. Then she said, "Don't worry, I'm not gonna leave you or anything. I'll be waiting when you get out."

My dad was waiting in a little room next door. He knew how bad the situation was. He didn't fear the Danish judicial system, but he did fear retaliation from Samir's family. At the same time, he was hoping for a swift revenge. As long as I didn't die, a swift revenge was preferable because then we wouldn't have to spend the rest of our lives looking over our shoulders. We would have paid the way tradition dictated. At one point, my father reached out to Samir's father and said that the family had the right to take revenge. But Samir's family had no interest in getting my blood on their hands.

Anna and my father drove back to Askerød. They had met before, and Anna was familiar with my family's violent history, yet the two of them got on well. When Anna went back home to her parents' house, she vomited. She had tried to hold it all together for as long as she could before it physically caught up to her.

I believe that the police tapped my phone. During the escape, I had made the mistake of inserting a new phone card into my phone to call a friend from Askerød. That might've been how the police got wind of my whereabouts. It's also possible that Anna's phone was being tapped. But that wasn't how the story was told in the Arab village of Askerød, where gossip spread once again.

Some folks fabricated rumors that Anna was the snitch because she always tried to keep me away from the streets. Shortly after, my mother invited her over. Anna had a meeting with my people and defended herself against the allegations before I confirmed she wasn't the one who snitched on me. Man, relationships are hard work.

20

THE LUNDIN FIGHT

I initially hoped the trial would prove that Askerød supported me. That all the witnesses would follow the code of the streets and refrain from testifying because they knew that my heart had been in the right place.

However, during the hearings, five months later, between thirty and thirty-five witnesses came forward, and with a few exceptions, they all testified against me. I still felt like I had acted in self-defense, but the hearings turned into a weeklong testimony of a neighborhood that so strongly wished to dissociate itself from one of its own that people were willing to go against customs and culture and take the stand. In the past, regardless of how egregious my offense had been, I still managed to have people willing to see the good in me. It seemed that Samir's stabbing was the proverbial straw that broke the camel's back.

On September 7, 2000, the verdict was read. I was found guilty as charged in the stabbing of Samir Hosseini and sentenced to twenty-one months in a correctional facility.

I had almost killed my childhood friend, but I didn't consider what I had done wrong. I only thought about escaping punishment.

Prison didn't teach me anything good. Nobody came out a better person than they came in. The county jail had the capacity for only twelve inmates. I shared a roof with a man named Jimbo, some guys from Århus, and some others from Copenhagen. Yogi, Jimbo, and Afni were among the prisoners with the most influence, and they invited me to sit with them during meals.

The four-time convicted killer Peter Lundin was housed in the same facility. He was convicted of killing his own mother in the United States in 1992. After his release, he went to Denmark, where in 2000, he murdered his girlfriend and her two children and then dismembered them. He is now considered the most violent and disturbed criminal in recent Danish history.

In the summer of 2000, Peter hadn't been convicted yet and was being held in isolation. The rest of the prisoners felt provoked by the ever-open door to his cell, which had a sign on it that said Not Guilty. We all agreed that he couldn't go unpunished, and we got the sense that the guards felt the same way.

When Peter went to the gym, no one else was allowed in there. One day, he was working out, and as usual, he left the door open. The guards had insinuated that they wouldn't interfere in the event we paid him a visit to teach him a lesson.

Jimbo was strong, Afni was extremely aggressive, Yogi was a six-feet-six behemoth, and then there's me, Sleiman. We entered the gym, and Afni and I launched the attack. We kept hitting Peter while Jimbo and Yogi tried to force him to the ground, but no matter how hard we punched and pushed, he remained standing. He hardly seemed to acknowledge the punches we rained down on him, and he somehow managed to push both Yogi and Jimbo out the door. In all my years of street fights and skirmishes, I've met a lot of guys who could handle three or four opponents at once, but none of them were as strong as Peter was. The fight should have been over in two minutes. But five minutes later, he was still standing.

Eventually, the guards had to break it up 'cause it would have been bad publicity if Peter had died in their custody. After the assault, he was transferred to another facility. The police told the media that it was because the correctional officers were worried about other prisoners wanting to harm Peter.

In my prison, life went on as usual. My new comrades took over the marijuana trade from a local criminal. He was a declared racist and had *White Power* tattooed on his arms. Yogi, a guy they called Nicko, and me, gave him a serious beating. Since Jimbo wasn't with

the whole White Power business either, we were now free to dominate the prison drug market. In reality, this just meant that we now
controlled White Power's junkie. He was the one who smuggled in
the weed by getting his friends to stash it in their prison wallets
when they came to visit him. He also did the actual dealing and took
all the risks while White Power just cashed in. The junkie was paid
in protection, plus he was allowed to smoke as much weed as he
wanted. We maintained the status quo, with the only new wrinkle
being we now controlled the junkie and made all the money.

After six months in county jail, I was transferred to a state prison.
I was only seventeen when the stabbing I was convicted of occurred,
which was why I was moved to a low-security prison so soon. Once
again, I expanded my network by befriending a group of immigrant
guys from Copenhagen. Luckily, I was placed in a good wing of the
facility. There, I was immediately invited to join the same dinner
table as a man called Grandpa, who was one of the most powerful
weed dealers in Denmark. I got to smoke joints, eat steak, and played
soccer. There was no hierarchy among the prisoners and no need for
extreme violence. I had a good time.

Anna was now able to visit me, and she wrote me three letters a
day. She wrote one in the morning before she went to work, one
around lunchtime, and a good-night letter telling me what she had
been up to. She supported me all the way, and I left prison with a
collection of four hundred letters. The only drawback was a lack of
conjugal visits, and being Muslim, I refused to watch porn like the
others did.

I also got smarter in prison. I had been caught several times now,
and I realized that when I went away to jail, everybody lost. In
prison, it was drilled into my head that there could be no witnesses
to my crimes. As many times as I've been locked up, I was fortunate
it wasn't for much longer than the sentences that I got.

21

BLACK COBRA

S hortly after the trial was over, Samir was driving home from his
apprenticeship as a mechanic when Bekir pulled up next to
him. Allegedly, Samir heard him shout from his window that Samir
would die. It has never been confirmed this incident occurred, but
Samir's family were worried that Bekir, his nephews, or his
associates would target Samir and his brothers in order to finish
what I had supposedly started.

Samir also felt that I deserved far more than only twenty-one
months in jail. Since the system had shown it didn't value his life
and wasn't willing to protect him, he had to seek security elsewhere.
He eventually found it in a neighboring city with a notorious immigrant gang who wore insignias on their backs depicting a snake
baring its fangs and rearing back to strike. They called themselves
Black Cobra.

Throughout the years, Samir has repeatedly denied being a
member of Black Cobra, but according to a national newspaper that
published a series of articles about him in 2008, local law enforcement officials had no doubt that he was affiliated with them.

Samir went from being the captain of the Banana Boys soccer
team that was created as a deterrent to gang culture and a strong,
positive role model in Gersager Park to someone who ventured
deeper and deeper into the criminal underworld. Maybe he did it

because he felt he had no other choice. It's also possible he just gave up being the good guy after realizing that it wasn't going to be his salvation, given the circumstances. Several teachers and policemen described Samir as a real light in the darkness who unfortunately ended up on the wrong path.

Samir has declined to be interviewed for this book, so this chapter has been pieced together by interviews of our own sources, plus thorough research of available documents and media coverage.

Now that Samir was connected to Black Cobra, Bekir faced a strong enemy. Bekir's original vision of a large gang under the name of The Iron Fist was no longer realistic, but the police still regarded him as the powerful leader of multiple Arab clans in Askerød. The police and the media dubbed the gang "the Bekir Boys" and estimated that they made their money selling narcotics and laundering money through online businesses.

Bekir has been convicted very few times, but one count of drug trafficking resulting in him spending three years in prison serves as evidence that he was involved in the drug trade. Even though I once ran with the Bekir Boys, I never dabbled in drug trafficking or dealing hard drugs on the outside. One of my friends, Hedgehog, who has close ties with the Hells Angels, once served a six-year sentence for dealing cocaine. I simply refused to have anything to do with the hard drug trade.

The enmity between Samir and Bekir was of a personal nature, based on more than just opposing gang affiliations. Samir's father was a strong man who refused to be bullied, and he passed that trait on to his sons. Samir and Zaki tried to lead normal lives. Sure, they got into fights, but they were decent people. We weren't. Our leaders could've helped make peace after what had happened between me and Samir, but they didn't want to.

I also made a big mistake myself. During a conditional release, I went to Hundige Mall. Here, I ran into Samir, his friend whom I had stabbed, and a third guy I had also been in a fight with once. What were the odds?

"How could you do that to me? I'm entitled to revenge, you know," Samir said.

"Then take your revenge. But remember, I was convicted and got locked up. I did my time."

Samir continued: "I'll never forget what you did to me."

"That's fair, Samir."

I still got the feeling that Samir was reaching out. He told me he was gonna be the bigger man, and I think he meant it. I think he was ready to forgive and not take revenge if I apologized. His father also tried to reconcile things between us. We were never gonna be best friends again. We were just supposed to tolerate each other.

I could've taken his hand right there and made peace. But I didn't, partly because the others were standing there screaming, and partly because I was stupid and felt some kind of twisted loyalty to Bekir and the others, who didn't want to reconcile. Listening to them was a big mistake. When Samir told me that he was the bigger man, I knew in my heart that I was the bad guy. Today, I realize that a lot of the shit that went down in Askerød later on could have been avoided if I had only taken his hand.

On May 13, 2001, back when I was still behind bars, the cold war between Bekir's family and Samir's family turned into a matter of life and death in a parking lot behind Hundige Mall. An incident occurred, resulting in Samir shooting Bekir in the face and then shooting Bekir's nephew who rushed to his aid in the chest and abdomen.

They both survived the shooting and Samir was taken into custody. He was only sentenced to two and a half years in prison largely due to the fact Samir seemed to be acting in self defense as he was surrounded by Bekir's men and likely could've died that day.

It wasn't possible to access the legal documents in this case, but according to the information available, the mitigating circumstances were based on the fact that Bekir was carrying a knife, which he used to threaten Samir's father. Samir was therefore not convicted for shooting Bekir, as he was defending his father, but only for the shots fired at Bekir's nephew. Bekir avoided conviction.

22

IT WAS MY BULLET

The day Bekir was shot, I was still in prison. In the spring of 2001, I was getting ready to be released and was filled with great hope. I hoped for a future devoid of crime and violence and, most importantly, one that included reconciliation with Samir. Anna convinced me that I should seek peace. Samir was my friend, and I was the one to blame for what had happened.

At the same time, I felt let down by my own. Gang members usually receive financial help while incarcerated, but my crew seemingly cut me off. Right after my verdict was read, Bekir slipped me fifty Krone, ($8 USD) and that was all the money I received for the duration of my sentence. Those fifty Krone felt like a slap in the face and a message from Bekir saying that I was no longer his right hand nor the prince of Askerød. On top of that, I got almost no visits. I began to suspect that Bekir was trying to isolate me and keep me at arm's length.

He took over the group while I was gone, you know. He had my friends served on a platter for him to control. He didn't give a shit about me. When I stabbed Samir, I did exactly what he had wanted me to do, and now I was just a chewed-up piece of gum to him. The whole gang scene was riddled with propaganda wars. I was isolated 'cause everybody thought stabbing Samir was wrong.

On the other hand, I had a better chance of leading a life on the right side of the tracks than ever before. I had an apartment, a family, and a wife who had written me four hundred letters while I was in jail. Lately, however, there had been trouble in paradise. Anna found out another girl had visited me in prison. Anna made it clear that if I so much as touched another girl after she had devoted her life to supporting me while I was locked up, she would end our relationship.

I convinced her that there was nothing between me and the woman who had visited. She had a crush on me, since I had been cut off by my gang and had limited contact with the outside world, it was flattering that someone else aside from Anna cared about my well-being. I might've been tempted, but nowhere near enough to cheat on her.

On a bright, spring night in 2001, Anna and I were hanging out at the halfway house where I was kept under supervision before my final release. We shared a late dinner, and she stayed overnight. The next morning, Anna was going to work as an assistant kindergarten teacher, and I was supposed to go to the polytechnic program, where I was studying to become an electrician. I hadn't attended school since I was kicked out of Tjørnely Elementary, but I was performing well in class. At 5:00 a.m. on May 14, my phone rang.

"Sleiman, you need to get over here. Bekir's been shot."

I got dressed and snuck out of a hole in the fence, which the inmates used to get in and out without the guards knowing. I wasn't under strict supervision at this halfway house, as it was just a formality. I was only fourteen days from being released, and this was an emergency. I wasn't upset that Samir had shot Bekir, but when my people had called and asked for me to come to Rigshospitalet, the largest hospital in the country, to demonstrate my solidarity with their leader, I was obligated to show my face. If I didn't, I would be regarded as the one who had failed the brotherhood. The code is the code, and it's to be followed at any and all costs.

In a situation like that, you don't leave your own behind. You just don't. In a way, I still loved him. I hated him too, but I didn't hate my friends, and if they were there, I had to go too. I would lose all my friends if I didn't show up.

I took the train and then a bus to get there. When I arrived, I saw all my people standing outside of Rigshospitalet. The cops wouldn't let us in. We were so agitated we thought they were gonna let him die, so we ran in from all sides. Some ran up the stairs, others used the elevators. The doctors and nurses couldn't do anything. If the cops can't stop you, doctors and nurses sure as hell can't either. They don't dare to. It wasn't exactly a friendly crowd that entered the hospital.

There are many floors, many long hallways, and hundreds of wards at Rigshospitalet, but we all had a pretty good idea where gunshot victims were treated, so after a while we found Bekir in a room with blood on his face and on his pillow. The bullet had passed through his mouth and exited through his neck. His nephew who had run after Samir was also hospitalized there, but I didn't care about him 'cause I didn't like him. He was new in Denmark and thought he was all that 'cause he knew taekwondo and Bekir was his uncle. He thought he could run the crew like some kind of lieutenant, so I had kicked his ass before.

I regarded Bekir as a man who kept the wheels of the war machine turning from his hospital bed, even while his family cried at his bedside. All of his relatives had come from all over Denmark. They made it abundantly clear that the bullet that had passed through Bekir's mouth should've instead been fired at me. "It wasn't his bullet," they said. "Bekir is your friend. He protected you from Samir's family."

They never told me in clear terms to seek revenge, but I can read between the lines. *In a way, they're right,* I thought. In their heads, this had all started with me, and therefore, it was my fault that Bekir had been shot. Forget that it was actually Bekir who had manipulated both Samir and I. I realized that I wasn't someone they loved. I was just a tool in their hands.

From that day on, I was never truly on Bekir's side. Unfortunately, I was too weak to completely sever my ties with him. For many years that followed, I ignored my intuition that constantly told me I needed to move on from him.

With Bekir wounded and Samir behind bars, Askerød was quiet on the surface. I was finally released from the halfway house and was living with Anna. Even though I was only nineteen and she was just twenty-one, we talked about starting a family together. Anna's father had connections in the façade-cleaning industry, and he managed to get me a job in Copenhagen. All of a sudden, we had an apartment and two steady jobs.

Anna's family was surprisingly supportive of me. They had initially feared I would be convicted of two counts of attempted murder because that carried a possible sentence of up to eight years in jail, and they didn't want Anna to wait that long for a spouse. However, when the charges were downgraded to severe assault, they embraced me in every way. I loved eating breakfast with her mom and dad. For the first time, I felt like I belonged, like I wasn't a homeless child anymore. Even though I had a family who loved me more than anything, Anna and her family gave me the kind of affirmation I had always longed for.

While I was in prison, I took up praying. Things really seemed to be looking up for me. Every morning, Anna prepared a lunchbox for me, and I was getting praised for my work. At night, when I snuck out to go see my friends, Anna would come and snatch me away from the weed, a habit I had fallen back into as soon as I was released from prison, despite all my promises to God, Anna, and my family. If I was at a friend's place, smoking weed, she would come knocking at the door and demand: "Where's Sleiman? He needs to come home with me right now!"

"What's up with your old lady? Are you whipped now?" my friends asked me.

"Why are you doing this to me? You're making me look like a fool!" I would tell Anna.

Anna didn't care. "You're the one making a fool out of me! You have to go to work at seven in the morning, and you're in there smoking weed!"

At this point, I was cleaning façades at the police headquarters in Copenhagen, and Anna insisted that I show up because her father was the site manager. For the first time, I had every chance of maintaining a decent, law-abiding life. I was finally an adult, responsible for my own life with a woman who packed my lunchbox for work. The infamous Sleiman was now a part of the workforce. If I chose the wrong path now, I could no longer blame the municipality, society, or anyone else. I knew that I would never have a better chance of proving everyone who said that I was destined to fail wrong.

In the end, all the skeptics turned out to be right, and I ended up letting Anna and her entire family down. Even though Anna and I had 3,000 kroner to spend each month after taxes, even though her and her family genuinely loved me, and even though she gave me a budget for clothing, food, and fun, I didn't have the self-control to resist once my people started calling again.

I was freaked out by the stability she brought into my life, and I was afraid that it would become boring. On the other hand, I was finally living the way I had always wanted to. I was sharing my life with someone who trusted me and accepted me for who I was. The thing was, I felt like the money I made wasn't enough, so I started doing smash-and-grabs again. I destroyed everything I had built. When I was locked up, I had made a promise to God that I was done. A few months after I got out, I had broken all my promises.

My crew had had their eyes on a store for a while. The merchandise we were looking to steal could easily be resold on the black market for upward of $75,000 USD. We knew when the new deliveries arrived, and all we had to do was wait for them. We had visited the store several times to learn the layout, so we knew exactly where the most valuable items were. We were pros. After the burglary, we drove off with the loot on innocent-looking cargo bikes. In no time, we pulled off four or five heists.

Everyone involved in the robberies were associates of Bekir, so while he never participated or even had any knowledge of them being carried out beforehand, he was still indirectly involved. We hid all the loot in an apartment that belonged to a Danish guy we convinced to let us use it as a stash house. He was rarely home, and since only my crew had access to the apartment, we hid the stolen goods behind a dividing wall. Even though it was our score, other people in Bekir's network knew the location of our stash house.

When Bekir recovered from his bullet wound, he once again had eyes and ears in every corner of Askerød. Bekir knew about my operation, and he demanded that I give some of the stolen goods to his son, who could use the money for school. I didn't feel I had the right to give away the loot to someone who wasn't involved with the operation without the consent of my accomplices, so I refused. Several disputes between Bekir and me followed.

What it all boils down to is I was the only one of the guys who dared to oppose Bekir, and because of that, Bekir didn't like me. I was a constant thorn in his side and an obstacle towards his dominance.

One evening, Bekir invited all the guys who had participated in the heists to dinner at a restaurant called Bali in Copenhagen—all of them, that is, except for me. Bekir told me that Anna was looking for me and was worried that something had happened to me. He also told me I needed to spend some time with her. In that sense, I guess he was still kinda fatherly. But when I got home, Anna told me that she hadn't been looking for me. She never talked to my friends. She hated them ever since they had accused her of being a snitch back when I got locked up.

It wasn't until the next day that I figured out what had happened. All the stolen goods stashed at the apartment were gone. The rest of the crew had been at the restaurant, and I was at home with Anna at Bekir's suggestion. In this world, you can't call the police, press charges, or file lawsuits, so they could never prove that Bekir's men had stolen our loot. But in my mind, there was no doubt.

Only cheap items had been left at the stash apartment, which angered me even more. I felt like they were mocking me by doing that. I picked up the leftovers and went to the clubhouse. When I got there, I dumped all of it in front of Bekir.

"Some bitches robbed our apartment. But they forgot something," I said to him. Then I turned and left.

Bekir didn't say anything, but a few days later, he left the country. No honor among thieves. I was the thief who was the victim of a robbery. Even though I was seething with anger over what had just happened, my dumb ass still couldn't summon the courage to stop dealing with Bekir.

When I first met Kira, it was at the mall. She was blonde and only seventeen. I was in a committed relationship with Anna, so I just flirted with her and left it at that. Anna had her shit together. She was a girl who knew what she wanted, and she wanted kids. Although our wedding ceremony wasn't fully sanctioned as legal, I didn't wanna risk losing that. Kira was just fun and games.

Next, I began to lead a cell phone double life. I spoke with Kira on my work phone and with Anna on my private phone. It was only a matter of time before things went south. And they did. Anna had a friend who also knew Kira. She chose to be loyal to Anna and told her that I was seeing someone else.

I had to get in front of this, so I did what I always did: fought regardless of the odds against a successful outcome in my favor. No one knows better than I that attacking is the best form of defense, so I handed my phone over to Anna and told her to call Kira.

Anna called her and asked if she had been messing around with me. Kira said no, but she admitted that we had talked. So, I said: "There you go! I've talked to her, but I haven't done anything!" But to Anna, that was worse than if I had fucked her 'cause she felt like there were feelings involved. There might have been, but not something that would make me leave Anna.

Not long afterward, my little sister Ayat was getting married in Århus. I was reluctant to go to the wedding because I felt like I was about to say goodbye to her for good. I had a hard time letting go of my younger sisters. I loved them, and they were my best friends, you know. I felt like I had taken care of them since our mother and Sarah were in the hospital and it was just the three of us in the shelter.

Just before the wedding, Anna had news for me: "I'm pregnant."

I was over the moon. I had been hoping for this all along. Anna really wanted to go to the wedding. It was also a chance for her to meet my father again. My dad and Anna had become friends, even though I wasn't on good terms with him. She didn't judge him, and she tried to mend things between us. My dad really liked her. He could tell that she loved me.

Anna wore a green, velvet dress at the wedding. She was more beautiful than ever. At one point, she was walking around with my baby cousin on her arm, and the image has stuck with me ever since. That really moved me. I had always felt like I was too Danish for an Arab girl and too Arab for a Danish girl, but I had found a Danish girl who accepted me for who I was.

We spent the night together, but just as we got home from the wedding, the two planes crashed into the World Trade Center on September 11, 2001. Anna's Danish girlfriends started talking ill of Muslims, and I began to sense a change in Anna as well. It became a huge deal in all of our lives—in mine, in my friends', in Anna's. After 9/11, the mood shifted. Everybody was like, "Immigrants are no good. Muslims are no good," and we were constantly targeted. With the new government in place, the laws just got tougher and tougher, and we began to get harassed regularly.

However, the wedding that I remember as a joyous occasion is something that Anna recalls as frustrating. According to her, I was only there for a short while, and when I was, I seemed distracted. To make matters worse, she had to present the married couple with the jewelry that you give the newlyweds at Arab weddings because I was nowhere to be found.

Anna's not stupid, she thought, 'If he can't even be at his own sister's wedding, what's he up to?' She got suspicious and a few weeks after the wedding, she did some sleuthing and found out I was also seeing a girl named Kira.

Anna got hold of Kira. and they promised to be honest with each other. After a short while, there was no doubt in Anna's mind: I was cheating on her. She went home to our apartment, packed up all of her stuff, and moved back in with her parents. Me cheating on her was the final straw.

She took the four hundred letters, which I had kept since my time in prison, with her. She went up to her parents' summer house where we had spent a lot of time and burned all of them.

During the months that followed, I tried to get her back so we could raise our child together. For a while, Anna wavered, but at the same time, Kira was using all the tricks available in the playbook of love and war. She was crazy about me and tried her best to win me over. Even though I hoped to get Anna back, I simply couldn't ignore Kira.

By the end of October 2001, my relationship with Anna was over. She sought to move on with her life and didn't want to start a family with a cheater and a liar, so she went to the hospital and got an abortion.

Sarah went to the hospital to try to convince Anna to keep the baby and forgive me, but Anna refused to let her in. She also didn't tell Sarah that she was moving to Copenhagen. I tried to find her, but she had changed her phone number. After some time had passed, she happened to run into some of my people. This prompted her to contact me again. She told me, "I just wanna live in peace. I found a new guy, and I live in Copenhagen now. Leave me be, Sleiman. And don't hurt my boyfriend."

That was when it finally hit me. It was over, and Anna was never coming back.

After the breakup, I smoked between ten and twenty joints a day. I committed one burglary after another, and I was either late for work or failed to show up at all. It didn't take long for this behavior to get me fired. The company was sad to see me go, but I just didn't feel like I was cut out for a nine-to-five. I preferred to earn my money through criminal activities.

I missed Anna so much that I bought a Pitbull puppy. One day, I left it alone for half an hour in the apartment where we stashed all our stolen goods to pick something up from the mall. When I came back, the loot was all gone and my puppy was lying on the floor, shaking and helpless after someone had mutilated it. It had to be put down. I had lost Anna, my unborn child, my job, and my dog, all one after the other. The worst part was I only had myself to blame. I could have chosen a different path, but every time, I was held back by greed, selfishness, lust, pride, or ambition.

Bekir didn't create me. He took advantage of what was already inside me. He exploited the fact that I would do anything to make sure that everybody knew who I was. I ran every single red light. I was willing to go through anyone to achieve my goal of conquering Denmark and assuming the throne so they would all say, "Look, there's the prince of the streets."

I became just that. But when I did, a lot of people hated me, and very few people genuinely loved me, largely because I had caused so many people so much pain and suffering in order to earn that title.

23

THE RISE OF A GANG

Anna was gone, but I still had my boys. Argon and Erion, the Balkan brothers I grew up with, remained among my closest friends. We all had rough upbringings, and the loyalty we felt toward one another was unlike anything I've ever experienced with anyone else. They were the brothers I had always wanted. They helped my mom find an apartment when she didn't have one. Erion stayed at my place when he had nowhere else to stay.

Erion was the youngest of the two. A short, strong dude who loved girls and smoking weed, he was a solidly built and was a talented boxer. He could have gone pro when he was eighteen had he not wasted his life on weed and women. Argon was a hard-working man who was a bit more cool-headed than his brother. One time, we were chasing after this guy because we believed he had snitched on our friends George and Wayne. When we caught him, I asked him if he was the one, they called The Convict.

"Yeah," he answered.

"Did you rat on George and Wayne?"

"What are you talking about?" The Convict asked.

"Oh, so you speak Danish?" I asked and spat my gum out into his face.

The Convict reached for an iron bar and tried to hit me in the head. (I know what you're thinking: Why are there always iron bars lying around like it's a stage of *Double Dragon*?) The easy-going Argon tried to calm down The Convict and convince him to drop the iron bar. But then Erion and I attacked him instead. If it wasn't for Argon, we might've killed him. We wanted to take the iron bar from him and bust his skull, but Argon stopped us, saying, "What are you doing? You're gonna kill him!"

If he hadn't been there, who knows what we might've done? Argon was a tough guy, a fighter, but he was more sensible than we were.

Argon and Erion were not fond of weapons, and when the young guys in Hundige started carrying guns and using them against one another, they opposed it. I mean, they got into fights and stuff, but to me, that doesn't make them criminals. I think Erion is working for the municipality now, teaching young boys to box. Argon cleans façades with his dad.

Abdul, Farid, Maxwell, Hamza, and Tarif were also part of the crew. Abdul was smart. A kind person, except when he got mad. He was big and strong with a head like a ram. We called him Ramhead 'cause he could bang his skull against anything without feeling a thing. He wasn't a criminal, though. He's a social worker now and makes a living off his big heart.

Hamza was the guy I became friends with after the first time we got into a fight. He's still a criminal. Farid was a troublemaker like I am. He loved to knock people out with his first punch. He was one of my best friends.

Tarif was the funny one. He would go crazy sometimes, sure, but he could make everybody laugh. He was a real comedian. He did the funniest impersonations ever. We loved to laugh at Tarif when we watched movies together. He could imitate every actor in the movie. He was a warm-hearted guy, a bit chubby, and you could always talk to him about anything. He was classier than the rest of us, and he didn't really fit in among hoodlums, but he ended up a criminal anyway. I think he still is.

Maxwell was a good-hearted but shy kind of dude. He never bothered anybody, and he hated it when people talked behind other people's backs. He got shot and almost died. That changed him. He became someone else. Someone worse. Today, he's right back to being the old Maxwell.

These were my closest friends. We regarded ourselves as soldiers on the battlefield of honor, but we grew up under rough conditions. We injured and maimed our enemies, and many people who got in our way still have the scars to show for it and stories to tell for the rest of their lives.

On our own, we were weak. United, we were strong. We each had a good side as individuals and could've done positive things with our lives that bettered our community, but together? Instead, we became evil.

The Askerød Housing Association owned a few run-down shacks that were to be used for a youth club. Meanwhile, my crew's reign of vandalism in Askerød had made all the social workers flee, and anyone who signed up to help was threatened to leave Askerød. We often claimed that we would act like well-behaved, upper-class kids if only the municipality would let us run a club on our own. Eventually, the housing association and the municipality relented and allowed us to take responsibility for the shacks.

In spite of my past, some people still trusted me, so Askerød's charming enfant terrible and prince of the streets was appointed keyholder and unofficial head of the club. I happily accepted this new responsibility. I renovated the place. Painted it and paid with my own money. I mean, I had made the money illegally, but I built a bar, an Arab-style living room, and a lounge area with slot machines. It was a place where we could all hang out.

I loved the club, but it also gave me the perfect opportunity to keep up my weed habit that my friends enabled. It got so bad that anyone who remembers me from that time recalls a moody, young man with a distant look in his bloodshot eyes wandering around in a constant haze.

The club was built on good intentions and nice words like *responsibility*, *independence*, and *trust*, but ended up as a place to store weapons and stolen goods and to deal marijuana out of. The club represented so much more than that to us. We began as a loosely organized circle of friends based out of Askerød and transformed into a strong, unified entity. At the clubhouse, we were able to plan our future criminal activities. In a word, we became a gang.

We were on a roll, and we were making money. Our pockets got deeper, and suddenly, we could afford to go clubbing, dining, and be flashy. We had parties, girls, and booze for everyone at the clubs. We funded our club through the sale of weed. This was more than a decade before the boom of the legal cannabis industry and weed started becoming decriminalized everywhere.

The marijuana market is huge. We're talking billions, and I don't think the average Dane realizes the scale of it. The marijuana culture in Denmark is widespread. Almost everyone I know either smokes or used to smoke, and the older generations still puff on a joint now and then without feeling like criminals. Even at fancy, upper-class parties, they often pass a joint around. Marijuana is part of Danish culture, the same as beer, and if the people selling it are criminals, then a vast part of the population is too.

The difference between Denmark and Holland, where weed is legal, is that criminal gangs fight to control the market in Denmark. It's more controlled in Holland. And because of our origins, we immigrants have good connections in countries that produce marijuana, like Lebanon and Morocco. It's kind of a way for us to create jobs for ourselves.

Christiania is an anarcho, hippie commune in central Copenhagen, where cannabis dealers have been openly plying their trade since the mid-1970s. In 2004, the police bulldozed Christiania's Pusher Street, but the dealers are now back in business. By 2012, the marijuana industry in Denmark was already a 1 billion Krone business ($152,000,000).

I served as the unofficial leader. Not because anyone appointed me, but because I was the most articulate member of the crew, the most instantly recognizable, and arguably the most skilled criminal. At the same time, the relationship between me and Bekir became increasingly strained. I was convinced that his soldiers were behind the theft of the stolen goods at our stash apartment, as well as the mutilation of my dog. The fact that I suspected Bekir of preparing a hostile takeover of our club didn't do much to improve our relationship.

Bekir never did things himself, but once in a while, he sent his three nephews to visit the club on his behalf. The three of them came by one summer day in an attempt to assert some kind of dominance over me to demonstrate to the younger boys that Bekir was still in control, even though I was the club's face.

"What's up, Sleiman? Show us what you got," one of the nephews said to me while I was playing a game of foosball with a younger boy.

I knew they were trying to get me to react so they could justify whatever action they intended to carry out, so I ignored them at first. They kept talking, so I finally confronted one of them, saying, "If you wanna play, then play. If not, get the fuck out."

"Who do you think you are?" he asked.

I decided to show him rather than tell him. I picked him up and threw him down on the concrete floor. Erion laughed because he thought it looked funny. One of the other nephews came charging at me with a metal chair, but I headbutted him and started hitting him once he was down to ensure I wouldn't have to worry about him.

Argon and Erion didn't feel like staying anymore. "Fuck it, Sleiman, let's bounce," they said, so we all just left.

To my surprise, Bekir was standing outside. "Who the fuck do you think you are?" he shouted.

"Fuck you," I said to him, and the three of us moved on, leaving Bekir's nephews in our wake and thwarting his plan to take control of the club.

The hostile takeover was unsuccessful, but this marked the beginning of a yearlong power struggle. I personally didn't consider myself the king of Askerød. At the time, I had no desire to be either. I just enjoyed the camaraderie and the sense of community at the club. I loved the independence and the fact that all the younger brothers in the neighborhood were welcome there. They were mostly between thirteen and fifteen years old, and just like I used to look up to Bekir, they now looked up to me. I had them perform tasks for me, but I made sure I treated everyone fairly, unlike how things often went when I was young or with some of the people on the lower tiers of Bekir's crew. I wanted them all to like me, and I tried to buy their love by taking care of the younger boys. I don't know how much crime they committed, but obviously, we had a huge influence on them. I don't think I was the new Bekir, but maybe I was starting to become like him.

The police were also frequent guests at the club. We weren't on good terms. They had this idea that we were big-time criminals now, and maybe they were right. We didn't just knock people out at the pub and pick their pockets for cash anymore. At one point, they had raided my mom's place so many times that she said, "That's it! Just take my keys. I'm moving out. I'm sick of this."

While I was in charge of the club, the war started to escalate. However, making me and my close associates responsible for the club had a positive effect on the community.

When the municipality stopped paying the social workers in the area, I took over the club. Even though it was turned into a marijuana den, there were still more pros than cons because when everyone was at the clubhouse, they weren't making trouble anywhere else. Of course, everything ultimately fell apart and once again our relationship with local officials, community outreach workers, social workers, and like deteriorated and it was all my fault.

24

JEALOUSY

One night out, I noticed a group of bikers at a club, sitting at a table filled with bottles. Some of the younger guys ventured onto the dance floor, where a couple of girls in short skirts wearing stiletto heels were dancing on a podium. I went over and started dancing with them as well.

I was enjoying their company until someone came up behind me and tapped me on the shoulder. I turned around slowly and found myself facing a short, muscular guy with glasses. Without hesitating, he just smashed a bottle over my head. Afterward, he just stood there looking up at me with a sinister sneer on his face before returning to the table with the bikers.

The man who attacked me was named Thomas. He was the son of a wealthy man. While he wasn't a patched member of neither the Hells Angels nor the Bandidos, he had strong ties to the biker scene in Odense. At the time this dude smashed the bottle over my head, I had no idea whom he was affiliated with. I was just aching for revenge.

I grabbed a beer glass from a nearby table and hid it on myself before I walked toward Thomas's table. I put a hand on the top of my head, saying, "Ow, ow, ow!" to give the impression that he had hurt me, and I was confused as to why he had, when in actuality I wanted to lure him into a false sense of security and get close enough to retaliate.

"What happened?" Thomas asked mockingly before I produced the concealed beer glass and attacked him. Everybody at the bikers' table got up and started hurling glasses and bottles at me and my boys.

When I had driven to the club, I had parked near the door in case I needed to retrieve any weapons from my BMW 320 convertible. With my people right behind me, I ran to the car and retrieved a baseball bat. When we turned around, the bikers were now standing outside the club, ready to rumble.

Now, if I had had any common sense, I would've just hopped in my BMW and fled the scene. There were now between ten and fifteen angry bikers ready to fight, and I only had about five or six younger guys backing me up. It didn't matter because I was hellbent on getting revenge. Stop me if you've heard this before . . .

When I get angry, my blood boils so hot there's usually a good reason to fear me. However, the biggest drawback to my rage is I almost completely lose touch with reality. If I fought those guys, it was highly probable I would lose badly. Fortunately, the police showed up. Imagine me being happy to see the police arrive. When they saw my face, they wanted to arrest me right away. My relief at seeing them was gone almost as soon as it had started.

"What are you arresting me for?" I asked for what seemed like the hundredth time in my young life.

"You're causing trouble."

"No, I'm not."

"Well, then you have to leave."

I was confused, but I honored their command and hopped in my BMW, and they let me leave the scene. Most of the officers knew me, and they knew I didn't have a driver's license. It was common knowledge around town I never had one, but in all the time I had a car, no one ever stopped me. As I drove off into the night, I was fixated on getting revenge on Thomas, but I had to think of another way besides violence.

I came up with an idea. If Thomas wanted to avoid my people beating him within an inch of his life, all would be forgiven if he paid me a one-time fee of $75,000, close to 500,000 DKK. If he paid, he didn't have to worry about me seeking revenge anymore.

I knew a couple of the guys who had been sitting at Thomas's table, two bikers named Madsen and Hedgehog. Neither of them was a member of a specific biker club, but they had close ties to a guy called Serge who ran one of the prominent biker gangs in Odense. I figured that I could make them the liaisons to collect the money from Thomas. I figured that Madsen and Hedgehog should have stopped this guy before he hit me, but they didn't.

After a few days, I tracked down Hedgehog's address and paid him a visit. I told him it was on them to get me my money. At this point, I figured my crew was strong enough to demand that price. I made it clear that if he and Madsen were unable to collect, I would instead send my people after *them*. At first, he didn't want to do it. After some protracted negotiation and him realizing that he didn't want to beef with an entire gang, Hedgehog accepted the terms.

While Thomas was partly under the protection of Serge and the bikers in Odense, attacking me in public unprovoked was such a colossal mistake that the bikers would probably agree to either hand him over or make sure that he raised the money. The conversations between me and Hedgehog went so well that it became the beginning of a close friendship.

We eventually made an agreement with the bikers that some of the immigrant boys would pick Thomas up in a van and bring him to the clubhouse in Askerød, where the negotiations would take place. If the negotiations broke down and Thomas refused to pay the $75,000, we had carte blanche to give him a severe beating, after which he was to be taken directly to Odense University Hospital so nothing could be traced back to Askerød.

However, our plans hit an unexpected snag. Serge was close friends with Bekir, so he went behind my back and contacted Bekir to find another solution. The guys from Odense agreed to give me a "present," as they called it, but they refused to pay the agreed-upon fee of $75,000.

Bekir was also close friends with my brother-in-law Karim. The guys from Odense requested that Bekir and Karim attend the negotiations, even though I totally opposed Bekir's inclusion in this matter.

He had only one purpose in getting involved: to make sure that he cashed in, and we never saw a dime.

We had a wild card in my crew named Sanchos who was notoriously violent, temperamental, strong as hell, and extremely loyal to me. He was the most dangerous one of us all. A loner. He was one of the first ones to start attacking pubs and shit like that. He loved me because he felt like I did things fairly. Once, he met a couple of guys at a nightclub who said they wanted to fuck me up. Later, he called me and said, "I'm hiding in some bushes. I just stabbed some guys who wanted to fuck you up. I let 'em talk and talk and talk, and then I finally stabbed them."

He was that kind of loyal to me. Eventually, I had to go pick him up after he had been hiding out for a while. He was completely covered in blood. I never found out whom he stabbed, but he was one of the reasons our crew became so feared and powerful. He had the capability to be merciless. As long as he was with us, we could be outnumbered five to one but still win the fight. However, everyone else knew this as well.

When the bikers from Odense arrived, Thomas wasn't with them. They had sent someone else to negotiate on his behalf. I wanted Sanchos to be present at the meeting, but Bekir opposed it. Sanchos was too unpredictable, he maintained. The meeting was going to be held at the clubhouse. In the end, it was Bekir who sat down with the representative from Odense by himself.

To this very day, I don't know if he got the $75,000, but Bekir had proven that he was the one who commanded the most fear and respect. The older, cunning man had outsmarted the young one. I was livid, but there were no noble reasons behind my rage. I was simply mad that I had lost my hand gambling in a game of money and power.

Perhaps Bekir *was* entitled to the money, according to the underworld's code of ethics, and Bekir *did* betray me. Even if Bekir got the money, in the end, he also kept me from beating a man with connections to a bloody pulp and possibly getting into even more trouble. A source who was present at the meeting and part of the inner circle in the gang scene at the time denies that Bekir got the money. Bekir kept Sanchos away from the meeting. While I considered him an asset, in Bekir's eyes he was just an unpredictable junkie.

From where I stood, Bekir had snaked me out of almost half a million DKK. So, we went back to the original plan in order to salvage things. Since we couldn't get the money from Thomas, we decided to hold Madsen and Hedgehog accountable. However, Hedgehog and I had formed a friendship, and I no longer wished to extort him. I felt like he was a good person, and it wasn't really his fault that Thomas had smashed that bottle over my head. The rest of the guys just wanted to him fuck him up and skin him for every penny. I get that. That was the original plan, but at some point, I had changed my mind. I didn't think it was fair to hold him accountable anymore.

The fact that I suddenly reversed my original position changed my crew's perception of me. They felt that I failed the brotherhood by allowing my friendship with Hedgehog to take precedence over the interests of the club. Some of them even suspected me of having taken money from Hedgehog without sharing. They were convinced that I had fucked them over. They didn't understand why Hedgehog was suddenly off limits. It had to be because he'd already paid me.

Another reason why my friends began to distrust me was that Hedgehog had close ties to the Hells Angels and Black Cobra. He was an enemy who had been spared for seemingly no reason. Could it be that I was also secretly in cahoots with Black Cobra?

In an environment where conspiracy theories gained traction every time someone opened their mouth, I had made myself vulnerable and open to scrutiny. Another internal issue was that I was also better at making money than the rest of the crew. Even though I enjoyed playing the part of the generous benefactor, some of the guys were jealous of me, and if I wasn't earning and sharing the spoils so others could benefit as well, they began to resent me for it.

Even to this day, that bothers me. Sure, I had money, but not as much as they thought. I had spent a lot of it on them: treating them to dinner, partying. If my friend needed a gold ring, I went and bought him a gold ring. I never considered them beneath me. In my heart and mind, they were my brothers, my equals. But I sensed their jealousy.

One day, I flat-out asked them, "What is it you want me to do?"

"Nothing," they replied. But after a while, they added, "You don't think of us as your brothers anymore."

I wasn't only putting out fires in-house. I was also at war outside Askerød. During the 2000s, a lot of the smaller groups that popped up in the western suburbs of Copenhagen dreamed of forming one large, organized gang. A gang that could finally compete with the older, more well-established, inner-city gangs. A gang so powerful it could simultaneously hold its own against the bikers. The Askerød Boys went from being an insignificant player to a force to be reckoned with in a relatively short amount of time.

While we were in the middle of a small-scale war with a competing gang in the outskirts of Copenhagen, that same group was making cautious proposals about an alliance. The gang, which is referred to as the Egyptians due to the ancestry of their leader (who is called The Egyptian), was at war with several other immigrant groups, especially a powerful gang based in central Copenhagen. The Egyptians wanted the Bekir Boys to enter an alliance with them and some other smaller suburban crews.

My people and I thought an alliance made sense. You can't start selling marijuana in Copenhagen unless you're strong. If you make a living stealing gold and selling it on the street, and someone who's not even from around here starts selling his gold on the next corner, he's not gonna do so in peace. It's the same principle with weed. You can't steal someone else's livelihood unless you're very powerful.

The Bekir Boys listened when The Egyptian first pitched the idea of an alliance. Back when I was a teenager, The Egyptian and I were friends. The main issue with him was he considered himself the godfather of all the suburban ghettos. He also wanted his gang to eventually surpass the Bekir Boys. This level of ambition didn't sit well with Bekir.

The Egyptian was too extreme. He wanted to be stronger than the guys from the city. Dealing with the guys from the city automatically involves the bikers, so we would have to fight them too. We didn't want to engage in all of that. Sure, we were doing things like running our own debt-collecting businesses, coming up with extortion schemes, and selling marijuana. But we also wanted to do so without sparking an unnecessary conflict. It seemed like The Egyptian had the intention of starting wars, and that seemed counterproductive to us.

The Egyptian was furious when my crew and the Bekir Boys

both balked at consolidating our forces. Eventually, he and his boys contacted me and demanded a straight answer. We met at our club-house and had a discussion to clear the air . . . at least, that was the hope.

"Are you with us in this war?" The Egyptian asked.

I told him I didn't know who sided with whom in these wars he was planning to jump into headfirst without any real forethought. I told him that we got on well with some of the guys from the city and that we didn't want to destroy those relationships.

The Egyptian claimed that I had been brainwashed by the enemy and that I was planning to kill him. He pulled out his gun and placed it on the table in front of me.

I told him that if he didn't put that gun away, I would shove it up his ass. He was a guest at our clubhouse, and he had better show some respect. In the end, we had to kick him out and tell him that he must be out his fuckin' mind if he thought we had been paid to kill him. Shortly after this meeting, the hostility between my crew and The Egyptian escalated.

The following case illustrates how often completely different people somehow end up in financial or moral debt to one another in the criminal underworld. In The Egyptian's ghetto, a group of immi-grant boys stole the equivalent of $4,500 in Danish Krone from a Danish man. The boys believed he had been dealing drugs on their turf. This man happened to know a biker, whom he asked for help. The biker refused to get directly involved but recommended Hedgehog.

Hedgehog was a family man who, most of the time, led a law-abiding life. However, he had a weakness for easy money, which he usually made from dealing cocaine. After he befriended me, he often asked me for help in various business matters. When Hedgehog was tasked with retrieving the $4,500, he asked me for help.

I knew the guys who had stolen the money belonged to The Egyptian's gang. Instead of calling them, I went over their heads and called The Egyptian directly, even though we were on bad terms at the time. Just to mock me, he told me to talk to the kids instead.

"Oh, so your little soldiers are in charge now?" I asked.

The Egyptian put one of the boys on the phone. "If you want the money, then come and get it," the kid said.

"Oh, I'm coming."

The complicated nature of my relationship with Bekir played heavily in this affair. I refused to go unarmed, so I tracked down Bekir in Copenhagen to ask him for a gun. He was at the gym with a mutual friend.

I said, "You have to help me get a gun. I have a problem with The Egyptian that needs solving. I'm gonna fuck him up. I have to go to his hood and get some money from him. Any of you wanna join me?"

"You're not getting a gun, and nobody's coming with you. We're not going to war with The Egyptian," Bekir answered.

"Fuck you. If you don't wanna help, don't. Anyone else wanna come?" I asked again.

"Let me talk to the Egyptian. I know him," one of the other guys said.

"Okay. Talk to him." But I quickly changed my mind. I wanted to leave right away. In my haste, I didn't even think to arm myself first.

I didn't drive just any car to meet The Egyptian. I rolled right into the heart of his turf in my Jaguar. I knew that I was playing with fire, but I was known for daring where others hesitated. What I failed to realize at the time was that I was driving straight into an ambush.

Three of my people followed in a car behind me, but when I arrived in The Egyptian's territory, I didn't bother to wait for him. I parked my Jaguar and walked straight into the heart of an unfamiliar ghetto. A group of masked men were waiting for me. I saw about forty guys with The Egyptian out in front. I walked right up to him and patted him on his stomach because everyone knew that he was always strapped.

"Are you packing?" I asked.

"What are you doing here?"

The Egyptian put his hand on his stomach and took a step back. From one of the rooftops, someone shouted, "Shoot them! Shoot them!"

Luckily, my people managed to catch up to me. The one who had the presence of mind to bring a weapon along was armed with a machine gun. He immediately opened fire at the rooftops where The

Egyptian had positioned his soldiers. They fired back, aiming at me. At first, I refused to retreat because I thought they were firing tear gas at us.

"What the hell are you doing? They're shooting live rounds! Run! They're trying to kill you!" one of my boys shouted at me.

I didn't know where to run. I had never been there before. If I ran blindly, I would get shot, so I sought shelter underneath a canopy roof. I knew I had to get back to my car, but I was surrounded.

My boy with the machine gun grabbed me up and got me to safety, then covered our hasty escape by continuing to fire his machine gun at the rooftop where The Egyptian's shooters were taking cover. We all managed to make it back to the cars, but now we had to drive out of The Egyptian's territory unscathed. This included having to drive under a couple of bridges on the way out. The Egyptian had shooters situated on the bridges who fired on us from above as we sped out of the ghetto. One of us got hit by the gunfire and nearly died. He was one of Bekir's Boys who had actually come to help. He quit the game after that day. The second we arrived back in Askerød, some of The Egyptians rolled in behind us, guns blazing. Gunfire was exchanged, but no one was injured, and everyone adhered to the code of the streets.

Once again, Bekir had proved a hard man to figure out. He had refused to help me because he didn't want to go to war with The Egyptian, but he had allowed one of his soldiers to ride into The Egyptian's ghetto with me.

That wasn't the end of it. The Egyptians had attempted to kill me because they suspected me of siding with their enemies. Mind you, I wasn't even personally involved in the case about the $4,500. The underlying issue was that Hedgehog had ties to the bikers and Black Cobra, so in the eyes of the Egyptians, I was in league with both gangs in their fight against the Egyptians.

The fight over the $4,500 (30,000 DKK) led the Egyptians to target Hedgehog. One day when he wasn't at home, they went to the house where he lived with his wife and children. They called him from inside the house and demanded a six-figure sum as payment for choosing the wrong side in the conflict. From that day forward, I became the protector of Hedgehog and his family. I risked my life for them, and Hedgehog will never forget how far I went to protect my friend.

Whenever people were in trouble, they called me. They were never my problems, but I didn't care about the danger.

Hedgehog had some trouble with some immigrant dudes who extorted him because one of his friends sold weed on their turf. There was no point in going after the dealer 'cause he had no money. Hedgehog had a house, a business, and drove a Harley, so they told him to pay them. My dumbass went out there and fought his battle, and it nearly cost me my life.

Not everybody saw me as a hero. They thought I put myself and my people into a bad situation to help a friend, which led to a misunderstanding that made myself vulnerable. If anyone had wanted to spread rumors about my affiliations, the timing would have been just right to sow seeds of discord.

In any case, the dream of one great, organized suburban gang that could directly compete with both the older, larger, more established gangs in the city and the various biker gangs, was laid to rest once and for all. However, The Egyptian ultimately got his wish of waging war.

25

HE'S GOING DOWN

S amir has never officially declared himself a member of Black Cobra. But since he was sentenced to two and half years behind bars for shooting Bekir's nephew, a long list of news sources and magazine and newspaper articles have described him as joining Black Cobra's fight against the Bekir Boys. The conflict between Samir and Bekir only intensified following Samir's release from prison.

Although Samir started out wanting to avoid any association with gang life or the criminal underworld, in the end, he decided to join Black Cobra. The fact of the matter was Samir didn't feel like he had any other choice if he wanted to protect himself from his enemies.

One hot day in July 2004, Samir came close to losing his life in a parking lot near the mall in Hundige, where at least twenty shots were fired at him from a machine gun. Samir was convinced that I was behind the attack. The police also shared his suspicions.

I was detained, and while I was in custody, Samir allegedly tried to have me killed. *B.T.* ran an article in 2008 with the headline "The Cobra-King: The Final Showdown," which reproduced an alleged conversation between Samir and another member of Black Cobra who was being detained in the same facility as I was. The newspaper maintains that it obtained the recordings from the police. Samir was supposedly recorded saying: "I know he's there. I know it, a hundred percent. Roskilde Police got him. Go for a walk at four, and see if you can find him. Keep an eye on his cell if he goes to the bathroom . . . He's going down in there. I want you to cut him."

Samir was right. I had been detained, but just an hour before he gave the order, the police derailed his plan by letting me go, so I avoided getting stabbed. However, it wasn't until *B.T.* published the article that I found out about Samir's assassination order.

No official suspects in the attempted assassination of Samir have been identified, but when it happened, the police immediately went looking for me. I had spent the night with friends at the clubhouse, and the police came to arrest us for suspicion of attempted murder the next morning. They had no evidence, but the circumstances pointed to me and my crew, mostly because Samir and I still had a score to settle and partly because I was part of Bekir's crew, who had yet to get revenge for the attack on Bekir two years earlier.

However, the police's suspicions in this particular instance were groundless. We had nothing to do with it. We had been to Nørrebro for dinner, and after that, we went to see a movie. Nevertheless, five of us were arrested on suspicion of having carried out the attack. Obviously, when the police arrest five guys, everyone will assume that one of them is guilty. The truth is they didn't have sufficient evidence to maintain my investigative custody, so my boys were released the next day. Oddly enough, the charges against them were upheld for a year and a half.

Two days after our release, a police officer came to the club. He approached me and one of the younger Bekir Boys named Jamil and said, "You're going to help us solve this case and put an end to this war."

"You've got the wrong guy," I said to the officer. "I'm not getting mixed up in this case, and I don't help the police. If you need me to do your job, I'm gonna need your fuckin' paycheck."

"You know what, Sleiman? You've got a car out there, a slick BMW. It's got a certain illegal look about it. If you don't help us with this case, we'll make sure your life gets really difficult."

"Fine, pal, make our lives difficult, and then piss off."

A couple of days later, the police made good on their threat. Sixteen officers stormed our clubhouse, where they found a sawed-off shotgun and some shells. At the same time, they paid my mother a visit and found a gun and some bullets in a room in her basement.

Hedgehog once gifted me a black BMW M5 with 507 horsepower, and I cherished that car more than anything else I had ever owned. Out of sheer frustration, the police started to employ the old Al Capone method. It had seemed impossible for them to bust my gang's members for their other crimes, but they attempted to go after us for tax fraud and the curious fact that many of us drove cars like black BMWs and big Audis, even though we were only receiving unemployment benefits.

One day, I was walking across a parking lot with Kira when a police officer called me over to him. Meanwhile, another officer was sitting inside my car. They had pried open the lock and entered my vehicle without my consent. They told me, "You're charged with unlawful possession of weapons."

"What are you talking about? Weapons? I'm not armed!"

"No, but we found a gun at your mom's place, a .45, and we're confiscating your BMW."

"Fuck you. Why would you do that?"

"It's illegal, and it's been modified to enhance the vehicle's performance!"

After that went down, I was put on a bus. Shortly afterward, the very same police officer approached me again. He said, "I'm going to make your life really difficult. I won't stop. I'll keep visiting your mother, I'll keep visiting the clubhouse, I'll follow you everywhere until you tell us who shot Samir."

"Are you stupid or something?" I asked him.

"You won't be released until one of you takes the blame for these weapons. If not, we arrest your mother because the gun was found in her basement."

I realized I was being painted into a corner and I had very few options left, so I decided to sacrifice myself. "You know what? Release my friends, then. I'll sign a statement saying both guns are mine. Then you release the others. But I want to see that they're released before I sign."

The lawyers said that as long as one of the authorities signed off on everything, they would all be released. I saw all of my people walk out of the detention center free and signed a statement saying the guns were mine. After that, the officer told me that I was free to go.

I figured it was better that one of us took the fall than all of us. I took the nine-month sentence that came with signing the paper. My people all thanked me for sacrificing my freedom for theirs and doing the time for everyone else's crime. None of those guns even belonged to me, but I was being loyal to my gang. Later, they all forgot I had stuck my neck out for them . . . again.

Just three weeks after Samir was shot, there was another standoff in the war between Black Cobra and the Bekir Boys. This time, Jamil, was the target. Everybody loved Jamil, and he had become like my little brother. I saw something in him that reminded me of myself. He had been dealt a bad hand. He was kind and full of life and innocent in a way. Sure, he was a troublemaker, but unlike some of us, he wasn't cruel. He was still a good person. Pure inside. He seemed like he would achieve more in life than I had. But the sad reality was Jamil's fate was headed in the same direction as mine. He had joined the rapidly escalating war, and the shots fired at Samir had to be avenged.

An attempt was made on Jamil's life. Even though the local media intimated that Samir was behind the attack on Jamil, the attempted murder has never been solved. Within the community, no one doubted that the attack was Black Cobra's revenge for a series of previous attacks on them.

I do think someone from our group was behind the attack on Samir, and to avoid retribution themselves, they pointed their finger at Jamil. Jamil was the new, hot-blooded kid making his way up the ranks, so he was blamed for carrying it out. The day Jamil got shot was one of the hardest days of my life. He was so happy that day. He had just gotten an Audi A3, and he was taking his girlfriend to the movies.

Jamil would come to play a central role in the gang war, and the last couple of years, he has been implicated in several serious police investigations. Back then, I wasn't the only one who had Jamil's back. Askerød Housing Association chairman Lone Binderup also had a soft spot for him. Like so many others in Askerød, he had been dogged by more misfortune than any young man deserves.

Jamil, his sister, and his little brother once ran through Askerød screaming, chasing after their mother, whose head had been sliced open by her ex-husband. His story is quite similar to mine. We both had violent fathers who disappeared from our lives. As a consequence, we were both forced to be the men of the family at a very early age, and deal with everything that came with taking on so much responsibility at a young age.

Jamil also developed a close relationship with Bekir.. No surprise as Bekir deliberately went after boys without fathers.

The attack on Jamil triggered a war that is still raging between the two gangs to this very day. He was only nineteen, he was popular among the young people in Askerød, and the attack on him felt like an attack on all of them. The war had gained a new generation of willing recruits, and the peace between Black Cobra and the Bekir Boys that I had originally wished for was no longer possible. It looked like Bekir had once again gotten exactly what he wanted.

After the attack on Jamil, Bekir won the boys over to his side and convinced them that Black Cobra was the enemy. I was the loser. I wanted to draw them away from Bekir, but now they were being drawn even closer to him. I could've just left the group. No one was forcing me to stay. But I was too weak, dug in too deep in my criminal lifestyle, and I honestly didn't know where else to turn.

Shortly after the attacks on Samir and Jamil occurred, the frustrated police force began to resort to unconventional methods in hopes of making progress. They had no evidence, but they knew that the big players in the war were Samir, Bekir, and I, so they initiated a group mediation for us all. The police were convinced that every single incident in Askerød had something to do with the conflict between me and Samir. They thought that if only we would make up, everything would settle down. They told me that Bekir would be there too, so I agreed to come. It was my opinion that only Bekir could resolve the conflict.

The meeting was set up at the police station in Karlslunde. In the morning, the police came to pick me up. It wasn't a question of whether I wanted to come or not. The police ordered me to go. However, when I arrived at the station, it was just me, Samir, and his brother at the mediation session. Bekir canceled on us at the last moment.

The chief superintendent, who had arranged the meeting,

promised me and Samir that the police would lay off pursuing our gangs so aggressively, if we managed to make peace that day. They would put an end to the constant raids, surveillance, and persecution. Unfortunately, neither I nor Samir were willing to grant them concessions, and I refused to tell them anything out of fear that I might be accused of being a collaborator or a snitch.

The police went into this entire process knowing that none of the groups would tell them who was behind the latest shootings, but they wanted peace, and they wanted it now. They informed us that they were authorized by the local politicians to spare no effort if Samir and I refused to make peace. Despite the threats, Samir and I did nothing but scowl at each other for the duration of the meeting as if we were at a pre-prize fight weigh-in. In reality, I simply didn't think I had the authority to make peace on behalf of the Bekir Boys. Bekir not being present was the main obstacle to reaching any peace agreement.

"Here's what's going to happen: You're going to shake hands and make peace today so we can finally put an end to all this. If not, you will learn what the full force of the police is capable of," the chief superintendent said.

"I'm not the one who doesn't want peace," Samir said.

"Well, it's not me either," I said.

"It seems like you're the one who doesn't want peace, Sleiman," the chief superintendent said to me.

I was confused by this. "Why would you say that? What are you attacking me for? It might as well be them who don't want peace," I responded.

"So, you and your friends are not going to shoot Samir as soon as he leaves this building to avenge the attack on Jamil?" he asked me.

"No, of course not. We don't even know who shot Jamil. Did Samir shoot Jamil?" I asked defiantly.

"No," the chief superintendent answered.

"Then why would we take revenge on them?" I countered.

The meeting turned into a complete disaster. I was cocky that day. I didn't have time to smoke before they picked me up, and it was so early that I wasn't really functioning. I just needed to smoke a joint and I couldn't, so I was pissed. It also felt wrong to be there without Bekir. In the end, the officer told me that if I took so much as one wrong step, I would have the entire police force on my back. So, I kept my mouth shut.

The war had been raging on for five years, and it had only just begun. No matter how many people were shot or stabbed or beaten over the course of our extended urban conflict, most of the cases remained unsolved.

Kurt Worsøe, who has been a local police officer in Askerød since the mid-1990s, is reluctant to provide critical information about the local criminal element. He doesn't wish to jeopardize the confidence his sources and informants have in him. The success of his work depends on their trust. He isn't the tough cop who investigates the shootings—he's the one they can turn to for help. If someone is to be arrested, he calls the families. Instead of the police going to Askerød, Kurt tells the person in question to come see him, and they almost always do. He also takes care of some of their paperwork. That's the way it has always been. At the police station, they consider it wise to have a man like Kurt, someone the young people don't have to hide from.

That doesn't mean he's unaware of how bad things have been. He has a good idea what happened when I stabbed Samir, when Samir shot Bekir, and when Samir was shot in his car. He also knows more than most about what happened when Jamil was almost killed and when I was ambushed. But seeing as how most of the events haven't led to any convictions, he keeps this information to himself, as do the other residents of Askerød.

Practically all the cases have been closed because the police have run their heads against the wall. Even when people shoot each other, they refuse to say anything, and if they do say something to the police, you can be pretty sure it's a lie. No one wants to be a snitch.

If we do, us and our families will pay for it. If somebody snitches, someone else has an obligation to avenge it. Kurt Worsøe once told me that during the twelve years he was an officer, nobody has ever revealed anything that could be used to get someone else in trouble. Not even off the record.

Even the people in the periphery of the periphery are silent. It doesn't matter if the police were talking to the twelve-year-olds or their grandparents, the reaction is the same: silence.

26

KIRA

When we first met, Kira had told me that she wanted to get rid of Anna so she could have me all to herself. In a way, that turned me on. And with that, a long, tumultuous relationship with frequent intermissions had begun.

Kira's entire family opposed our relationship from the beginning, and the subsequent years became one long battle between me and Kira's parents. They had never had an immigrant in their home, but I suppose Kira thought it was exciting because I was a bad boy, and she was a nice, Danish girl. I could tell that her family didn't like me, but she was persistent, and I respected that.

When I met her, Kira was a young, virtuous girl. Shortly afterward, she bleached her hair blonde, giving her a more provocative look. Not too long afterward, my friends began supplying me with salacious gossip about my new girlfriend.

"She's a slut. She's cheating on you with other guys," they said.

Even though I wasn't sure they were telling the truth, I slowly began to suspect her of infidelity. Kira was an accomplished ballroom dancer and participated in the national and European youth championship, and I could hardly control my jealousy when she left for competitions. I thought about all the men she was dancing with and how she exposed her body, looking all sexy and fit and tanned for everyone to see in her competition dresses. I also hated it when she went to the beach. Other guys could look at her well-toned dancer's body in swimwear.

She started lying to me. She told me that she had to stay home with her family and that they didn't want her to be with me, but she wasn't at home. She was dancing at the national championship. I had to learn about it from other people. I think she did it to spare me a bit. She also had a hard time because she wanted to maintain a relationship with both me and her parents. I couldn't trust her anymore, and that became a problem.

The Arab gossiping culture is even more bitchy among the men, and it's worse because you actually believe them. They're your brothers, your friends, and I didn't question what they said about Kira. My friends knew how to pull me away from her. I don't know why that was their plan, but they probably felt like I should be focusing my attention less on her and more on them.

The combination of jealousy, interference from friends, and hostility from her family resulted in a toxic and often abusive relationship. Sometimes, she would disappear for two months straight because her parents forbade her to see me, so I began to hate her family. Her parents had pinned their hopes on Kira giving them grandchildren, but there was no way in hell I was gonna be the father in their eyes.

Kira's dad was a craftsman, and her mother was a personal care worker. Her mother was familiar with my reputation from her job at the municipality, and you could hardly blame them for disapproving of the relationship. No normal family would want me for a son-in-law, and they did what they could to protect their daughter against me. Kira was also aware of what was going on because we were together during the time of the shootings between Black Cobra and the Bekir Boys. Her best friend was dating my close friend Erion, who was just as involved in the criminal underworld.

Her parents' disapproval of me was never more evident than it was on one unfortunate Saturday night. Kira and I met at the mall that day. We agreed to meet up later for dinner. She had just gotten off work at the drugstore and was going home to talk to her parents. After that, she would come back, and we would head to the restaurant.

At 7:00 p.m., there was still no sign of her. I called her several times, but there was no answer. I then called her parents' house. Her mom told me that someone else had come to pick her up. "I think she went on a date," she said.

I was furious. If they had only accepted Kira and I dating, then we would have figured out by ourselves if we were supposed to be together or not. Instead, we had to hide when we went grocery shopping so that we wouldn't risk bumping into her parents. She had to bow her head in the car so that no one would see us out together. It made me hate them.

Driven by anger, I went over to Kira's house with a hammer in my hand. I was determined to break down the door if her parents didn't open it.

Her father was a hefty man of almost six feet five, and he wasn't afraid of me. At the crux of everything, he was a Danish father who simply loved his daughter too much to have a man who was a Muslim, an immigrant, and a criminal for a possible son-in-law or father to his grandchild. When he opened the door, he said, "She's not home. She's on a date."

"That can't be true. Bjarne, let me talk to Kira."

"She's not home."

"I'm sure she's home. Let me talk to her!"

He slammed the door. There was my answer. I began making one of my trademarked bad decisions in the heat of anger and started beating on their door with the hammer.

"If you do that one more time, we're calling the cops, Sleiman," Kira's father said when he opened the door again.

"I *will* do it again. I want Kira to come outside."

"Kira's not coming out!"

He closed the door again, and I went right back to knocking on their door with the hammer until Kira came running and opened the door. "Sleiman, please just go," she told me.

"Why? What's wrong? Why would they say you're on a date when you're right here?"

"Sleiman, please just go. I don't want to be with you anymore," she told me.

"You don't mean that, Kira."

Her father asked us to leave the house and talk outside. After we had talked for a while, he suddenly came outside, grabbed Kira by the hand, and told her that it was time to come inside. In the meantime, Kira's mother called the cops, so while I was arguing with Kira's dad over him reversing his previous position, the police showed up and asked him if he wanted to press charges against me.

Kira's father said, "I don't want to press charges. Just take him to the station so he can cool down."

So, they arrested me for disorderly conduct and drove me to the station. Kira didn't do anything. She just said that it was over between us.

You would think I would learn my lesson or that we would be over after that incident, but Kira came back time and again. Spiteful breakups were followed by joyful makeups, which once again clashed with her parents' hopes for their daughter's future.

I thought it was fine living the way I did, but then I realized that I would have to do something legal. Something that would earn me respect, something her parents wouldn't sneer at. Something that would prove to them I was as good a boyfriend for their daughter as any man was. I didn't want to be lower class. Why would I stay down there? Why were they middle class? I wanted to be better than they were. I wanted a house that was bigger and more expensive than theirs was.

Hedgehog and I had our eyes set on a sewing machine shop at the local mall, but I knew that they wouldn't allow me to own a store in the very mall where I had stolen from and vandalized the shops for ten years. The shop cost about $15,000 USD. We decided that Hedgehog should call and pretend like he was the one who wanted to buy the store. But when we got to the rental company, the lady was surprised to see that I was the one who signed the lease. She didn't say anything, so the store was ours.

This was the beginning of a success story. I redecorated the store and, through a company in Aalborg, obtained the rights to sell a French clothing brand. Financially, these were good times in Denmark, so it was easy for us to make arrangements for overdraft facilities at the bank. Hedgehog's wealthy mother also put up a solid financial security, and I had some money saved up from an unnamed source.

I got a good deal from the guy who imported the brand. He was having a hard time selling the clothes and offered me advantageous terms for the deal. When I bought clothes on credit, I could turn around and sell them for over double what I paid for them, and we averaged about $25,000 a month in profit. It was a hip-hop brand that I'm not going to identify any further for legal reasons. In the end, the store earned a handsome profit during the first six months it was in operation.

The store was a legitimate success story, fully vetted by the police and local law enforcement. When the legal money started rolling in, Hedgehog encouraged me to invest in certain things, and I followed his advice. I had this dream about buying a house with a garden, so I bought a small house for $340,000 with a down payment of $65,000 (408,000 DKK). At the same time, I paid off all my debts to the state. Because I was making $25,000 a month, I was removed from the list of people with tarnished credit histories and bought a Jaguar with financing.

Everyone wasn't thrilled about my success in business. At the clubhouse, my absence was felt, especially because my departure also meant the club lost its most valuable source of income. While I became richer, my friends and associates became poorer. While I always shared the money from my criminal activities with the group, I didn't feel obligated to do the same with my legal income.

I became more and more dependent on my company, so I tried to stay away from crime and keep my distance from the crew. It wasn't because I was suddenly against doing illegal stuff. I just didn't have time for it. I was working day and night in that store, and many people started to hate me a bit, as well as people within my group.

Eventually, they started smashing up my cars—lit them on fire, keyed them, and poured brake fluid over them. I don't know exactly who it was, but people tried to get to me that way. I went from bum to businessman in no time, and suddenly, I was driving fancy cars and owned a house. Some people couldn't handle that.

I desperately wanted Kira to move in with me at my new house. I wanted to prove to her and her parents that I was just as good as they were. I was doing everything for all the wrong reasons. She wasn't ready, and I wasn't stable enough. Our relationship was on again, off again. We would be good to each other, then we would be cruel. It seemed like cruelty always won out in the end. It was the same with the battle raging inside of me.

She still had doubts about us, and she lied about her birth control. I wanted to have a child more than anything, and she told me she was off the pill. But I caught her taking them anyway. I don't think I've ever been so disappointed in my life. She didn't trust me. When I think about how I was living at the time, I honestly don't blame her.

27

THE AMBUSH

One night in January 2007, I was at a club across from Tivoli in Copenhagen with Kira and her best friend, Tina. Normally, I can drink quite a bit, but that night, for some odd reason, I was blind drunk after just one drink. Next thing I knew, I was in the bathroom, where a fellow immigrant and a gigantic guy were offering me cocaine.

The club was dark and jam-packed. In the bathroom, it was light, less crowded, and less noisy. Perhaps that's why I remember this detail. It was a strange duo. One of them was a huge, pale, Danish-looking guy, while the other one was short, sturdy, and dark-haired. They were both elegantly dressed in all white. It was all very strange.

I turned down their offer, but they kept insisting I have some. They kept on pushing until we got into a fight. When I came out of the bathroom, I ran into Samir's little brother, Zaki. He asked me if I needed help, which made me even more suspicious. He was my enemy, and how did he know what had just happened in the bathroom?

I went over to Kira and Tina and told them, "We have to get out of here."

We all walked toward City Hall Square and turned a corner to get to where the car was parked. On the way, Tina wanted a burger at McDonald's. A narrow alleyway lead into this McDonald's, but when we tried the door, it was locked. When I turned around, I was standing face-to-face with the same dark-haired guy from the bathroom.

I wasn't waiting for him to move, so I attacked him to gain the upper hand. Just then, three hooded men came running toward him and tackled me like I was the quarterback still holding the ball. I was now on the ground, and even more men showed up out of the night. About ten guys were now stomping on me relentlessly.

"Don't kick him in the head! You're gonna kill him!" Tina yelled, ran over, and threw herself down to cover me. She made sure to protect my face with her thigh so no one would kick me in the face.

After Tina jumped to my aid, the battering ceased. I was lying on the ground unconscious while Tina was making futile efforts to wake me up. One of my own attackers had reservations about jumping me and returned to the scene. He attempted to get me to come too. When I woke up, I thought he was still beating me. His face was just inches away from mine, so I grabbed him by the ears and pulled him down so I could headbutt him until his blood was pouring down on me.

"I'm trying to help you!" he yelled. The reluctant attacker got up and ran away.

We ultimately ended at Glostrup Hospital, where Kira and Tina insisted that I should be checked for internal bleeding. Physically, I was fine, but there was something I couldn't quite put my finger on that began to trouble me. There was no doubt in my mind the entire ambush was planned, but by who and did my own people help set me up?

I began to wonder if my relationship with my friends and my crew had become so strained that they were the ones who had ordered the girls to drug me and hired the other guys to beat me up. And if so, who made the call to whom?

I wasn't sure if the guys I considered my friends were in fact my enemies. After that, my old friends also started questioning who I really was. They overheard a phone conversation I had with my bank and misinterpreted it to mean that I had made $435,000 selling my house. They refused to believe that the outstanding mortgage had to be repaid. They thought I had hidden something from them, and I had way more money than I did. When they started accusing me of these things, I thought: *Who the hell do they think I am?*

The incident at the club made me see things in a different light. I used to be close to Samir, Bekir, and The Egyptian, but now they had all become my enemies. My oldest and closest friends mistrusted me, and in return, I suspected them all of trying to bring about my downfall without even knowing if any of them were truly to blame.

I had always considered my friendships as something bigger and stronger than other people's friendships because we fought together as soldiers and risked our lives for one another. It had always been us against the world, us against the system, us against the Danes, us against the racists, us against xenophobia. Now even these friendships were crumbling. "One for all and all for one" had turned into "All against all and nobody for anybody." Love had turned to hate. Even Jamil, whom I considered to be a little brother, had slipped out of my life, and I didn't even know why.

They tried to make bad blood between Jamil and me so they could isolate me from the group. How did they do that? By telling Jamil that I was living a double life. That I was a multimillionaire, that I was betraying them for Hells Angels, and I didn't care about the group.

I felt it happen, but I still hoped that some of them had love for me. But none of them did because nobody really loves anybody in that world. On the streets, there's no real love. There are friendships based on mutual interests, but when those interests are no longer aligned, then the friendships disappear. They wanted me to go to war and kill Samir or Samir to kill me because that way they could get rid of us both. If I died, then the other boys won because Samir would be in jail. And if Samir died, the boys still won, because then I would be in jail. That was how cruel and cunning they were.

On the periphery of my group, there was a young man they called The Bornholmer because he hailed from the small island next to Sweden where the sun always shines. He was a weak and deeply indebted man who was always desperately short of money. He was trying to distance himself from the group, and I decided that this merited a punishment. The Bornholmer was running his own business on Christiania and didn't include the group, and I decided he should pay before he left us. So, when he told me that if only, he had

$7,000 in his pocket, he could produce something worth $14,000 in two weeks' time, I gave him the money knowing there was no chance he would be able to repay it. I added a special condition: if he wasn't able to double the investment, his debt would balloon to $70,000 (461,275 DKK).

He fell right into the trap. As I had expected him to do, The Bornholmer failed to fulfill his obligations. This led to me and my associates Omar and Baasim chasing him around Copenhagen. He gave us the slip a couple of times, but one day, we caught up to him. Someone intervened, so he was able to evade us again. He obeyed the code of the streets and didn't report to the police that we were after him.

We drove out to see one of The Bornholmer's gang-related friends, who was going to tell us where he was hiding out. The friend pretended to help, but he gave us the runaround. While I can respect him not snitching, he was in the way of us handling our business.

I punched and stomped on The Bornholmer's friend in hopes he'd reveal his whereabouts. Mid-punishment, I noticed I was the only one putting in work and demanded the other two guys get their hands dirty as well. They hesitated because they usually left the bloody work to me. But this time, I wasn't having it..

They resented me for forcing them to get their hands dirty too because I always had to do the heavy lifting. I was always suspected of being involved in every crime, even when I had nothing to do with it and everyone else either got to avoid suspicion or benefit from my handiwork. They wanted the money, but they also wanted to appear innocent when it came to the violence. They couldn't have it both ways anymore.

My own friends began to fear me. They thought to themselves, *if he's capable of those things, then what will he do to us if we get on his bad side?*

28

THEY TRIED TO MURDER ME

K ira and I broke up again in Spring 2007. It would be easier for me if she just stayed away for good. That being said, we still hung out from time to time hoping to preserve some semblance of a friendship.

I was with Kira and her friend Tina one night, I gave one of their mutual friends a ride home in my BMW. Kira had a license, but she was always too scared to drive. Tina, on the other hand, was always eager to grab the wheel. Tina and I were joking around, and Kira thought that we were enjoying ourselves a little too much for her taste.

"You have more fun with Tina than you do with me, and I get jealous, Sleiman," she said. Then she started hitting me and saying that she didn't want me to hang out with Tina anymore.

I was pissed. "You know what, Kira? If this is the way it's gonna be, then I don't think *we* should be hanging out anymore!"

She started crying, and when I dropped her off, she was still crying.

Almost exactly a month later, Kira called me again. This time, I was in the hospital, doped up on morphine after being shot four times.

At four o'clock in the afternoon on September 5, 2007, I was sitting at the Italian restaurant in the shopping mall Field's in

Copenhagen with twelve other high-ranking or elite members of the Bekir Boys. Despite the hatred, internal power struggles, the distrust, and the jealousy, the Bekir Boys finally agreed it was time to make peace with all of their enemies, us included.

The so-called Bekir Boys finally wanted to cease their conflicts with Ishøj, Taastrupgaard, and Black Cobra and sought freedom from Bekir's regime. Bekir wasn't there to protest or scare the others into changing their minds, as he was out of the country and none of his representatives were at the table either.

While the general public and the police knew them as the Bekir Boys largely due to the press and the local media, they never used that name to describe themselves because Bekir was hardly ever there when they conducted their daily business. Unfortunately, even though Bekir wasn't physically present, his spirit still hovered over the group.

We felt it was time that Bekir decided if he wanted peace or to end it once and for all with Samir and his family, and Black Cobra. The rest of us were tired of the conflict. The cops were after us, we were losing our lives, our money, our cars, everything. I had lost my business and my house and the whole life I had built for myself. I had lost all of that to the group. It was time to put an end to it. It was time to live.

I wasn't as close as I used to be with my old friends Erion, Argon, Jamil, Baasim, and Omar. I began to run around with two other guys from the crew called Pepe and Lefty instead. We thought the war with Black Cobra had lasted so long that we had almost forgotten how it had even begun. We were very inspired by General Sun Tzu and his thoughts on the art of war. Especially the part about how, if you fight an enemy for too long, both grow accustomed to each other's methods. So, if you fight the same enemy for too long, you start to adjust to each other's strategies and then nobody wins.

The younger guys who had entered the group also refused to just adopt this war. I was the only one left from the old guard. The rest of the group I was rolling with most of the time were newcomers.

A rumor was spreading around town. Supposedly, it was a guy they called The Mexican who had started it. The Mexican was close to Black Cobra, and he claimed that Bekir and my brother-in-law Karim had made peace with Black Cobra without telling the rest of the Bekir Boys. If that were true, it could be considered treason and possibly shatter the newly recovered harmony between us. In order to find out if there was any shred of truth to this rumor, I spent a couple of weeks searching for The Mexican.

When we left the restaurant, we found out that The Mexican happened to be working out at the shopping mall's gym, and I went in to have a word with him. I asked him to join me outside.

"Why should I come outside? I'm way outnumbered," The Mexican said.

"I just want to talk to you. Just me and you. Forget about the other guys. I'll be the only one talking to you," I said.

When The Mexican agreed to come out, I asked him the question that everything hinged on: "Did you tell people that Bekir and Karim made peace with Black Cobra behind our backs?"

"That's what I heard," he shot back.

"Who told you?" I asked.

"Samir."

I paused for a minute before continuing with my line of questioning. "I don't fuckin' believe that. Can you point out Bekir and Karim?"

The Mexican had no idea who Karim was, nor did he know Bekir personally. He was only repeating what he was supposedly told by Samir to anyone else who would listen.

"If you don't even know who they are, how can you know if they made peace?"

The Mexican didn't answer the question.

"You need to mind your own business," I told him. I was getting frustrated at the thought that everything we were trying to build might fall apart due to the gossip of a nobody, so The Mexican and I started fighting.

"Samir told me, I swear on my mother's grave," he said.

"Come on, Sleiman! Cut it out!" some of the others shouted and pulled me away before I did something I might regret later.

The Mexican ran out of the mall, and I decided not to follow him, as I had already said my piece. I just wanted to go home to Askerød. The others in the group advised against it because, having gone after The Mexican, it was highly probable that a counterattack would be waiting for me if I went back. I didn't care about the consequences 'cause as far as I saw it, I had done it for the group. I felt like I was fighting for something.

Against everyone's advice, I drove back home to Askerød. Later, I was standing in the parking lot, contemplating my next move, when I spotted Kira's car, but I didn't see her around anywhere. I was a bit disappointed, so in order to salvage my night, I borrowed a James Bond DVD from one of the neighborhood kids. It was *Die Another Day*.

I walked home, and when I stepped into my apartment, my little sister Alaa was visiting from Århus. Our mother asked me to stay awhile. "Let's have tea. It's been a long time since we had tea and cheese," she said.

Back when we were a real family, eating my mother's homemade cheese was one of my favorite things in the world. *My night has turned around after all,* I thought to myself. "All right, let's do it."

I barely had time to sit down before the phone rang. It was a girl named Maja. The two of us used to have a thing, but I, of course, screwed her over. She was salty that I had chosen Kira over her. I was afraid she wanted to hang, but instead, Maja asked me if she could borrow cash. I said yes and agreed to bring her the money.

She was standing in the parking lot by the clubhouse where the Bekir Boys usually hung out. When I came down, two of her girl-friends were with her. Now Maja had changed her mind, and she wanted to buy weed from me. I didn't have any on me, so I gave her the address of another dealer. Then the two other girls got in their car, peeled out, and left Maja behind. There was something strange about the whole meeting, and I asked Maja what the hell was going on.

"Where are your friends going? Aren't you going with them?"

She glanced over my shoulder. "Are those your friends over there? Do you know them?"

I turned around to see whom she was referring to. From the heart of Askerød, roughly twenty-five guys came running toward me. Maja had been a diversion to lure me out in the open, and she could've been sent by a number of people I was presently at odds with.

Five minutes later, I was lying on the ground in front of the club-house, smoking a cigarette like Solid Snake, covered in blood after being shot four times. I was surrounded by paramedics who were feverishly working on me and telling me to put my cigarette out. Then my phone rang. I picked up. It was Kira.

A paramedic leaned over me, trying to find the bullet in my stomach. No luck. He wanted to give me laughing gas to relieve the pain, but I declined.

"You're an idiot," the paramedic said. At that point, however, he must have realized that I was going to survive because he couldn't help laughing at the title of the DVD with the bullet holes in it: *Die Another Day*. He thought it was fuckin' hilarious.

The place was swarming with doctors. They checked the reflexes in my legs and toes to determine if the bullets had left me paralyzed, but my limbs were functioning just fine. I was freezing, though. Later, they moved me to a warmer room."

I always thought there was a price to be paid for the life I led. I had proven my loyalty. I had come close to killing in the name of the group, and now I had almost died for it. I was always on the front line, but I had never been shot or severely injured before this night.

Some people suspected that I was secretly on Black Cobra's side or that I had an alliance with one of the biker gangs. At least, that was the rumor that was circulating. Others suspected me of making a killing doing business on my own without including the group. After this, how could you possibly question my loyalty?

Kira kept calling, but I didn't feel like talking to her. Later, the police came in to question me. "Who shot you?" they asked.

"I don't know who shot me. I didn't see. They all looked like dwarves, and they were wearing masks."

"You're lying, Sleiman. You're full of shit. We know who it was, and we know it was Black Cobra. We have wiretaps."

"Well, then do your job. I can't help you."

"Who shot you?" the police asked again.

I gave my same answer: "It was a dwarf!"

The police left the hospital, but the next day, the criminal investigation department returned. "Who shot you?" they asked.

"A group of dwarves wearing masks," I responded. Stick to the story.

"Listen up, Sleiman. We just want to put an end to this conflict. It started with you, and now it's going to end with you," the cop said.

I remained consistent. "They were dwarves!"

I obeyed the code of the streets. I didn't want to involve the police, but I had no intention of backing down either. That morning, I had been an advocate of peace. By the time the night was over, things had changed.

All through the night, Kira kept calling me. She desperately wanted to visit, but I refused to talk to her. When she finally managed to get through, her voice broke as soon as she heard my name. I was hurt because in all the time we had been together, I had never heard Kira cry straight from the heart. She had lied to me and said that she wanted to have kids with me while she was secretly on the pill. Now suddenly, she was saying all the things I had always longed to hear. She wanted to move in with me. She wanted to have kids with me. She wasn't gonna let her parents control her anymore. I almost cried as well. Was that what it took? Did I have to almost die before she realized that I was good enough for her?

"Oh, so now that I'm almost dead, you want kids," I said, and once again, I was an asshole.

Then she said, "Shut up, you big idiot! I'm coming to visit you at the hospital."

Kira did come, and for probably the first time, we had something resembling a healthy, adult relationship. She bathed me, pushed me around in my wheelchair, and told me how much she loved me. It was the polar opposite of our previous chaotic dynamic.

Even with Kira by my side while I was on the mend, I was aching to go to war. I didn't even care if it cost me my life this time. I was discharged from the hospital prematurely because I wanted to go home to Askerød and show everyone I was still alive. In the war I was about to enter, there was no room for Kira. While I loved her more than anything, I also began to wonder if it wasn't better to let her go so that she could live her own life. I began to question if the life I was living was the right one for her.

When I was discharged from the hospital, Kira followed me to my apartment. Later that night, she was walking home, but she was afraid to go alone, so we talked on the phone the entire way.

"Sleiman, I'm coming over tomorrow, and then I want to talk about our life together. The people you call friends are not your friends, and what you call a life is no life," she told me.

Kira came over the next day and helped me down the stairs so that I could go for a walk around Askerød. After we hobbled around the block for a while, she helped me up the stairs to my apartment. We talked about how she had always been torn between me and her family. If she chose me, she lost them, and if she chose them, she lost me. She told me she was ready now. Somehow, she was going to make it all work. I began to wonder if she was really serious about wanting to finally settle down, and I started to get worried. There's no place for love in war.

The next day, Kira was supposed to compete in a dance competition in Slovenia, but for the first time, she was willing to cancel. "You need me," she said.

I insisted that she go. I made her think that when she finally returned, we would become a real couple. If there's one thing I regret, it's not telling her that I was sorry for being cruel to her. It was a terrible goodbye. A goodbye filled with grief because it felt like she knew what I was doing. For many years, I had treated her like a substitute for Anna.

The next day, Kira went to Slovenia. She texted me constantly, hoping to receive passionate and loving texts in return. They were never reciprocated, but she kept sending them, nonetheless. I texted her back, but there was no passion in my messages. When she got to Slovenia, she called me up. I promised to call and write her, but I didn't. I was already sowing the seeds of war. I was walking around the block to prove to everyone that I was still alive.

After two days with no correspondence from me, Kira called and said, "Sleiman! Don't tell my parents that you're the one who got shot because I told them that it wasn't you. If they find out it was you, they're never gonna let me come back to you."

I promised her I wouldn't tell. Immediately after I hung up the phone, I called her mother. I told her that I was the one who had been shot and that Kira shouldn't come back to me because it was too dangerous. I said, "Susanne, make sure she doesn't come back to me. I promise you I won't contact her again. Just make sure she never contacts me."

Kira's mother was grateful that I cared enough to be honest with her. "Thank you, Sleiman. I'm really sorry you were shot, but it means the world to me that you're doing this."

That was the first time I felt like Kira's mother thought I was a good man. Her parents had always told me, "We don't wish you harm, and we want you to have a happy life. Just not with our daughter."

Later that day, Kira called me up again. "You're a bastard, Sleiman! You've killed us, and we'll never get back together."

It was over. I no longer needed to worry about Kira. I could focus on the coming war. The final stage of the game had just begun.

29

CHASING THE ENEMY

While the old rumors about me being a covert operative for Black Cobra died when they shot me four times, the very same failed assassination attempt buried my old reputation as being "the untouchable one." For all the years I had led the charge into the teeth of battle and wreaked havoc throughout Denmark, I never once was seriously injured. When everyone saw me hobbling around Askerød, it cemented that no one was safe from facing repercussions for their previous actions and that Black Cobra feared no one.

Among my longtime friends Erion, Argon, Bassim, and Omar, I had high hopes that they would be willing to back my play against Black Cobra. To my surprise, they weren't on board. At all.

"We're tired of your wars, Sleiman! One day, you're at war with the bikers. The next day, you're at war with The Egyptians. We're done with your wars. We just wanna make money!"

Bassam told me this when I had a meeting inside a local McDonald's with my four oldest and closest friends right after I got shot. They abandoned me at my lowest point and my most critical moment. They all told me straight up that they wouldn't support me. That broke me.

The hope was that I would abandon my plans for war without

their backing. I had already drawn first blood in the conflict with Samir, so if I just stopped now, we could call it even.

Even my beloved sister Sarah tried to talk me out of pursuing revenge: "No more", she told me. "No more! If you take revenge now, one of you is gonna end up dead. I don't care who your friends are, and I don't care who Samir's friends are. This fight has gotta end. You stabbed Samir because you felt you had to, and he stood in front of you at the clubhouse because *he* felt he had to."

It all began as Bekir's war against Samir's dad, but it ended up being me against Samir. The younger kids started hating each other because of it. It had gone too far now. Whose war, was it? Why were they fighting? Sarah reminded me that we used to be best friends, and insisted our conflict had to end.

I was listening to Sarah, but the voice inside my head screaming for revenge was louder than hers. The thought of being the bigger man and not taking revenge hadn't even crossed my mind. I always believed that someone who doesn't avenge himself is weak and vulnerable. This was the lesson my father had taught me as a child, and that had been reinforced throughout my entire life in Askerod. How could I possibly let everything go and just forgive?

As soon as I healed up enough, I started driving around the neighborhood looking for the guys who had shot me. First off, I didn't know who they were, but I knew that Samir was around. I didn't need to be a detective to know all I needed to do was split the difference and go straight to him. I didn't even care that going after Samir was essentially the same as going up against the entire Black Cobra gang by myself.

Not too long after my search began, Erion and I were driving around Hundige when we spotted Samir. Even while injured, I set off in pursuit of him.

"Stop! Let me out!" Erion said.

"But . . . it's Samir!" I pleaded.

"Sleiman! Let me out. I'm not fighting your war."

I let him out, but Pepe jumped in the car to ride with me in Erion's stead. "Let's go," Pepe said. He and his friend Lefty were both wanted by the police and had to stay under the radar, so I helped them out with food and money. For that reason, Pepe felt obligated to be there for me.

As Pepe and I rolled around following leads while looking for Samir, we began to put together pieces of the puzzle from everyone we spoke to. At this point, the crew consisted of myself, Lefty, Pepe, and Tarif. We began eliminating possibilities and getting new information until we suddenly discovered a new lead suspect in my shooting, a Danish guy who was known as The Hippie. He was an outsider, someone who hadn't previously been a part of the gang wars in Hundige. I had no clue who he was, but he was affiliated with Black Cobra, and according to our information, they had decided to outsource rather than use any obvious candidates for shooters. Before long, we were driving around Copenhagen in search of The Hippie as opposed to Samir.

Sources told us that The Hippie was last seen at a downtown department store. We went and saw he was still there. My people chased him up and down the escalators. I didn't take part in the chase because I had been shot in my legs, and I wasn't up for that quite yet.

They chased The Hippie everywhere in Hundige and all throughout Copenhagen. Lefty has since moved away from Askerød and is now a small-business owner, wanted to find him, and was armed at all times. Had he found him, Lefty would've likely executed him for me.

My other trusted friend, Tarif, was my best friend when I was young. He used to follow me home every night because he was afraid, I would get jumped or shot if he wasn't watching my back. He kept guard and looked out for me early on in a way I'll never forget.

Since I never cooperated with the police, no one was going to be arrested for the attempt on my life. However, in late 2007, several Black Cobra members were sent to prison regardless. Law enforcement had analyzed a series of recorded phone conversations among them, and during the trial, they used the recordings to discover that The Hippie had, in fact, been summoned from Copenhagen to carry out the hit on me. He wasn't present when the verdict was read in July 2008, as he had already hanged himself in prison before the trial.

Samir, Zaki, and The Mexican were found guilty of aggravated assault, as well as for using lethal weapons. Samir was sentenced to two and a half years in prison. Zaki was sentenced to one and a half years, while The Mexican was sentenced to one year.

By coincidence, I got background information on what went down with The Mexican and The Hippie through the unlikeliest of sources, a biker chick named Mille I was messing around with at the time of the 2008 trial. Mille told me about her sister, who was married to and had a child with The Hippie. She told me that her brother-in-law had killed himself because he had been involved in a murder attempt on a *perker* from Hundige.

She didn't know it was me, and at first, I didn't tell her. But I started to understand what he had been going through after he had shot me. She told me that he began sleeping with a machine gun under his pillow. Apparently, he became suicidal because he believed that people were coming for him. He felt like certain people in Black Cobra wanted him to take the fall for this, and he couldn't stomach the idea of spending ten years in the joint constantly fearing for his life. He also had a drug charge hanging over his head, so he was looking at serious time.

Shortly after finding all of this out, being with Millie just felt weird, so I let her go. I called her a couple of months later, and she told me that she was back with her ex. What's surprising is she's a Muslim now. She wears a headscarf and is married to a Muslim man. I honestly didn't see that coming.

30

BLOODZ

L efty was five years younger than I was. He grew up in Hundige but was never a part of the criminal underworld. All of that changed one day when he was wounded and almost killed in a confrontation with members of Black Cobra. He immediately joined the Bekir Boys, even though he was from Gersager Park.

Lefty was a former military sergeant, but he quickly transformed into a skilled swindler. He worked with fraud in general but specialized in tax fraud because there's a lot of money to be made in that department, and the sentences are pretty light. Lefty, has now long since left the gang scene behind.

It took him a long time to get there, though. Lefty teamed up with me when he and Pepe were wanted by the police and needed to lie low.

One thing my new crew all had in common was all seven of us felt the need to distance ourselves from Bekir. We never liked the fact that the media called us the Bekir Boys, and the only way to get rid of that name was to come up with a new one. I decided on Bloodz. The message to Bekir was simple: you don't define us, we're not under you, and we don't need you.

Bloodz was a brotherhood. The name was a reference to the guys who had shed blood for one another in the same conflict. We were blood brothers. We wanted to liberate ourselves and just live. If

Black Cobra wanted to fight us, it would be because of us and no longer because of Bekir. If they wanted peace, we were ready to make peace.

That said, Bloodz wasn't solely founded on a noble vision of confronting the sins of the past, and the name didn't exactly promote peace, love, and harmony to the general public. We didn't immediately desire to abandon our criminal endeavors. We were just free and independent of Bekir with no obligation to do anything on his behalf or to cut him in on anything we did.

As long as we were busy fighting one another, we didn't make money, and when we didn't have money, we didn't have wisdom. 'Cause with money comes a new form of understanding. When you've got money in your pockets and you're able to buy stuff, you begin to learn a few things about life. I wanted nice clothes, a house, a car, and to grow as a person, even though I was a criminal. But as long as your general keeps you hungry, you're only concerned about making ends meet. As long as Bekir kept us in that mindset, we were never gonna be anything but failures.

I wanted Erion, Argon, Omar, and Bassim all to join our ranks, but there was one requirement you had to meet in order to become a member of Bloodz. To confirm your membership, you needed to do it with a tattooed signature on your skin. They all declined to join, and it hurt me, but I made this a requirement because I was done being a part of so-called brotherhoods where I was always doing the overwhelming amount of dirt and the rest of the crew was benefiting from the reputation, I had built for us.

Bassim and Omar were smart and really tight. They didn't mind violence as long as they weren't the ones getting their hands dirty. So, I told them, "If you're gonna be a part of this, you have to pay, same as the rest of us. You have to get a tattoo. Then you'll be a part of all for one and one for all." They didn't want to go through with it.

Some of them also felt that I was initiating war with the guy who had given them security and an identity. Not choosing sides early on seemed like a sensible thing to do. However, the time may come where you'll need to change your allegiances.

One night in early 2008, Pepe, Lefty, myself, and four other guys went to Tattoo Joe's in Copenhagen and got our Bloodz tattoos. I opted to get mine placed on my wrist. Bloodz don't have an official leader, but I was a founding member and the most infamous one. Eventually, the Danish gang underworld took notice, as did the Danish authorities. According to them, I was now the head of his own gang at twenty-five years old.

When Bloodz first surfaced, everyone in the criminal underworld knew about it. We were among the first to actually name their gang. Back in the day, that was considered corny and wannabe American. It wasn't how we did things in Denmark. The ones who claimed to be members of a gang were just punks. But suddenly, you had these grown men who all had Bloodz tattoos and just went all fuckin' in. Other criminals were intimidated by this, but eventually, everyone else copied us.

The name Bloodz may have referred more to blood brothers than bloodshed, but it sounded hard, and it legitimized the adoption of the Los Angeles gang culture. A crucial part of warfare is to brand yourself as someone who's capable of extreme violence, and it's easier to create that kind of aura around a gang. And the media fanned the flames. Now you had Black Cobra and Bloodz, for the media it was even easier to frame the immigrant gangs in Denmark being equally as dangerous as the bikers.

Others just shook their heads in disbelief at the news of Bloodz breaking from their former affiliation. Bekir was dead certain Bloodz couldn't make it without him.

In early 2008, Bloodz had already presented a united front, made money on debt collections and theft, and we had fun doing it. We went clubbing together, partied, and relished our independence and growing reputation surrounding the name.

I had the best connections in the marijuana scene in Christiania, and I was also the best at innovating new ways of doing business. I temporarily got myself an apartment close to Blågård's Square, smack dab in the heart of Copenhagen gangland. Bloodz wouldn't dream of operating there, but we hung out with all the heavyweights from the area. Meanwhile, the gang grew, and throughout 2008, more and more guys could be seen with Bloodz tattoos.

Bloodz's first test actually came at the hands of a financial dispute and a power struggle with Bekir.

I made $55,000 selling a Mercedes to Hedgehog. Discord had already begun to rear its ugly head within the gang. A gang without capital is like a company without capital. You're unable to pay cash or purchase in bulk, and you can't expect credit or discounts in return. Some members felt that $55,000 belonged to Bloodz, but since it was was my sale, it was my money. I was through with being the only one who contributed while others just profited from my work.

A couple of the other members pulled off a heist, but the original idea to pull it off came from Bekir. They stole $45,000 worth of goods, but Bekir felt entitled to a cut because it was his idea. They tried to avoid a direct confrontation with Bekir and asked me to stash the goods for them so they didn't need to involve him.

"'Don't you fuckin' do that! Don't give him any money! Just because he came up with the plan doesn't mean it's his money. It's your money. Don't give him a dime!' I said.

I was adamant that Bloodz had to be independent from Bekir, so I agreed to hide the stolen merchandise as some members wanted to compensate him to avoid a confrontation. This pissed me off.

They wanted to give Bekir 50,000 DKK ($7,600). I don't know what they were scared of. He hadn't done shit but scream and shout for the last twelve years. They thought I was stirring shit up again, and in a way, they were right. I did try to cause controversy between him and us because the guys weren't ready to cut the umbilical cord yet. They still depended on him, but I was dead set on keeping him out of our business. I didn't have any plan for how to wean ourselves off Bekir, but I was more than ready to make one if I had to.

In September 2008, I went on a short trip to Flensburg, Germany. I had a friend who had ties to one of the biker gangs. He was an errand boy for one of the heavyweights and was possibly on his way to becoming a full-patch member. We went with this biker they called Stepdad. It was more pleasure than business. We wanted to expand our circle of friends a little, visit a few strip clubs, and party.

We ended up at a fancy apartment with two other biker gang members. While they were drinking, one of the bikers explained how he used to fight other bikers to gain recognition and eventually membership. Later, we all went to a high-class brothel where they showered, put on bathrobes, and each picked a girl on the bikers' dime. I wasn't in the mood to put myself in a position to possibly be ambushed again, so I just waited for the others to finish. When they came out, we all went to a bar, where we partied with a group of girls. I went back home the next day.

When I got back to Askerød, I met up with a couple of the other Bloodz, who accused me of running my own side business, spending too much time with biker gangs, and associating with Black Cobra. According to them, I hadn't been a team player, but I could make things right by investing more money in Bloodz. I had to have some money left from the sale of my house and my Mercedes. They accused me of being greedy, but I accused them of the same sin. If I had to invest money, so did they. They had just made $45,000 on the heist idea they had stolen from Bekir!

At the same time, the old Bekir Boys and the newly tattooed Bloodz members were beginning to merge into a united crew without me. No one said anything, but slowly, I was being phased out of the same gang I had founded.

The day I came back from Germany, we had a direct confrontation at one of Askerød's shared laundry rooms. I was being accused of swindling them. They had been working a debt collection case, but once they found the slow payers, the debt had already been settled. The other members of Bloodz were convinced that I had pocketed the reward without telling any of them.

"Don't lie to us, Sleiman!" Baasim said.

An argument began that resulted in several Bloodz members' hands reaching for their waists as if they were going for their guns. That really set me off.

"Oh, so that's how this is gonna play! Give me a minute while I go grab something really quick. Then we can settle this once and for all," I said as I went to go get a weapon.

When I returned, they were all gone. "We didn't mean it like that," they said on the phone later when my brother-in-law Karim called them up to hear what the problem was.

"How did you mean it, then?" he asked.

"Chill, Karim. Tell him we'll always be there for him when he needs us. We'll always have each other's backs. We're just not gonna be doing stuff together anymore."

After that incident, I was effectively expelled from the gang. The group I had imagined as a way to get out from under Bekir's thumb once and for all was crumbling before my very eyes. Bekir was taking over, and at the same time, yet another rumor was spreading that I was a snitch. Was there a glitch in The Matrix?

An older lady hired me to recover $75,000 (almost 500,000 DKK) owed to her by a shady businessman. If I managed to collect the money, I would get to keep half of it. I felt pressured by my old friends who thought I was out for myself to make them aid me in the case.

"There's gonna be no standing on the sidelines while I get my hands bloody," I told them all.

I took the lead when we met with the businessman at the harbor in the neighboring town of Vallensbæk. He didn't have the $75,000, but we convinced him that he had better pay us with goods from his warehouse to help settle the debt. In the end, we made off with merchandise worth about $65,000 USD.

After the goods were delivered, infighting arose among the crew. One of the participants didn't think everyone had earned an equal share. The conflict escalated because I had a potential buyer lined up already who was willing to pay us $60,000 USD for the entire lot. The others thought we could get more than that. If they forced the guy, they had squeezed to report all the stuff stolen, they thought they could also cash in on the insurance payout. I thought that was a stupid idea. It was obvious that the loot should be sold immediately for the highest amount of money available.

Things didn't go the way I had hoped. They decided that Baasim should stash the goods in his apartment. At the time, Baasim and I had had a falling-out, and after a couple of months where the gear didn't move, I had had enough. We arrived at an agreement. I had to send someone else in my stead to pick up the goods at Baasim's because we were on the outs, and I might hurt him if I saw him face-to-face.

Instead, the police beat us to it. They visited Baasim and confiscated everything in his apartment. Making things worse for him, they found a receipt he had kept as proof of the retail value of all the gear in order to get top dollar for it from a potential buyer. How exactly did Baasim get the money to buy all these electronics? They also found a gun. This was during the middle of the gang war, and illegal possession of firearms was a serious offense in Denmark.

The rumor soon spread that I was the one who had ratted

* Instead, We Became Evil

Baasim out to the police as punishment for not going along with my original plan. The story seemed plausible on the surface. Everybody knew that Baasim and I were on bad terms because he only wanted to plan things and play Mafia while he left all the dirty work to me. Everybody also knew that Baasim had declined my offer to join Bloodz, providing a good collection of motives supporting me as the likely snitch.

The rumor stuck, and the gossip on the street about why I would do it finished the job. I went from being crowned the prince of the streets to being accused of violating the code, so I was kicked out of Bloodz. Not even Pepe and Lefty backed me up, and over the following months, I became a pariah.

The question I asked everyone was, "Why would I send Baasim away for only four months for possession of an illegal weapon when I could've had you all locked up if I wanted to?" I had been in the game for thirteen years, over half my life! I could send my entire generation of criminals to jail for years with the information I could provide. Why would I suddenly go from being the man who never cooperated with the police to snitching over something petty? It simply didn't add up.

The rumor that I was a snitch was the worst thing that could've happened. I was isolated and had a target on my back. Again. Nobody was willing to defend me. Eventually, I even challenged Baasim to a duel, man to man. First, I would allow the Bloodz and Bekir Boys to interrogate me or find definitive proof that I had given Baasim up. If I was revealed to be a snitch, I would die. If Baasim was revealed to have spread false rumors, he would die. He didn't agree to the duel, but that didn't stop the streets from talking about me.

The snitch rumor was replaced by other ones. Suddenly, I was a Hells Angel. The next minute, I had been a secret member of Black Cobra the whole time I had been part of Bloodz. Samir and I had made a deal. We weren't Muslim—we were Jewish, and it was all part of a Jewish scheme to break up the Palestinian community in the neighborhood. Later, they claimed I was part of the AK81 gang, charged with pointing out every immigrant that needed shooting in Copenhagen. All these rumors were baseless. That was the name of the game. It was a power struggle, and I lost. I didn't deserve to be branded a snitch, but I knew I was playing a game with a low likelihood of a positive turnout. There's no honor among thieves.

Even Pepe was persuaded by the rumor for a while. It wasn't until later that he realized that it was all false. They were saying I was making exorbitant amounts of money and I was holding out on the crew. But then people started accusing me of ratting out Baasim, and when you hear something like that every day, eventually you're gonna end up thinking there's some truth to it. Over time, more and more of them succumbed to the lies.

Bloodz continued to operate without me. Throughout the entire conflict, Bekir lurked in the shadows. Right after I had been excommunicated, Bekir came home from one of his many trips abroad and took over. My friends who had refused to be tattooed when I had first offered them membership now suddenly lined up to become members of Bloodz. The whole gang was handed to Bekir on a silver platter, and he regained his position as the leading figure of Askerød.

My expulsion from Bloodz was also the beginning of my journey of leaving behind a life of crime. Had I won the internal power struggle, it's unlikely I would've ever quit the gang life. I'm thankful this all happened to me because if they hadn't betrayed me, I never would've quit, and I never would've realized that everything I had been fighting for all along was wrong and ultimately meant nothing.

31

THE PEACE AGREEMENT

O n September 5, 2007, at 11:00 p.m., as I was sitting in front of the clubhouse in Askerød receiving medical attention after being shot four times, my sister Sarah decided: she was going to do everything in her power to stop the war between me and Samir.

When I got shot, an opportunity presented itself to seize the moment and sign a peace agreement. Sarah managed to convince me that I should finally make peace with Samir. She had lost our father when she had stopped him from trying to kill our mother, and she wasn't about to lose her little brother too. Sarah also reached out to Samir's family through mutual friends in Askerød, who also longed for peace. The problem was that if I took another step toward peace with Samir and Black Cobra, I would also be one step closer to a war with Bloodz.

For Sarah, the war had another dimension to it. In 2000, she and Karim moved from Fredericia in Jutland to Askerød, where Karim became best friends with Bekir. They hung out every day and engaged in criminal activities such as extortion, debt collection, and selling marijuana. Sarah was aware of her husband's dealings with Bekir, her brother's sworn enemy and main rival, but she didn't interfere because everything was very complicated. For one, Karim is the father of their three children.

Bekir is good at making bad blood between people, but he's also good at patching things up again. He creates problems, and then he makes money solving them. Karim got to witness Bekir do this time and time again throughout the years.

Bekir and Karim would occasionally spend stretches in prison, but there was more to Karim than just being a criminal. He was also a charismatic and kind man who generated a positive atmosphere around him. After his release from prison, Karim got the chance to be landlord of the Askerød houses sometime between 2002 and 2003. He worked hard, and when the young people came to him with their issues, he knew their families and could talk to them. People were so happy with his work that he was offered permanent employment. Multiple sources confirm that Karim was a popular and respected landlord in Askerød for several years.

Eventually, Karim's friendship with Bekir turned sour. When they ran businesses together, Karim didn't feel like he was in an equal partnership. Karim also refused to let Bekir decide who he was and wasn't allowed to be friends with. Despite his affable nature, Karim isn't the type of man you would want to pick a fight with. He is tall as a crane and broad as a castle gate. In early 2008, he was sent to prison. He suspected that Bekir was behind it because he was angry with Karim for running his own criminal enterprise without including him.

After his release in December 2008, Karim confronted Bekir with his suspicions, and the argument turned into a violent fight. The former friends and business partners had become enemies, so now both Karim and I were seeking peace with Black Cobra. Sarah had had enough and wanted better for her brother and her husband and their young children.

Karim had never been a member of Bloodz, but he had lived in the periphery of the gang. When they ostracized me, Karim and I became each other's protectors. We both sought out a middle ground where we could all coexist without needing to be affiliated with the Bekir Boys, Bloodz, Black Cobra, or another gang.

During 2009, our beef with Bekir and parts of Bloodz became more and more pronounced. Our cars were repeatedly being keyed up or our tires were getting slashed. All over the buildings and common areas in Askerød, people had spray-painted the phrases *Sleiman Die* and *Bloodz Rules*. Our families were being harassed. The windows to Karim and Sarah's apartment were smashed, and one night, when the whole family was hanging out on the balcony, they were shot at.

Eventually, Sarah went down and told the young men of Askerød that if they didn't stop, she would have them locked up. "I've had it. You can call me a snitch. I don't care. You're dealing with people's lives, and it has to stop. I don't care what you think about my brother, but he's decided to do the right thing now, so let him do it. If you were real men, you wouldn't write that shit about him on the walls," she told them.

The harassment stopped, but only temporarily. Around Copenhagen, the war between Bloodz and Black Cobra became an actual war. In Hundige, members of the two gangs came to blows daily all throughout 2009.

At the highest level of government, people had their eyes on the conflict from the outset. They fully expected for things to come to a head, it was only a matter of when.

Their prophecy came true. One day in the late summer of 2009, Karim received an urgent phone call. It was Samir.

"Someone is driving around outside our clubhouse threatening to fuck us up and shoot us. People are saying it's Sleiman. Is that true, Karim?" Samir asked.

They agreed that Karim should come over to Black Cobra's clubhouse in Gersager Park. After he hung up, Karim called me. "Can you come over?" he asked.

"Sure," I answered.

Shortly afterward, I was standing face-to-face with Samir. He said, "People are saying that you're the one driving around here yelling at us."

"Listen up. To me, this war is over. You were stabbed. I've been locked up; you've been locked up. You were shot, I was shot. Right now, we're square. There's nothing left," I said to him.

"That's fine by me. I've always wanted us to be friends. You're the one who never listened, Sleiman. You're the one who's been running down the wrong tracks."

"You're right. But that's in the past. I was blind. I listened to the wrong people," I offered to my old friend. Then we looked at each other, and we both shook hands.

All that time I was at war with Samir, I tried my best not to see him as a person. He was Black Cobra. He was the leader of the enemy. He wasn't my childhood friend. He wasn't Samir. But I realized that we were still the same people.

A couple of days later, Samir, Zaki, Karim, and I all went out to dinner at a local Italian restaurant. We talked about all the things that had happened over the past few years, and we all agreed that we had made some unforgivable mistakes. We didn't become close friends again, but we weren't enemies anymore. Once again, Sarah was the hero of another chapter of my story.

Of course, not everyone was happy that we had made peace. To them, Karim and I were traitors, and making peace with Black Cobra was the same as declaring war on Bloodz. The police made a note of the peace agreement. This was what they had wanted us to do years ago, but it seemed almost too good to be true. Had the two childhood friends truly patched things up? Or did Sleiman feel so threatened by his former Bloodz brothers that he was forced to seek protection from his worst enemy? The police weren't sure, but then again, that's not new for them.

32

THE MURDER ATTEMPT

On September 15, 2009, Karim and I were driving home to Askerød when his phone rang. It was Haashim, a good friend of his whom I didn't trust. Haashim is also Bekir's nephew, and I didn't think he would allow his nephew to be friends with his former friend Karim unless Haashim was spying for Bekir. They often partied and smoked weed together. Haashim asked Karim if he wanted to smoke a joint later that night.

Whenever they had phone conversations, I would monitor them. Karim is deaf in one ear, so he always keeps the volume on his phone turned up to the max, so I could hear the entire exchange in case anything ever went left. Karim told him he would have to pass on the joint because we were supposed to visit Sarah and spend a quiet night with her, their kids, and their friends.

Karim and Sarah were now divorced, but they still hung out sometimes. She still cared about him. Most importantly, he was still a good and loving father to their kids. After the divorce, they attempted a reconciliation, but even though Sarah became pregnant with their third child, they split up again soon afterward.

Karim and I kept the lights on as we drove into Askerød so we could spot a potential ambush hiding behind the hedges. We even parked the car up against a wall to ensure the best possible protection from attack, and we got out of the car one at a time while keeping a close eye on each other and our surroundings. In the wake of our peace dinner with Samir, the rumor that we might be snitching had gained more traction around town. Not everyone in Bloodz saw us as traitors, but enough did for us to take every precaution going forward since our enemies were quite literally our own neighbors in Askerød.

Around 9:00 p.m., we headed up to Sarah's apartment. We heard noises coming from outside but paid no attention to it. Haashim called Karim again.

"Wanna come down for a smoke?" he asked.

"Can't we do it later?" Karim replied.

"Who was that?" I asked.

"Haashim. He wants me to come down and smoke a joint."

"Forget about it. We're here now, having coffee."

A little later, Haashim called again and asked, "How about now?"

"I'll be there in five," Karim said.

Sarah was annoyed that Karim looked like someone who wanted to be elsewhere. They had friends over, and he had told her he wanted to come spend time with his kids. She found it strange that he was so eager to leave. She wanted to yell at him and tell him to go for a walk with his children, but she was reluctant to cause a scene while they had company that included our mother.

At about 10:00 p.m., our mother took Sarah's children over to my apartment. Karim asked Sarah if she would make him a cup of coffee, but she refused because he was being a jerk. Karim was restless, and after a while, he just got up and left. "I'll be back in a bit," he said, which worried me because I thought the repeated phone calls had left an uneasy look on Karim's face.

Karim went downstairs and opened the door to the street. He had only taken three steps outside before the sound of gunshots echoed throughout Askerød. The first bullet hit Karim's hand and penetrated the bone. The next bullet hit him in the stomach. He managed to get a look at his shooters because even though they were wearing masks, they didn't have enough time to make them fully cover their faces.

Sarah had barely noticed that Karim had left before she heard the loud bangs and the sound of Karim crying out in the street. She immediately knew what had happened. "They shot him! They killed him!" she screamed.

"You fuckin' dog!" Karim shouted in Arabic and stumbled back into the building. He was bleeding from his hand but more profusely from his stomach.

Sarah was so in shock, the only thing she could think of was to go get some water. The attackers knew that he was visiting his children. How could they also have known that she had just sent her kids off with their grandmother? Karim could have taken them with him. They could have killed the kids.

Karim managed to stumble into the hallway of the apartment building before he collapsed. A Danish neighbor came over and said to Sarah, "Giving him water might be dangerous. Wait for the ambulance." The neighbor had first-aid training and tried to stop the bleeding, but the blood kept gushing out of Karim's hand and stomach. It was clear where the bullet had entered, but they couldn't find an exit wound.

I immediately called Samir and his people from Black Cobra. "They shot Karim!" I shouted into the phone.

As he lay on the floor, Karim gave me the names of the two men who had shot him.

Before I could exit the premises, Sarah ran after me and blocked the door. "Stop. You can't. I'm pregnant! I'm gonna lose the baby. You want me to lose you, Karim, *and* the baby?" she screamed. She refused to let go of me.

One of Sarah's friends and her husband aided Sarah in restraining me. I made it seem like I had listened to reason, but the second they relaxed, I tore off down the stairs and into the night after the gunmen. When I first came downstairs, I saw a group of people near the building hooting and cheering, so I yelled at them. Among them were members of Bloodz. More and more people joined them outside until a crowd formed.

Soon, Haashim and his brother Baashar arrived on the scene. They tried to force their way into Sarah's apartment, saying that they wanted to talk to Karim. I was convinced that Haashim had lured Karim into the ambush and that he and Baashar would try to manipulate Karim into believing that Black Cobra was behind the shooting. To prevent them from entering the apartment, I attacked them both. Both of them were bigger than me, but I had faced way worse odds and walked away unscathed in the past. I was so blinded with rage that I beat both of them into the ground and continued hitting them even after they had relented until Samir and his people from Black Cobra arrived and finally pulled me off them.

"You're gonna kill them," they said.

Haashim took advantage of the confusion, got to his feet, and managed to enter the apartment. "I had nothing to do with it. I love you. You're my brother," he said to Karim before the guys from Black Cobra came and pulled him back outside. Just then, other members of Bekir's family arrived on the scene, cheering, whistling, and clapping with joy.

The ambulance arrived, but the paramedics wouldn't enter the dangerous Askerød crowd before the police arrived. Instead, Samir and his people carried Karim down to the ambulance through the chaos outside.

Finally, the police showed up. Someone told them that I had just beat the living daylights out of the two brothers, and the officers arrested me and locked me up in one of the other buildings off my reputation alone. They said, "Sleiman, don't you move."

"Why am I the one being arrested? I'm going in the ambulance with Karim!"

"You're staying here while we figure out what happened."

One of the officers spotted a bullet casing and sealed off the area.

"Why don't you arrest the people cheering out there? Why are you arresting me?" I asked the policeman.

"You're staying here. You're coming to the station for questioning."

The police started searching for more shells. The windows of the apartment below Sarah's had been hit with a bullet from a hunting rifle. Another shell was stuck in the wall. A third one was later surgically removed from Karim's back, but he survived.

The police arrested Bekir and his son, only to release them two weeks later. They had a bulletproof alibi, and no one has ever been convicted in the case. Once again, the code of the streets was obeyed, and Sarah, who had helped make peace between Samir and me, realized that peace on one side meant war on the other. Neither my life nor hers was any safer than before we had squashed our issues. Moreover, the father of her children had almost died.

When Karim's life was hanging by a thread, not one of his old friends came to his aid. Help instead came from Samir and his brothers from Black Cobra in Gersager Park. In Askerød and among Bloodz, there was no longer any doubt: Karim and I had sided with the enemy. When the papers wrote about the shooting, they reported that a member of Black Cobra had been shot. It's impossible to tell whether the information came from Bloodz, the police, or a third party, but it was wrong. Karim and I never sided with Black Cobra. We just were no longer at war with them, but to some, it's the same thing.

Bekir wasn't the one who pulled the trigger because the one who shoots is always the one who gets screwed. I know who shot Karim. I know who used the hunting rifle, I know who shot the gun, and that night, they were gunning for us both. I've seen them hide in the bushes and behind dumpsters. I've seen them running away when they were waiting for us but realized that we were with our families. They had waited a year and a half for the right moment to shoot us both.

In the period that followed, several messages were written on the concrete walls of the housing development meant for Karim and me. On the building where my mother lived, right in front of her door, it said, *Askerød = Bloodz. We're painting the town RED. Welcome to the DEAD ZONE.*

Bloodz have also left their signature on the wall, signaling to my entire family that they better leave Askerød if they want to stay alive. Around the time Karim was shot, Bloodz had at least seventy members, half of which lived in Askerød. Most of them were between eighteen and twenty-two years old, far younger than I was. They had no part in the original conflict, but their hatred for Karim and me was as fierce as mine had been when I was younger and felt that someone had betrayed the group in favor of the enemy—the difference being that they didn't even know me personally to hate me so much!

Three weeks later, the police reported that a man had been shot and wounded in front of a nearby train station. Eight patrol cars chased the perpetrators. The media was unable to disclose who the victim was, but it turned out to be Samir's little brother, Zaki. Around the neighborhood, word spread that if it happened again, Samir was going to war for real this time.

Twelve days later, on October 20, 2009, Karim and I were driving down the interstate in Copenhagen, headed north. Traffic had come to a standstill, and cars were barely moving. By unhappy coincidence, we ended up driving right next to Bekir, who was sitting in a car with two bald men riding in the back seat. We made eye contact, and I made a finger gun and pulled the trigger. I wanted to jump out of the car and confront Bekir right then and there.

"Don't," Karim said.

I got out and walked over to Bekir's car. "If you wanna do this, then let's do it," I said to Bekir, who had rolled his window down.

"Not here. Drive back and let's meet in Hundige," Bekir said.

"All right," I responded.

I took the next exit and headed back to Hundige. Karim tried to talk me out of it, but my temper had taken over at that point. I told him to get out of Askerød for a while. "Stay out of this and go home. You've got kids. I don't want you to come along."

When I came home, I put on a bulletproof vest and walked into the heart of Askerød, but Bekir was nowhere to be seen. I called up two friends who were not from Askerød and were neither Bloodz nor Black Cobra to back me up. They were two guys I knew I could count on. For the next three days, we walked around Askerød looking for Bekir. I told everyone I wanted to meet him 'cause we weren't leaving. I wasn't gonna let 'em beat me in a cheap and cowardly way like they had gotten Karim. I would rather be gunned down and die a horrible death than die in a cheap way. If Bekir had shown up during those three days, he would have been killed 'cause we had had it. He was the one creating the conflict.

"You're not welcome in Hundige anymore," was the general consensus.

The young boys had left threats for us on the walls with markers and spray cans, they had shot at our homes, they had told everyone they weren't allowed to talk to us. Even the police had been by to warn that things were bad. We wanted to move our entire family to Gersager Park, but the municipality wouldn't let us. They were afraid we were just gonna bring all our problems with us across the way.

Even Sarah and her kids, who were completely innocent, weren't allowed to move out of Askerød for their own safety.

If that's the way it's gonna be, then we're staying here like a thorn in their side, we thought. We weren't gonna let them win. We had fled from Palestine, from my father, from women's shelter to women's shelter. We had been mistreated because of our reputation as the butchered woman's family, and now I was supposed to flee from the people I used to call my brothers? Hell no. I would rather die. And I knew that everyone who was against me didn't know the truth. They were against me because they had been brainwashed. There were maybe thirty to forty members of Bloodz, and I told all of them that this was not a fight between me and them. It was between me and Bekir. Many of the young members didn't see it that way. In their eyes, I was a traitor, a snitch, nothing more.

On October 22, things went south. I was walking around outside Bekir's building with my two escorts trying to provoke a reaction. After a while, I went back to my own block and was sitting outside when about twenty young guys came running toward us and shots were fired. They say I was the first to shoot, so they only fired back in self-defense. That's all I can say about that. But I can say that shots were fired at me with a machine gun, so I ran, and a friend drove me out from Askerød.

Later, the media received information that a group of young people had fled the scene using the system of paths running through Askerød. It was the guys from Bloodz. It was also revealed that a dark-colored car had been seen heading away from the scene toward Godsvej in Greve. A young man was later arrested in the case. The police also questioned me, and I again declined to cooperate with their investigation. If nothing else, I'm consistent.

Initially, no one spoke to the police after Karim was shot, but eventually, a charge was brought forth—not against Karim's attackers, mind you, but against me for beating up Bekir's nephew by pistol whipping him. I maintained that I didn't hit him with a gun, but that I was wearing heavy, square rings, so I pleaded not guilty.

In court, my defense attorney argued that I had been placed in the worst situation imaginable. She said, "When does the right to defend yourself apply? What is the craziest situation you can find yourself in? In this case, we have a man who has been shot and is lying on the floor, bleeding. Nobody knows if he will survive. Then someone comes and tries to force their way into the apartment before the police arrive. The accused believes these men were behind the ambush. Karim and Sleiman did not seek them out. It's the other way around. What would you do, Your Honor, in that situation? What would the lay assessors do if they believed that those who were closest to them were in immediate danger of being killed?"

I was acquitted by a 2–1 vote.

Apart from being kicked out of Bloodz and not being jailed for preventing the brothers from entering Sarah's apartment, 2010 was also the year where I got a job as a personal assistant for a handicapped family member. I began to spend a lot more time with my family. Now that I didn't have my friends anymore, I had to face the sacrifices I had made. My sacrifices had mostly been my family 'cause they had been left at home, worrying whether I was coming home alive or not. If I hadn't been kicked out of Bloodz, I think my mom would have eventually died from grief and worry.

33

A TRAGEDY

In the middle of December 2010, a royal-blue, armored BMW was headed down the highway toward Askerød containing Prime Minister Lars Løkke Rasmussen. He had a lot on his mind: lousy opinion polls, constant meetings with the opposition, and an American ambassador who thought it unlikely that Rasmussen could make a comeback on the international scene after the disappointing outcome of the climate summit the previous year. When he had given his inaugural speech earlier in 2010, he had spoken of twenty-nine ghetto holes on the map of Denmark. Askerød was designated as one of these holes, and the residents were furious.

After the speech, Rasmussen went on a trip to Askerød to meet the inhabitants of a place he'd just publicly derided.

When the Danish prime minister and his escort of bodyguards stepped out of their cars and into the mud of the construction site in front of what used to be our clubhouse, the boys could hardly believe their eyes, as most people had no clue the prime minister was visiting that day. Was he lost?

The boys in the community showed him around Askerød and Jamil took point. When the prime minister visited Askerød, nobody, except the other boys, knew that twenty-five-year-old Jamil held a prominent position in Bloodz.

In the basement of the clubhouse, Lars spoke to the young men, and Jamil told him about his life. He told the Prime Minister that he owed the state $225,000 for robberies, vandalism, and other related infractions, but now he had a job as a kindergarten teacher.

Jamil told Lars Løkke Rasmussen about when he was seven, he was a soldier for Saddam Hussein. When his mother heard they wanted him to join Saddam's personal guard, she didn't like the idea, so she fled Iraq. That's when his family arrived in Denmark.

"'What happened then?'

Next Jamil relayed the story about how his dad stabbed his mom because he wanted all her money. He was then kidnapped by his father and for two years, no one in Denmark even knew where he was. Ultimately, his mother went on a mission to track him down and brought him back to Denmark at age eleven. However, by the age of fourteen he'd dropped out of school due to the lure of the streets and fast money.

Fifteen days later, the very same Jamil would play an important part in what might be considered the greatest tragedy in the history of Bloodz and Askerød so far.

When I was expurgated from Bloodz, his new and close friend Pepe was next in the line of succession, and the other members respected him because he was smart.

Pepe was no altar boy, but he wasn't a serious criminal either. Pepee and Lefty are couple of years younger than me and belonged to the same generation as Jamil. Jamil and Pepe grew up in the same building and had been friends since they were kids.

Pepe was also there the night we had *Bloodz* tattooed on ourselves. His intentions were good, but Pepe suffered from the same problem as I did. He didn't want people to be at war anymore, but for them to still have the freedom to be criminals. We wanted to steer the younger boys away from crime, but we'd been criminals for so long, we had no idea how to live on the other side of the tracks. Sure we all wanted to put an end to the war, but in our eyes, general criminal activity was almost a legitimate business in and of itself.

It was impossible to separate the war from the crime, and suddenly, Pepe found himself in a serious conflict with one of the other members. He got the feeling that Bekir somehow orchestrated the conflict. Shortly afterward, he gave up his ambition to be a positive influence in Askerød. He felt that his life was in imminent danger and decided to quit Bloodz altogether once the gang began gearing up for war against myself and Karim.

Pepe's family knew Karim's family from Lebanon. They stayed in the same refugee camp, and his dad loves Karim. Pepe's dad was upset when he fell out with Karim and I, and it got to a point where his dad told him he was in the wrong and gave him an ultimatum: Either you choose your family, or you choose the shit you're in now.

Pepe subsequently tried to steer the young boys away from crime and Bekir. But he also bad-mouthed Bekir behind his back, and that backfired on him. "I truly believed I could get that man out of the picture and slowly turn our town into something good," he says.

Pepe also made peace with Black Cobra, resulting in threats against his family. His little brother was accosted, and hooded men assembled in front of his parents' home. The fact that Karim had been shot also frightened him, so in order to avoid a similar fate, Pepe decided to move away from Hundige with his wife. It got to a point where he told people that he didn't want to do it anymore. He simply didn't want to start shooting guys he used to hang out with and risk them shooting him in return.

But the persecution did not stop. On several occasions, members of Bloodz got a hold of him, and Jamil was among the guys who were after him.

Pepe was living with his wife, and we started talking because he thought the persecution he was being subjected to was similar to what I'd been through. We became close again, but things just got harder and harder. Pepe was told that people were waiting for him outside his house. They had caught his little brother and tried to threaten him into telling them where Pepe was. They told him he was a traitor. They always rolled up in big groups, and Pepe was always alone.

After that, Pepe saw no other option available than to arm himself for protection. Pepe had his gun on him on December 30, 2010, when he went to get a haircut at a barbershop in Copenhagen where he was a regular customer. The salon was completely empty, yet the hairdresser told him that he didn't have time for him and that he should come back the next day at 1:00 p.m. Pepe thought it strange, but he didn't analyze the situation any further and left.

The next day, he returned with two of his friends. They parked right in front of the barbershop and went inside. Jamil was waiting with about eight other members of Bloodz and several other guys from a different gang. Pepe had barely set his foot in the door before Jamil punched him hard in the face twice.

Pepe had no idea what to do. Imagine walking into a place and realizing that it's filled with people who want to kill you? Once Pepe heard them say 'You're coming with us.' He knew what that meant. He was going to disappear from the face of the Earth, and his mom and dad would never know how it happened. He said, 'No, I'm sick of this.'

They jumped him. Pepe pushed them away and grabbed his gun but suffered some blows to the head as they tried disarming him. He dashed out of the salon towards his car. One of his friends was with him, so they got in the car and tried to drive off, but the engine kept stalling. The men then ran out of the barbershop, caught up to them and started kicking the idle car while they shouted.

Next, they pried open the passenger side door and grabbed his friend and used him as a human shield so if Pepe took a shot, it would go through him. Pepe was cornered, and knew they had guns in their cars. He couldn't use his car to escape anymore, so instead, he got out and ran away since luckily none of them went to get their guns out of their cars while he was trapped.

Pepe didn't just run away: he shot four times into the crowd of pursuers as he ran to ensure he got clear. Aside from the guys from Bloodz, other people had joined the crowd outside. One of them was twenty-eight-year-old Ali Mohsen, a regular guy with a family who was just there for a haircut. He never made it inside. One of the bullets penetrated his left eye, went through his head, and out the back of his skull. He died instantly.

Pepe fled the scene. He ran down Vesterbrogade, a main street in Copenhagen that doubles as a shopping district, and into a back-yard, where he dropped his gun in a dumpster. Shortly afterward, he was arrested by the police as he walked down the opposite side of Vesterbrogade.

On March 22, 2012, fifteen months after Ali Mohsen was killed in front of the barbershop. In Glostrup Court, closing arguments in the trial against Pepe were made, who was charged with manslaughter and faced fourteen years in prison. During the trial, he told the court he feared for his life. The press has covered the story extensively.

During the trial, the victim was described as a man who had nothing to do with the ambush. Meanwhile, the question of his connection to the assault has never been solved. Why, for instance, was he standing in the front line? A man who had absolutely no connection to the incident should've kept his distance when it looked like a bunch of men were trying to kill another one in public.

Pepe also relates how the members of Bloodz were furious to hear that he had made peace with Black Cobra. During the trial, Jamil admitted, "We're not very happy about it when people try to leave Bloodz."

Pepe has now been in prison for fifteen months and has lost forty-five pounds. It's hard to recognize the once muscular young man as he sits there, a shell of his former self, while his defense attorney, Michael Juul Erichsen, demands his release.

In his opinion, there is no doubt that Jamil and the other members of Bloodz were there to do Pepe harm and Bekir was lurking somewhere in the back of it all.

Five days later, High Court Judge Jette Marie Sonne steps in to pronounce the sentence. In a way, she speaks in favor of the defense, for the court has no doubt that Pepe's life was, in fact, in danger. Based on the evidence presented, the court takes into consideration that the accused, during the months leading up to December 31, 2010, attempted to resign from Bloodz. In this connection, the accused had made peace with Black Cobra and notified the police's gang unit about his plans. The accused knew from his time in the gang and others who had left the group that the other members considered making peace with Black Cobra an act of betrayal. The court, therefore, maintained that the accused had a well-founded reason to fear for his life during the months leading up to the shooting.

But that was only a consolation. Even though it was a dissenting judgment because one judge and one juror didn't believe that Pepe intended to kill, nor that he was aiming at anyone in particular when he shot his gun, the majority was of the opinion "that the accused must have realized the probability of his shots hitting one or several of the people standing on the sidewalk with the possibility of the shots being fatal."

The court didn't find sufficient evidence to support a claim for self-defense either. Furthermore, the parliament passed a bill in 2009 stating that a sentence may be doubled if the crime happens in connection with a gang-related showdown. This also applies if someone is carrying firearms in the street and has connections to the gang world. The law does not apply directly in Pepe's case, but it does encumber his ability to claim self-defense.

The court sentenced twenty-six-year-old Pepe to twelve years in prison.

One would expect Pepe to be filled with a thirst for revenge and hatred toward his childhood friend Jamil, but that's not the case. Despite all the crimes Jamil has committed, and the fact that Jamil hunted him down and might possibly have wanted him dead, Pepe still regards him as a man with a big heart. Jamil was just seduced by Bekir and the end result was incarceration. The vicious cycle of violence, death and jail time followed so many of us Arab immigrants in Denmark.

34

2012

Some may say that May 2012 was truly spring for Sleiman. When he was a kid, he won hip-hop contests in Vejle with his friend Aiman. Throughout his career as a criminal, he has often tried to make something of his music, and it has been his life's dream for music to help him escape the world of crime. Others have also noted that he may have something that could attract a larger audience.

Sleiman recorded a couple of tracks with the hip-hop group Kaliber, who have made quite a name for themselves in the Danish underground scene and won radio station P3's up-and-coming artist prize in 2012. Along with his friend, Kaliber member, Jesper "Livid" Helles, Sleiman writes the lyrics that are about life as a criminal and an immigrant in Denmark. Their song "Alt Det Øjet Ikke Ser" ("All the Things the Eye Doesn't See") was recently picked as February's best track by the hip-hop site Det Sorte Får (The Black Sheep) and has become a hit on YouTube. For the first time in his life, Sleiman has gained respect for doing something good.

August

It is the most beautiful August evening one can imagine. Hundige is bathed in a soft, golden sunset, and seven men are driving around the streets of the residential neighborhood while shooting a music video for my new song called "Bad Boy."

Kaliber was the hot, new name on the Danish hip-hop scene.

Their song "Vest for København" ("West of Copenhagen") now has over 5.2 million views on YouTube, they've enjoyed huge success on the Danish festival stages by that summer, and had a record deal with Sony. The details of the contract remain a secret, but it was the largest contract ever signed with a rap group in Denmark, allowing the members of Kaliber to live off their music. That's the same path I dreamt of following, and suddenly, that dream wasn't a distant fantasy.

Jesper is an intelligent man with tattooed biceps without a single ounce of fat on his body. He's still as broad as he is tall. He earned his mass working out to fend for myself when he was living that gang life.

At the time, he wrote most of the lyrics to Kaliber's songs, and was considered one of the promising talents on the Danish rap scene. Back when Jesper was a teenager growing up in Ballerup, west of Copenhagen, and on his way to becoming a career criminal, he heard about me.

I was already considered a legend. Every town west of Copenhagen has guys like that. I had a reputation as a brutal guy, but I was also respected because he knew how to make money. My peers viewed me as a jet-set gangster who drove big cars and went to all the fancy clubs in Copenhagen.

Jesper and I met for the first time in 2009. People had heard my music and contacted Jesper because they thought I had potential but I didn't quite know how to improve on my own.

Jesper's job was to make my music more accessible. My lyrics were a bit too wrapped up in clichés about the light at the end of the tunnel. Jesper told me my lyrics need to be concrete and create images in people's minds. People need to understand my story 'cause nobody wants to hear about my struggle when they don't know what that struggle is. I had to make songs that were concrete, relevant, and intelligent.

We recorded a song called "Alt Det Øjet Ikke Ser" together. Jesper became a role model for my life. This time, our friendship wasn't based on a continuing criminal enterprise or a code that states we can only be true friends if we're each prepared to take a bullet for one another when push comes to shove.

All of the members of Kaliber came from violent backgrounds.

Jesper grew up in a regular family of schoolteachers and engineers, but during a teenage rebellion that lasted way longer than it should have, he became part of Ballerup's underground. All his friends were from the streets, he didn't have much contact with the ordinary world, and he still feels like a guest in it.

Jesper's own attempt to escape the criminal world was a mini version of what I was trying to do. He backslid once. In 2005, after he got his first record deal, he returned to the street once that initial deal ran its course.

While I wasn't a member of Kaliber, we shared certain commercial interests and I brought them authenticity and street credibility while they helped to develop me and aided me in improving my craft.

There was a drawback in trying to integrate me into Kaliber as they were on the way up and finally finding success. Most of Denmark at the time saw me as a man who helped brutalize and change Denmark for the worse. Even though the immigrant gangs have never achieved the same level of power as the biker gangs, from the perspective of the general public, I helped make the already pervasive gang culture in Denmark more vicious.

We came with our Middle Eastern traditions and a different approach to revenge due to our honor system. As a result, the violence became more brutal. Suddenly, there was no more man-to-man fighting in the club. Now, we rounded up all of our boys and stomped on the guy outside. Now it was all about being flashy and flamboyant, about being recognized in the streets and showing off your success in the media.

Normally, criminals try to stay under the radar, but it became more brutal and more glorified at the same time because the immigrants took pride in it. In turn, the bikers also had to escalate their level of violence to match us. This ultimately resulted in the amount of gun violence skyrocketing. I was often used as a scapegoat for this shift in culture as if I singlehandedly made it all happen as opposed to just being involved with the era.

Because of my reputation and my many enemies and detractors, Jesper initially had his doubts about letting me become too closely linked to himself and Kaliber. That made it difficult to appear as my ally.

It was a difficult situation for me, but we continued to work together as I tried to turn my life around and in the process, inspire others that seek to do the same thing. If I managed to change some people's minds about me in the process? That would be even better.

Bekir has been the most important figure in the gang war in Askerød. Without his influence, Samir and I never clash, the boys of Gersager Park and Askerød never would've turned into Black Cobra and the Bekir Boys, and peace would have settled in Hundige much sooner.

At one point, he was like family to me. I called him uncle, and I looked up to him because I thought he was going to save us. I thought he would take us to new places and make our lives better. But when I got older and saw the truth, I realized that he wasn't fighting for me. My friends and I were like a piece of barren land that no one wanted. He ripened us, and he could have sown something good and turned us into beautiful flowers that others could have enjoyed. Instead, he planted evil. Everything was about his revenge. About his attempt to make himself known as a king.

After Pepe and I both left Bloodz, Lefty stepped up and became the leader of the gang. For some time, he was wanted by the police abroad and couldn't return to Denmark, but Bekir provided him a place to stay, and for a while, they were close. Eventually, things went south between them, and in 2011, Lefty attacked Bekir's son and served a sentence for aggravated assault.

Bekir didn't create me, nor did he make Samir the president of Black Cobra. Even if Samir did turn to Black Cobra to be protected from Bekir, Samir subsequently worked his way up to become the president.

His activities in the gang suggest a personal motivation for which Bekir can't be held accountable. During the period where Samir has been the dominating figure, Black Cobra has been involved in several homicide cases, and Samir himself has multiple assault charges on his résumé. While we're all in the shadow of Bekir, we are the architects of our own lives and build our own futures.

During the last couple of years, gang-related crime rates in Denmark have dropped slightly. The Hells Angels have been temporarily weakened because many of their leading figures have recently been incarcerated. In the meantime, Bandidos have rearmed and linked some of the immigrant groups to the gang, forcing Hells Angels to do the same. This is an example of how the process of integration within the criminal world has, sadly, proven much more successful than in the rest of society. Danish gang members and new Danish gang members are fighting one another from all sides and constantly creating new alliances. Within that space, people are waiting for the cold war between Hells Angels and Bandidos to explode into something that could become very serious. Then it will not merely be the Hells Angels at war with the Bandidos —the two biker gangs will have each of their support groups among the immigrant gangs.

During the summer, it was as if peace had settled in Hundige for a while. Perhaps it was because Bloodz had been weakened and were now without a leader. Sleiman had been ostracized, Pepe and Lefty had walked out, and apparently, Bekir had lost his status. Sleiman's old gang is currently like a snake without a head. The gang is no longer as visible, and in Køge, where the war between Bloodz and Black Cobra claimed several lives, the two parties are apparently talking to each other.

Last summer, there was even talk of an evening meeting, with the objective of making a peace agreement between everyone in Gersager Park and Askerød. Young and old, friends and enemies, Bloodz and Black Cobras were supposed to have dinner together. Sleiman has talked vividly about how amazing such a night would be. But sadly, the meeting never came to fruition. The past has left its brutal traces in Hundige, and while a peace agreement sealed with the breaking of bread under the open summer sky is a beautiful notion, too much blood has been spilled for it to be settled with a barbecue.

Besides, there are many indications that Bandidos is slowly swallowing up Bloodz. Whether that will result in the end of the conflict or, if the homeless, leaderless Bloodz members will continue the war against Black Cobra from within Bandidos, is a question in need of answering. Small conflicts keep arising, and on August 31, things were smoldering once again. A large number of Bandidos gathered in Gersager Park, where Black Cobra still have their headquarters.

There have been several incidents since then, and the sense of peace that ruled last summer was ruined by ten to twelve gunshots on October 5. At around 10:30 p.m., the shots were fired at the club-house that Sleiman once helped establish and Lars Løkke Rasmussen visited back in December 2010. On October 5, shots were fired from a bridge on Anders Plougs Boulevard and from a dark BMW driving down Godsvej.

No one was injured, the police turned up with dogs to search the area, and the residents of Askerød were uncomfortable. The police couldn't say for sure if the attack was gang-related, but according to Jensen, it appeared to be a well-staged operation.

Three days after the shooting, the clubhouse was closed. Jørgen Fahlgren, former head of the Askerød housing department and a strong advocate of the clubhouse, is sad to see it go. But there was no other way.

Things were not looking good in Askerød. The atmosphere was tense, and people fear that the young people will run wild in protest against the closing. The clubhouse didn't close because of the shooting. It closed because unfortunately the young people in the community were so self-destructive.

In 2010, Askerød was removed from the official list of Danish ghettos, but now the area has been readded to the list. According to the new specifications, more than 50 percent of the area's fifteen hundred residents are from non-Western countries, and the number of criminals in the neighborhood is on the rise.

On October 11—the police searched three apartments in the area looking for a group of men suspected of having stabbed a member of Black Cobra.

The Black Cobra member is thirty-four years old and from another suburb west of Copenhagen. He was filling up his tank when a dark Mercedes rolled up beside him. Several people jumped out of the car, and one of them stabbed him multiple times. Per usual, no one saw anything and no one came forward with any infor-mation regarding the crime.

35

TWO SIDES OF THE SAME COIN

When Sleiman stabbed Samir, he crossed a line that swept Hundige up in a tornado of evil that continues to wreak havoc to this very day. In *Politiken*'s library, nearly four hundred newspaper articles have been published about the conflict between Bloodz and Black Cobra in the span of a decade, not to mention the thousands of articles posted online about the same gang war.

"It's possible that there'll always be a whiff of crime surrounding me. After all, I'm from the ditch. I'm from Askerød; I'm from The Scrub House, The Ditch House, The Dam House, The Pond House; I'm from the undergrowth. I grew up in a place named after shrubbery and ditches, and I'll never be able to wash that out of my veins, my blood, or my sweat. It's where I was shaped, where I was molded. Askerød was where I was destroyed, but it was also where I became a person and a man. That's why I have chosen not to leave it. And I'm proud that I'm still there. I'm proud that I put up a fight instead of running away."

Sleiman talks to people who belong to criminal groups, and if anybody thinks that prisoners in Denmark are cut off from contact with the outside world, they can think again. Sleiman is in constant communication with friends on the inside. They call him, and he calls them. If they're in trouble, he tries to help. In order to get by in the joint, you need friends on the outside.

Right now, two of his closest friends, Hedgehog and Pepe, are behind bars, and they each still have plenty of years left to their sentences. Hedgehog is still haunted by the same group who tried to squeeze money out of Sleiman for the business with the car. The blackmailers say that if they can't get the money from Sleiman, they'll have to get it from him.

Sleiman once said that if they go after Hedgehog, they'll have to go through him first. It sounds more like the guy who wishes to pay at the counter but refuses to take his wallet out of his pocket as opposed to a man turning over a new leaf.

"I can't turn my back on a friend who's in jail for seven years and another who's in for twelve and now a third who's in for ten. I have my family and a small number of people whom I love, and I will do anything to protect them."

It has been six years since Sleiman was last convicted for a felony. He doesn't wish to comment on it further, but after having talked to several other sources, it's clear that he has still found himself on the wrong side of the law on several occasions during those years. As mentioned earlier, the police encouraged him in as late as 2012 to wear a bulletproof vest everywhere he went. Meanwhile, there's nothing to suggest that he has been criminally active the last three years.

He says, "I'm no longer active, but there's a risk I might end up in a situation where I'll be forced to defend myself. And I will. There are people out there who think you're weak when you're not a member of a group, and they're trying to take advantage of that."

Is it possible to speak with two tongues and still tell the truth? Sleiman is a man who tries. He tries to hang on to his old world and leave it at the same time. Once in a while, he speaks so fondly of the bond he shared with his brothers that one begins to suspect he might return to the fold if invited.

"The streets took me in. When nobody else wanted me and all my flaws, the streets embraced me. They embraced me as a whole human being, an ugly one, an imperfect one, but a human being, nonetheless. While other people said, 'Monster,' and 'Beyond repair,' the streets said, 'Welcome, brother.'

"I have spent my entire life searching for love, and I never found it in the environment I was living in. I found it through Anna, through Kira, through Birger, through my family, through Jesper, in my relationships with the people who have somehow met me with honest intentions. Through them, I found love, but from all the people I expected to receive love, all I got was hatred, and a lot of the people who expected love from me got hatred as well. I was not an evil child, and I was not an evil person when I came to the streets. But I turned into one. My friends weren't evil kids or evil people when they came, but instead, we became evil."

The burden of responsibility lies with Sleiman and his friends. In Sleiman's eyes, the fathers in the ghettos bear some of the responsibility. Many fathers and some families were simply too weak to stop the young men, while others participated in and incited the war. Far too many merely looked on with glee and did nothing, and their sons became gang members and criminals.

Sleiman says, "They did nothing to stop us when we chose the path of blood. There's an old Arab saying that goes, 'When you see someone else's misfortune, your own troubles seem much lighter because now you have someone to point fingers at.' And evil thrives when good men do nothing."

Sleiman doesn't claim that it is all society's fault. He's also well aware that it would be public suicide for a man with his track record to say so. Yet he insists on his right to criticize. Society *was* to blame for some of the things that happened. He insists that the Hansen family would've received more help than the Sleiman family did when the family arrived in Askerød and his father had tried to murder his mother and sister. He insists that his mother was a woman but was treated as a *foreign* woman while he and his sisters were treated as *foreign* children, and this resulted in poorer treatment. He also insists that what happened to him and his friends also happened in the other large ghettos in Århus, Odense, and Copenhagen.

"I turned to violence because I grew up in a society, in a ghetto, where violence was the only thing people understood. If I had grown up in a local community where the influential people were academics, doctors, and lawyers, I would have become an academic. But I grew up among criminals, among thieves, among hustlers, among people who blackmail other people. I'm not saying it's society's fault, but I'm a product of that. I'm not a product of Palestine. I don't know Palestine. I'm not a product of my mother and father's escape from Lebanon. I'm a product of Denmark."

"I've just tried to describe how a normal boy can become a serious criminal and how a father's violence and a father's hardships in a new country, a new society, while having to learn a new language, can end in tragedy for that society and for his family. I hope the young people of Askerød and other ghettos will read this book and ask themselves if they're on their way to wasting their lives like I wasted mine.

"I hope they understand that they shouldn't follow the Sleimans or the Bekirs of their world because that road only leads to defeat for everybody. None of the guys I grew up with are happy today. The same goes for me. Some of us are still locked up. Some have killed people, and some of us have to constantly look over our shoulders because we're scared that someone will sneak up and shoot us in the back. None of us will ever really be free."

So, does Sleiman regret the life he has led? Yes and no.

"I regret a lot of my actions, but they're also the things that made me the man I am today. And I can't regret who I am. I can't regret my own life. I'm still the same person. I'm just trying to be a better version of myself." Now Sleiman will tell the rest in his own words.

36

GENESIS

Back in 1998 in Grieve, I began having dreams of rapping and decided to try to pursue it, so I started going to DB King's house, where he had his own studio, and we started working on editing my poetry and turning it into songs and raps.

At this point, I was working with Ameena, Dave, Bongo, and DB King. They were good at what they did, they had flow, and they knew how to record a song. They were miles ahead of me, and I wanted to be as capable as they were.

I was continuously writing and rapping, but I was having a hard time finding my flow and confidence in my delivery. I didn't get it. I was putting so much time and effort and emotion into it, and I really felt the music and loved being musically creative, but I somehow still couldn't connect my feelings to my voice. I just sounded monotone. At times, my confidence would take a hit when hearing their constructive criticisms, even though I knew they were trying to help me improve. They genuinely wanted to see me succeed, especially Ameena. She would always tell me I was the Danish Tupac and to believe in myself. Seeing how much she truly believed in me would help boost my self-esteem.

I started trying to dance in my delivery—switch among different emotions. I suddenly started feeling like something was going my way. They would say, "Stay on the mic. Keep recording. Practice makes perfect. Rap as if you are trying to convince us. Make us believe every word." I started doing that, and I began making progress.

Ameena could always see the struggle raging within me and told me to not be afraid to show this part of myself to the world at large, knowing that a part of me felt embarrassed and hated showing weakness of any kind. She told me this because being connected to the music meant that I had to embrace my own vulnerability.

In my neighborhood, you looked weak if you had big dreams because it meant that you weren't 100 percent committed to the streets. I didn't think you could ever get away from the stigma that follows you from a lifetime commitment to the streets. So I felt like I had to keep my rap dreams a secret. I was spending all this time with normal people who dared to dream big, dreams that were on a whole different level than I ever thought possible for someone like me. I started understanding a lot of my mother's problems, and I became more aware of the traumas and tragedies that had affected my family. I also became more conscious of my own behavior. Music became my therapy, an outlet for all my boxed-up emotions.

So now I was living a sort of double life: I was in that home studio dreaming, hoping for something greater for the future, but I was simultaneously getting deeper entrenched in the street life. None of my hood friends even knew about my secret life, but every time I left the studio, I went right back to the same problems and the same hopeless friends and felt like I was in a paradox—I loved the music, but I also hated it for giving false hope 'cause what seemed so attainable in the studio always seemed so unattainable in the streets.

I became angry for allowing myself to get lost in the dreaming, so I started staying away from the studio and the crew. I would meet Ameena and another good friend, Monica, and they would ask me why I had stopped coming. They told me that I should come back because I had an important message to give the world through music.

I knew I wasn't going back. I wasn't going to let myself dream big anymore. No more false expectations. I wasn't going to become anybody anyway! It was shameful to even mention having any big dreams in front of my hood friends, so I didn't go there anymore after that.

37

MY FIRST SHOW AND THE START OF MY MUSIC CAREER

I did my first, and only, show in a long time in 2007 that was fateful for my music dream. The second I stepped out onto the stage, I saw nothing but folded arms and cold glances from my people. None of them showed support or applauded after my songs.

For the first time in my life, I was afraid of my own group, and I felt insecure among them. I had a feeling that something bad would happen. Shortly afterward, I was shot. That's why I stopped making music, because I felt like music had gotten me into a fantasy world where I didn't see the real danger around me during the ongoing street wars to become the next boss. I didn't even recognize that I might be betrayed by my own in the very same group I had once founded.

It wasn't until after the assassination attempt on both myself and my brother-in-law Karim that I returned to music. In 2011, I suddenly had a beat sent to me from Kayreem, who was both a singer and a producer. I didn't even know how he knew I used to make music! I hadn't released any material; I had only shared a few songs from the 2007 show on MySpace with a group called Street Corner Poets.

I sat for several days thinking about whether I should get back to him. My situation was far different than it was back in 2007, when I still had a leading role in Bloodz. Now I had been at war with them for the past four years. I figured that with everything I stood to lose, I had already lost. I had lost my position in Bloodz, and my friends had now become my enemies.

Eventually, I decided to get back to him, and he invited me to a session in his studio, TrackMansion, in Nørrebro with his partner, Jan. After almost two months of work, I released a song titled "Regn-dråber" ("Raindrops") that was more traditional poetry than rap.

After the release of the single, Jan and I fell out because the initial agreement was that TrackMansion was going to sign me, release the music, and cover the expenses in a 50/50 deal. In the end, I paid for all of it myself. Because of that, I wanted the rights to my own music, which they had merely helped distribute without paying a penny out of their pocket, as we had initially agreed. It ended up costing me 50,000 DKK ($7,600), while the song only made 4,000 ($610). It didn't appear on the charts or even get played on the radio, but I didn't lose heart. On the contrary, I was eager to get back to it. I felt like I could do something better. It couldn't end here because I still had a story to tell.

I continued to collaborate with Kayreem, this time without Jan, who at one point had introduced me to Jesper "Livid" Helles. At the time, Livid was a part of Kaliber, which was participating in a competition in the Career Cannon on Denmark's radio. The prize was 250,000 DKK ($38,000) and a record deal with Sony Music.

Livid and I quickly became good friends. He was a strong critic of my music, which he felt like I wrapped up too tight. He thought it was too metaphorical and poetic and that I should just tell my story in as simple and natural a way as possible. Livid thought I had the wildest story. He said that there was no one in the industry like me.

I personally didn't feel special. If anything, I felt like a failure. Livid believed in me so hard that he made me believe in myself. That led to us making the song "Alt Det Øjet Ikke Ser" ("All the Things the Eye Doesn't See"). The song was poetic because it was about voicing those internal battles people struggle with that others don't immediately see. That way, we started unpacking the metaphors and saying things plainly.

Livid was still very busy with his music career with DB King, Face It, and Mr. Mo in the group Kaliber, and it looked like they were actually going to win the competition. Turns out that they did, along with the 250,000 and the record deal.

During that period, I started a consulting firm, SS Consult, where I lectured about my life and how I broke out of the gang culture to secondary schools, institutes of higher learning and businesses. At the same time, I was offered an education in management, which would usually cost 60,000 Danish Krone ($9100) for free at Mindjuice Academy by its founder, Pernille W. Lauritsen, whom I met at a talk I gave at the publishing company Politikens Forlag. It's an education that only high-ranking people in the largest companies in Denmark receive. I asked for Livid to get the same offer. We were each other's shadows in everything. I felt like he should be involved in anything that could provide financial or personal gain in the long run.

Everything I learned during that course, combined with my experiences, made me highly knowledgeable in terms of crime, action patterns, motives, solution models, and personality types. I gained insight into my motives dating back to my childhood, my parents' schism, and what later became the whole family's misfortune. I thus felt like it became my diploma in terms of crime and preventive work.

No social authorities had tried to help me, or my family leave the gang life back then. We weren't offered the existing exit programs because it meant having to name someone. That wasn't an option. I would fight to stay in Hundige without having to rat anyone out. I had played a part in destroying my neighborhood and therefore owed it to everyone to help rebuild it.

Everything I earned in the company, I shared with Livid, whom I took with me on a lecture tour for social workers, the Ministry of Integration, municipalities, juvenile prisons, schools, and other crime-prevention institutions. He was my support in music, and in this way, I supported him by letting him share in my personal and financial success. I felt like I owed him that.

Meanwhile, Kaliber's career began taking off. They got hundreds of gigs, released their first EP, and were in the process of negotiating another album with Sony. Despite all of this, Livid continued working with me, to the great annoyance of the rest of his group.

While they saw me as a burden, Livid considered me an opportunity to expand Kaliber into something bigger.

Livid told me they were afraid to be seen with me. They believed that he put Kaliber's safety at risk by working with me, for they were afraid of being killed by my enemies as a means to reach me. . Livid asked me to stay close and not say anything to them about it.

While Kaliber was about to release their second album, Livid and I completed my next two singles, "Gadeprins" ("Street Prince") and "Bad Boy." I found out that DB King also wanted money out of my pocket for "Bad Boy," which he had produced. I thought it was about lifting each other up and supporting one another, but it was all about money in the end.

He became a stranger to me, even though I had known him since I was fourteen or fifteen years old, but I didn't want to fall out with him because of it. He felt the same way as Face It, who in turn wanted money from me for "Gadeprins," which he had produced with Hooman. I ended up paying 70,000 DKK ($10,700) for the two songs, which didn't become hits either. I only earned around 6,000 ($915) back from the TuneCore account Face It set up for me, while the expenses for production, music videos, mixing, mastering, and cover art exceeded 150,000 Danish Krone ($23,000) in total.

I had always believed that it was easy to make music. I didn't know, how much time and work really went into it. I just thought you went into the studio, wrote a song, and then, suddenly, it would be released, people would stream it and share it, and then you would become famous from one day to the next. But I got wiser.

38

LAILA AND MOHAMMED

On August 2, 2013, I became a father for the first time to my daughter, Laila. I was still in conflict with myself over the loss of my brother, Mohammed, and his fate that he had been in a wheelchair for his entire life while I was given every opportunity possible and had wasted most of them. I had never been able to process my grief or my guilt. Now I suddenly had a daughter, and I should have been delighted about it. I always felt that Mohammed had been a better person and a better son than I. I'm sure he would have made far better choices than I did, for I was hopeless and an eternal pessimist, while he was always happy and an eternal optimist—even with his disabilities.

Everyone knew that Mohammed had loved life, whereas I was perpetually unhappy. This gave me a bad conscience. How could I allow myself to be unhappy with all the opportunities I had when he was always so happy without having any opportunities at all? How could I be happy that my wife had given birth to our first child when I had just buried my big brother? It didn't feel fair, but I also think it was a mercy sent from God that I should now be the father of this pure, beautiful, and innocent creature.

There was a greater meaning in the fact that she was born right after his death. I felt obligated to become a better person, a better father, a better son, and a better brother. I felt obligated to be a little bit more like Mohammed. It shifted my focus and prevented me from falling into an even deeper hole.

Laila saved me.

39

MY BEDROCK AND MY LIONESSES

My mother was nearing the end of her life. Her condition began to deteriorate over time until she was eventually declared terminal.

I remember one night, when my wife was two months pregnant with our second child, we were sitting around my mother's bed. We talked about children, Hanin's pregnancy, and what gender the baby might be while Laila lay playing with some Kinder Surprise chocolate eggs on my mother's bed next to her. My daughter tried to give my mother one of the eggs, but she couldn't eat solid food anymore.

The moment Hanin went to take Laila away, my mother pointed with her finger and tapped Hanin's belly, signalling that it had to be a boy, although we knew nothing about the gender at the time.

I especially remember one time when I was looking for Laila and my mother in our home. I heard some plastic rattling from inside the storage room. I opened the door and found my mother sitting on the floor with her granddaughter on her lap with a whole packet of tea cakes. They both had chocolate around their mouths and all over their fingers. My mother started laughing because she had diabetes and wasn't allowed to eat such things. I loved their relationship and the fact that she got to see my child.

After my mother passed away in her room, my sister Sarah came to the apartment when she heard our cries after we had found her dead. Next, my father came to the door. We didn't understand how he knew our mother was dead and how he could've come so quickly. I had forgotten that several months ago, he had told me that my half sister was going to court in Copenhagen that same day to testify against a person who had sold her a stolen camera.

It seemed almost unimaginable that my father would come to our house on that exact day and see my dead mother being carried out of her apartment before his eyes. They had never reconciled, but my father collapsed at that moment. He was completely inconsolable. I could see the tears rolling down his cheeks. I never thought that my father would shed a tear for my mother, but for the first time, I saw that he loved her. He was crushed. Maybe he had never forgiven himself, and maybe he'll never get there. It seemed like our whole lives passed before his eyes. All his guilt and unprocessed feelings made him burst into tears. He cried silently. It made it all the more sad to hear my dad cry that way.

I don't think my father would be able to look into the mirror of the past if I held it up in front of him. If I did, I think it would kill him. As we buried my mother, we were going to bury the past too. His heart was broken. I don't think he will ever recover from that day.

My dad stayed throughout the ceremony. My sisters, my lionesses, prepared her for her funeral by giving her a last wash and wrapping her in white, cotton robes. I can't imagine how hard it must've been for them and how crushed they must have been while they were doing it. I never would've been able to do that myself.

My relationship with my mother had always been poetic. As fate would have it, she would be buried on the day I was born September 21. After her passing, I was inspired to make even more music with all the emotions her death dredged up.

On the streets, we called ourselves generals and soldiers, but no one told us how long a soldier's life was. Most of our generals were not at war, but we were, for we were the soldiers, the useful idiots, and other idiots could easily come along and replace us. There were many lost souls like us, and that was why I made music. All the boys from the block could've turned into something. The ghetto was filled with lost stars. We were all part of a game where we made the rules ourselves, but we couldn't control the consequences. When we started seeing them, it was too late to back out. You were now part of the game, and you had to finish playing. If you were dishonored today, then you had to fight to retrieve the honor tomorrow. There was always vengeance to be had or payback to seek out. You couldn't just walk out of the game without risking your entire team would leave you all alone in the field.

No one was untouchable. Everyone could get hit, and there would be no one to catch you or give you a new life. I know because no one ever caught me. There were no Replay buttons or do-overs, so when it was over, it was over. We were the simultaneous inflictors and receivers of violence.

It was all about being strong with our hands, so no one taught us to use our heads. Why would you need a wise soldier anyway? Preferably, we should just be constantly high and never think independently. We just needed to follow orders. That's what a good soldier did.

My mother gave birth to me in a bunker in Lebanon. I had to lay her into the ground on my birthday, exactly thirty-two years after the day she gave birth to me. Just as she carried me into the world, I carried her for the last time down to her grave and turned her head toward Mecca.

My wife gave birth to our son, Mohammed, on February 18, 2015 —a boy, just like my mother had predicted, named after my beloved brother whom I had also lost.

40

EX-KALIBER

I was on tour with Kaliber after they released their second EP in 2014. They were living the lives of superstars. It was all about the parties, the drugs, and the ladies.

Meanwhile, they all began flirting with dreams of solo careers so they would no longer have to split their earnings. DB King, Face It, and Mr. Mo felt that Livid had already gone solo because he was collaborating more and more with me on the side. They could also see that people were starting to recognize my music while I was touring with them. There were major financial problems in the group because the money was being spent on wild nights out, expensive taxi rides, girls, and whatnot. Livid was unaware of all of these issues, and that was one of the reasons he started thinking more about himself and less about Kaliber. As I saw it, he felt betrayed and cheated by his own groupmates.

Things got so wild that it eventually went wrong one night in the studio, where they regularly held parties. They were all so fucked up on drugs that someone forgot to put out a cigarette, and the whole building caught on fire. Everyone managed to escape except for Steven, who was from my hometown and with whom I had started the music dream with Ameena, Street Corner Poets, and DB King back in 2007. Steven died that night, and so did Kaliber shortly afterward.

The jealousy, greed, and debauchery had overshadowed their love of music and creating something cool. They had had all of Denmark behind them and were Denmark's music media darlings at the time. They were simultaneously ahead of their time because they had used the sound of the 1990s to create something new. Unfortunately, they squandered it all away in one fell swoop.

One day in 2015, I heard that Mr. Mo wanted to get out of the song we made for my mother, after I had paid all the expenses, because he was afraid to be seen in a music video with me. Mr. Mo had sung the hook while I did the verses. That song was the most important one to me, so I couldn't let it happen because the video had already been shot. After explaining the importance of the song, Mr. Mo relented and allowed it to be released, but the damage had been done. That was the last night I saw Kaliber as a group

41

SUCCESS

Now that Kaliber was over, the rest of us had to put the past behind us. It was now or never, and we all knew it. We needed one another, and we completed one another. DBKing was perhaps the best rapper and Livid was the best songwriter, while I was the best at melodies, catchphrases, and themes. The three of us needed one another in different ways to achieve our goals, so we had to work together. Livid and I needed DBKing as a producer, while he needed us as artists and songwriters, so we all continued to collaborate as solo artists while we each worked on our own albums.

We started again from scratch. We had no studio, so DB King converted his garbage shed into one, and we began working on new material. We were determined to build our solo careers together, but we had a kind of competition among us that could be both healthy and unhealthy given that it could possibly lead to resentment, jealousy and hurt feelings in the event I began to surpass him.

Livid and I created the first four songs with my traditional rap delivery for my EP in hopes of getting me signed to a major label. The first was called "Fundament" ("Foundation"), featuring Gilli and Young, who were upcoming artists at the same time we were. Gilli was from Copenhagen, while Young was from Århus, and both were popular artists in Denmark. The second song was called "Brorman" ("Bro") and featured Livid, as well as MellemFingaMuzik and Sivas, who were also popular acts. The third song was called "Drømme" ("Dreams"), featuring Stepz, who was one half of MellemFinga-Muzik. Other songs included "Nabolag" ("Neighborhood"), "Kome-ter" ("Comets") with Livid and DBKing, and "Bomaye."

"Bomaye" was much more melodic than anything I had ever made before. It was a whole new style for me, but I was afraid it was too flimsy and sweet. We sent the EP to Ali Sufi, who was the owner of Grounded, a Sony Music sublabel, where we chose "Brorman" as the lead single. Grounded/Sony offered me a contract with a non recoupable 30,000 DKK ($4600) signing fee and a 300,000 ($46,000) DKK marketing budget.

However, Sony did not think that "Brorman" should be the lead single. They all gravitated to "Bomaye" and thought "Fundament" should be the preview track before the EP was released in March 2016. "Fundament" created a strong expectation of what would be in store for my EP. Sony had high expectations, especially Ali, who signed me there. Just like Livid, he believed in me, my story, and my mission as a true artist.

It scared me because I didn't see myself breaking through. I had tried for so many years and never succeeded. I was afraid to disappoint all those who had high expectations of me. I was afraid of being a flop and being dropped as abruptly as I had been signed. I would disappoint Ali, who had taken a chance on me; Livid, who had spent years of his life building up Sleiman as an artist; and my family, who were hoping and waiting for me to have just a little success for a change. I dreaded ending my career after only managing to release a solo single.

Everything I had done before hadn't resonated on the streets yet. I dreaded the results when Sony chose to release "Bomaye" as the lead single. I got the same feeling in my body as I had during the show back in 2007 and when I had to release the song for my mother. I was afraid people would laugh at me and say, "Now he wants to not only rap but also sing and make melodies."

At the same time, DB King began to make unreasonable and costly demands concerning my budget at Sony. He wanted an advance on royalties and 30,000 ($4600) for the beat, while the best producer at the time only charged somewhere in the region of 12,500 DKK ($1900). The original idea was to shoot the music video in

Zanzibar, but he didn't want to travel because he had a street shop, which he wouldn't leave.

At the request of Sony, we included MellemFingaMuzik on the song instead of DB King and shot the music video in Marbella, Spain. Sony also suggested removing Livid from the song and inserting Gilli instead, but I couldn't let that happen. We had created that song together before I was even signed. I considered giving it to DB King for fear of being ridiculed, but my family stood up and said no, even though they didn't know anything about music. They thought it was my song and that I should stand by it. We released it as a single and the entire EP on March 12, while the video for "Bomaye" came out on March 18.

The first week after the EP was released went pretty well. I entered the top fifty in Denmark on Spotify and other music streaming services. It was the first time I had ever been on a hit list, let alone in the top fifty. I climbed up to the top twenty in a week. On the way to a radio spot on *The Voice*, Ali heard children in a schoolyard playing "Bomaye," and he heard it blasting from other cars on the road as well. He was sure it was already a hit by then.

In just under a week, "Bomaye" was number one in Denmark with one hundred and eighty thousand streams a day. I held that position for six straight weeks. Before the month had passed, the song had gone gold after 4.5 million streams and was on its way to platinum, which is achieved after nine million streams.

I started being contacted by booking agencies, one of which was The Night, which was owned by Danish singer/songwriter and businessman Jon Nørgaard.

After I signed with The Night, Jon offered to take over my management for a payment of 20 percent of everything I earned from that day on. I signed with him, and he ended up getting me a better deal at Sony of about 2 million Krone ($305,000), plus an advance of 500,000 DKK ($76,000) from bookings.

Before long, my EP went gold after ten thousand albums were sold. Shortly afterward, it went platinum in Denmark with twenty thousand sold. "Bomaye" now has over 11 million views on YouTube. After years of false starts, disappointments, and doubting myself, I was finally seeing real progress.

42

ALL OR NOTHING

The next song I released was "Alt Eller Intet" ("All or Nothing"), featuring Gilli. The song went gold within the first month after release. We wanted to go with another song called "Don Diego" as our next single, but Sony pushed for For Evigt Ung" ("Forever Young") instead. We argued back and forth, but ultimately, Sony got their way. It turned out they were right because "For Evigt Ung" made it to number four in the top ten against American artists who charted just above it. It eventually moved down to seventh, then stayed in the top twenty for several months on its way to gold, then platinum certification in Denmark.

We revisited "Don Diego" with a set of fresh ears, and I ended up choosing a different verse to put on it. Sometimes, you just have to get away from things and return to them later. I played "Don Diego" for my boy Diego, who inspired its creation, and I introduced him our friend to The Iraqi. Diego loved the song and wanted to pay for the video. I told him that Sony didn't want to release it, and he exclaimed, "Fuck Sony! I'm paying!" He asked me to take The Iraqi to Spain so he could star in the video

We went and made the video. He chose The Iraqi to star in the video because he was a well-known actor in Denmark. I went back to Denmark to perform at the New Year's Eve party at TV2 in

Aalborg with a fully completed video for "Don Diego" in my back pocket while "For Evigt Ung" was still in the top twenty.

After New Year's, I wanted to release "Don Diego" right away, but Sony refused. When I told them that I already had a video for it and they didn't need to pay for it, they finally agreed to release it. Immediately after it came out, "Don Diego" entered the top fifty at number two. I was one of the hottest acts in Danish music now that I had two songs in the top twenty. "Alt Eller Intet" was still in the top fifty, and "Bomaye" was still in the top one hundred. After years of failure, I now had four hits at the same time.

This all came at a cost, unfortunately. The three biggest urban artists at Sony, who all had ten times more followers than I did on social media platforms and who had all worked with me before, showed up at Grounded to complain. They demanded to know how "Don Diego" could be at number two while they were at the bottom of the top ten.

I had to strike while the iron was hot. My producer, Kewan, and I made the songs "Laila," "Caliente," "Sicario," and "Chico," then stashed them away in hopes of keeping our hitmaking streak going.

Kewan began telling Jon, Pepe, and myself that we should all move from Sony over to Warner Music and start our own label because things at Sony were becoming toxic. Kewan had been attacked by some other Sony artists who believed that Ali hadn't supported them and I was being favored. Given the hostile work environment at Grounded, Pepe, Jon, and I began negotiating for a label deal with Warner.

43

PROBATION

P epe had just been released from prison and came with me on tour during his probation before his final release. He had become more and more interested in making music, and I put him on a song for the first time by letting him sing the hook on "Caliente." With the help of Livid and Kewan, we were able to get Pepe to lay down the hook even though he had no previous experience

I moved all my future releases to Warner and entered an override agreement between Sony and Warner. Meanwhile, my last four songs released at Sony were made into an EP that was garnering significant streaming numbers in Europe.

Our negotiations with Warner were finally done. I had negotiated a 2.5 million DKK ($381,000) contract for the group Camo that I was a part of; Probation, our own label; and for myself, the artist. One million of which were earmarked for Probation, half of which would be used to sign new artists, production, et cetera, which still had to be approved by and paid for by Warner in the end. The rest of the money would be used as we saw fit, but the priority would be for overhead to run the label.

I still hadn't released either "Caliente" or "Laila," but I had them in the stash as pre-produced songs with finished music videos when I began my Warner run.

44

CAMO

Camo was a supergroup consisting of me, Livid, and a kid we called The Moroccan. Livid was already a solo artist with Warner, while The Moroccan was Pepe's protégé whom he pushed to get into Camo. The Moroccan was bad at showing up for our studio time slots, and when he did, he was always unprepared. We quickly realized that all he had was a cool voice.

Pepe felt like he could do better and deserved it more, so he began to push to take his place. It made sense to throw The Moroccan out because Pepe wanted to rap in Danish. The Moroccan didn't step up and produce, so Livid and I made the switch official.

Pepe was under the supervision of the Danish Prison and Probation Service and wanted out of financial aid, which required a job. He therefore asked if we could hire him to run Probation for us, which would help him out. But it wasn't long before Pepe began to complain about his salary. He didn't think there was any difference between what he received in financial aid and what he received from us.

It bothered me because he was never meant to get rich from my dream. I was just trying to help him move on from his supervision. I had made sure that he would get somewhere around 400,000 DKK ($61,000 USD) the first year without delivering anything, and 150,000 of that amount was The Moroccan's signing fee. The other

250,000 was just for running Probation, but it was me who ran everything and signed artists for the label while he got paid for it. It didn't bother me, however, because I felt like I was helping a friend. Pepe still felt it was not enough for him.

I started releasing my ten songs at Warner. The first was "Chico," which was a tribute to Pepe getting out of jail. I then released the remaining songs in short intervals because I wanted to fulfill my contract with Warner as soon as possible so I could renegotiate a new one with them.

Livid, Pepe, and I started writing songs for Camo while I released my singles. When I was about to release "Laila," Jon negotiated a separate agreement with Warner that they should pay the costs for both "Laila" and "Caliente" because in my exit agreement with Sony I had freed the songs up by paying an amount that covered Sony's expenses. Warner bought the songs from me for around 300,000 DKK ($46,000), which made them a part of the original override agreement with Sony.

In January 2018, I released a song with Pepe as a feature. It was the first time he was on an official release, and it didn't do as well as we expected it would. Pepe's dissatisfaction led him to start negotiating with Jon and Livid about where he could land a solo deal. He started flirting with Sony, with whom I was not on good terms. Shortly afterward, Camo went to Greece, to shoot music videos for two songs named "Havana" and "Mentirosa."

In Greece, I started writing a song while listening to one of DB King's beats. Sebastian, who was a producer, recorded my hook down there, but Pepe also wanted to record something. He thought it was supposed to be a Camo song, while I thought it was a Sleiman song. Livid became angry with me during the video shootings over trivial reasons. I began to feel like things with us weren't going to end well.

When we got back on the plane to leave, Pepe and I didn't speak a word to each other. When we got home, Pepe started slandering me to my own family members. I felt betrayed.

Pepe reached out to me later and told me that he was sorry, but that he was angry that I wouldn't make the song from Greece into a Camo song. I had done everything I could to help him, but I couldn't forgive or trust him anymore for breaking an unwritten rule between brothers and friends. I stopped contacting Pepe, Livid, and Jon and left them everything. The only thing I took with me was the money for my equipment, which they kept in the studio; the deposit for the studio; and the name Probation. It was my life's work and my name, but they could keep the rest.

I left my dream there. Even though I left of my own volition, I felt that they had taken everything from me because I was forced to go. I could tell that it wouldn't end well if I stayed.

45

REQUIEM FOR A DREAM

After two months without any contact with my former associates, Pepe got in touch with me through a mutual friend because he wanted a meeting at a café in Amager. I heard that Pepe wanted to sign with Ali Sufi at Sony. Grounded and Sony removed all my songs that Sony had released from Sony's playlists on Spotify since I was on Warner now. To make matters even crazier, it was Pepe who made me aware that it had happened.

At the meeting, he wanted me to give him my last three songs, especially "Caliente," which I had recorded with the German rapper Kontra K, and let him release it because, in his opinion, I was done in the music business and now the time was his. I refused to give him my songs or cease my career for his, so our meeting was over.

We walked out toward the parking lot, where he got into his car and called me over. He told me he and Livid had been down and lost for several months, but they had been working on some songs. He also said that some mutual friends from back home had told him that I wasn't doing right by him and that I should get out of his way so he could succeed. Pepe then said that he was sad, and he wanted to take a trip to Germany to get away for a few days.

When the conversation ended, we both had tears in our eyes. The air wasn't completely cleared when we parted, and Pepe left for

Germany. The next day, I got a call. I was told that Pepe had just died of cardiac arrest in a hotel in Hamburg.

I thought it was a lie. Pepe couldn't be dead; I had just spoken to him yesterday! I ran over to see his family, to see if I could get confirmation, but when I reached the parking lot, the entire older generation of boys from the block were all crying. That was all I needed to see to know what I had been told was true.

After Pepe's death, I ran away from the gray, concrete blocks of Askerød. I had experienced too much loss in such a short time. I lost Pepe after we had seemingly gotten clear of our pasts and were headed to success. Unfortunately, we lost sight of what was important and got seduced by the trappings of fame. Everything we had fought for, hustled for, and used leverage to negotiate for was now in danger of crashing down all around me. However, there was a way I could come out ahead: record a new hit.

46

6IX9INE

I wanted to finish all my business in Denmark first before I went to Spain to meet with my boy Diego to strategize what to do next with my career. When I contacted Warner to get out of my contract, I was asked if I had any objection to the "Havana" video being removed from YouTube at the request of Pepe's family because of certain scenes in it that they took issue with. Livid had already accepted, and so did I.

Warner told me that I owed them approximately 280,000 Danish Krone ($43,000). I only handed over some of the songs agreed upon in my contract, and because of the fourteen tracks Warner had brought over from Sony and prepaid for, 300,000 DKK ($46,000) had been used from that previous budget.

Warner didn't want any more money from me and let me keep the remaining songs I either hadn't delivered or finished yet. However, they chose to arrange with Kewan to use the work that he still owed them for me to instead be used for other Warner artists. This arrangement would leave me free and clear of any obligation to them, and all the demos and sketches I had were mine and mine alone. They let me go without obstacles. They treated me like a human being, and I will always have great respect for what they did because not everyone is that good to you in the industry. They treated me better than I had treated them.

I slipped off to Spain in mid-August and expected to return to Denmark before my fifth child's due date, which was on October 4, 2018. That September, a DJ who ran an agency in Europe for international artists contacted me. He had heard my song "Mac II," which only contained one hook, and asked me if I would like to record it with American rapper 6ix9ine.

I thought about it for a long time because I had put my music on hold after Pepe's death. I talked to my sister Sarah about it. She didn't know 6ix9ine, but her daughters overheard the conversation in the background and shouted, "Do it, Uncle! Do it! He's famous!" A big hit was what my career needed more than anything, so that swayed me.

A few days later, on the morning of September 24, 6ix9ine's agents and I agreed to collaborate on "Mac II." However, our impending deal contained a catch: I had to fly to Milan, Italy, the same day to close the deal with $100,000 in cash.

I couldn't get that money in such a short amount of time. However, Pepe's friend wanted to be a partner in the song, so he gave me 24,000 euros ($27,000), while Livid and another investor Mike Lowrey each flew to Milan with 10,000 euros ($11,500) . Diego's friend, C, and I flew to Milan with the 24,000 euros. It was the first time in several months I had spoken to Livid besides briefly seeing him at Pepe's funeral. Despite everything that happened between Livid and me, I felt like he should be involved in this deal. He had been there since the beginning, so he deserved to be there for the end.

In Milan, we met 6ix9ine and his team after a Philipp Plein fashion show. We went to the Westin Hotel, signed the contracts, and gave them the 34,000 euros ($38,500) in cash while the rest was sent via bank transfer. We then went to a party in Milan, where 6ix9ine was to perform. His security guards asked us to help them keep the fans away from him because no one was allowed to go near him. C and I were fucking annoyed at having to become bodyguards for the night after agreeing to collaborate with 6ix9ine on a song. We had thought we were going to party and have fun. 6ix9ine also made us all wait over half an hour for his red Ferrari to pick him up in front of the hotel to go to the party.

At one point, DJ Pvnch told us that they were only supposed to be in Europe for fourteen days but were instead there for three weeks. They were next going to Dubai for fourteen days because 6ix9ine had problems with the FBI after a search of his apartment in New York City. DJ Pvnch lost his shoes on the European tour, but 6ix9ine didn't want to buy new ones for him, so he ran around in flip-flops the whole trip. I was next told that the only reason 6ix9ine performed that night was to cover the 10,000 euro hotel bill at the Westin. It told me everything I needed to know about him.

We went up to his hotel room after the party, where they asked if 6ix9ine could rap my Danish hook for "Mac 11" in English. I thought, *Why not?* After a few hours, the song was done, and C and I traveled back to Spain with 6ix9ine's song, which we also owned the rights to. Now I had a potential hit in the bag and was ready to return to Denmark and attend the birth of my child.

Later, Maria K from Universal Denmark, who had asked if I would enter a fifty-fifty collaboration between them and my company Probation, contacted me. Maria asked if I was able to make more deals with international artists, considering the contacts that I had. Next, my former collaborator, Gilli, came to Spain and showed up with C at a restaurant where Diego and I were eating. He asked, "Hey, don't you think I should be on that 6ix9ine song? Sleiman, I have nothing against you. I've always only had respect for you." I had promised C and Diego not to mention anything to Gilli about his lack of support for my music throughout my career, so I just replied, "Yes. Of course, bro."

We recorded Gilli's verse very quickly, and I went ahead with two new feature deals that I had agreed to with Maria. That turned into two more songs, one with Lacrim and one with Marwa Loud, both of whom were French artists. Those songs, including the 6ix9ine song, cost me a total of 220,000 euros ($250,000) in expenses and advances on royalties. I got the master rights for them, which I then had to share with Universal. Once the songs were recorded, I would release the 6ix9ine song first, which we renamed "R.E.D." The song with Lacrim was called "Totorina," and the remaining song with Marwa was titled "TIK TOK."

I sent a bill to Maria for about 50,000 euros ($57,000) for half of the rights to "R.E.D" because I had paid for it all to begin with. Universal told me I couldn't release the song because 6ix9ine had a deal with a sublabel under Universal USA, 10k Projects, which was owned by the son of the director of Universal USA. If I released the song, 10k would sue me. Instead, I chose to sue them with the help of Romano Law in New York City.

Universal Denmark then told me that I wasn't allowed to release *any* of the other songs I had produced and owned the rights to, including "Totorina" and "TIK TOK." Universal had sent me 300,000 DKK ($46,000), which they felt made them co-owners of the songs, so according to them, I wasn't allowed to release them. They wanted to end the collaboration with me because I had sued a Universal artist in the United States. They were told by the director of Universal USA that Universal Denmark wasn't allowed to continue working with me. They next demanded that I either return the 300,000 DKK or that they buy the songs back from me for 200,000 DKK ($30,460). I saw that as a mockery because those songs cost me all my money I had left to record. I felt robbed, and I recorded the conversation we had as evidence because it was a breach of contract, according to Danish law.

Universal Denmark didn't keep our agreement because they knew from the start that I had made a song with 6ix9ine. After all, that was why they had contacted me in the first place. They had known for months that I was suing 6ix9ine and 10k, but it wasn't until I wanted to release the songs that it became a problem. They knew that 6ix9ine was a Universal artist, as there was a previous conflict with Sony and Universal Denmark over another song that 6ix9ine had made with Jimilian.

In addition to all of this, there were another six songs made with six different artists from Europe that had been agreed to in the same manner. 10k and Universal USA must've known that 6ix9ine ran around Europe and made these kinds of one-off, money-grab deals. Difference being all the others had had their songs released because they had never asked for permission to do so. I did, and therefore, the door was shut on me.

At that moment, I lost everything. All my money was gone, and I was left with three useless songs and a bill of 220,000 euros ($250,000) for music I could never even release. In the end, I got Gilli removed from the song and hoped that the 6ix9ine team would accept it now that the song had gotten a lot shorter. They put me in touch with a producer, Wizard Lee, who was the producer on 6ix9ine's album and was going to make the new version with me.

Prior to this, 6ix9ine had apologized to me via a Zoom call for the hell he knew he had put me through. He told me that if the song was included on his album *TattleTales*, that would be the best solution for me. It would be a win-win. However, when the album was finally released, my song wasn't included. I was crushed. It was too close to the release date for Wizard to put it on the album. Eventually, my lawyers were promised that there would be an extended version of *TattleTales* that would include the song.

When the extended version of *TattleTales* was released, my song was indeed used. However, the album was a massive flop. My song was received even worse than it had been when I had initially released it myself. I had pinned all my hopes on an American rap star and European artists to give me crossover hits and riches, even though my pursuit of superstardom in music had come at the expense of my marriage and my family. It was over. I could now finally close that chapter of my life.

47

BEL SALAMA (THE EPILOGUE)

I could now end my career and say goodbye to music. I had no
more to give. I had said everything I wanted to say. Now I just
had to gather all the remaining songs I had lying around, put them
on one last album, and get them out on all platforms as a means to
say goodbye. That's why I chose to call my last album *Bel Salama*.
Translated from Arabic, it means *Go with peace*.

I wanted to say goodbye to the fans who had supported me since
day one and helped me reach goals I could've never dreamed of.
Thanks to their support and love, I received a two-times platinum
single, twelve gold singles, four platinum singles, a two-times platinum album, and a three-times platinum album. I reached over one
hundred million combined streams on various DSPs and forty-five
million combined views on YouTube. I became the most-played and
most-subscribed-to Danish-speaking rapper on YouTube in March
2021.

I managed to play around one hundred shows and give about
thirty talks during that same time period. It's a very special feeling
when you are surrounded by fans who sing along to your songs and
know all the lyrics. That rush, that feeling of euphoria, is the wildest
thing I've ever experienced in my life. It closed the empty space I've
had inside me all my life, but just for a while, because when the

music stopped, the lights went off, and the voices were muted, it all disappeared again.

The loneliest place in the world was in the car on the ride back home. Livid and I shared that loneliness, but we also shared the money. The only thing I always looked forward to on the way home was seeing my kids again. I felt like I had done something good because I had something to bring home for them so that all the nights I spent away weren't for naught.

I felt like I was a father they could be proud of and could look up to. I loved the look they gave me when someone stopped me on the street and wanted a picture. It didn't matter to me to get that look from anyone in the world more than it did to get it from my kids. They would say, "Why do people want to take a picture with you, *baba*? Everyone knows you. We are lucky that Sleiman is our father." Even my kids saw me as the man with the double life, as I was either their father or that Sleiman guy from the videos on YouTube. I always answered them with: "No. It's me who's lucky because I have you."

People always talk about their experiences and memories in retrospect because you have to make mistakes before you can learn from them. I hope I have learned from mine. Perhaps my mistakes will serve for others to learn from them instead?

Despite how this chapter closes, this still isn't the end for me. There's something else I'm destined to succeed in and find happiness in.

I played the cards I was dealt in life as best as I could, but I always felt like I had one card less than everyone else. I was always one step behind. I always felt like I was missing something because even though I was successful, it never filled the hole I had inside of me. I never got to relax and enjoy it. Maybe I can't live in peace, so I'm constantly seeking out the storm on purpose?

I don't know if my children will love me or hate me or how they'll see me when they're old enough to read this. I hope that they don't judge me for the battles I went through or how I fought them, but rather for the good person I strived to be. I hope my kids will respect me for my struggles and that they can manage to see how hard I've fought, especially so they could have a better life than I, or at least a better beginning. My biggest wish is that my children don't inherit my negative social legacy and that history doesn't repeat itself after all.

I hope they'll make better decisions than I did and that my divorce from their mother doesn't create a hole in their soul like the one I had in mine. What I want more than anything is for them to love themselves. I have always sought recognition and love from others but never had love for myself. If I have to be completely honest, I think I'm the architect behind many of my own failures. Sometimes it seems like I sabotaged my own progress. Maybe I just need to forgive myself once in a while?

Ultimately, that's why I wanted to share my story in a book where I acknowledge my actions and take responsibility for them. It's important for me to share my story because when I was a young boy, no one took responsibility for me. My hope is that my story will help others in whatever way they need it. As this book was being finished, Palestinians have endured evictions and airstrikes in Palestine, Israel, and East Jerusalem that resulted in hundreds of Palestinians being killed, including children and thousands more being displaced that resulted in protests the world over.

I have spent so much of my life in survival mode, just hoping to carve out a space of my own to exist that I haven't been able to ever dedicate time to matters like politics. I never received much in the way of a proper education as it merely served as a pipeline to incarceration. I can relate to never feeling like I had a proper home or was ever given a real opportunity to become a citizen of Denmark since I served prison time as a young man. I've been profiled, harassed, surveilled, and treated like a second or third class citizen my entire life. While I can't confidently talk about the Isreali-Palestinian conflict, I do believe that Palestinians have the same right to live, exist, thrive and have a home as anyone else does. I want my children to have every advantage and opportunity I wasn't afforded.

Our stories are so scarce and our visibility on the world stage is so low that there's presently no other book like the one you're presently reading on the market. I hope this book can become successful and inspire book publishers to allow for a variety of Palestinian experiences to be told aside from the stereotypical ones that pervade mainstream media today.

So where am I today? I still live in the same city, on the same block. I love my kids, and I hope they love me. I'm still the same guy who came from the gutter but occasionally got to sit in first class.

SLEIMAN
December 2021

KINGSTON IMPERIAL

Marvis Johnson — Publisher
Joshua Wirth — Designer
Roby Marcondes — Marketing Manager

Contact:
Kingston Imperial
144 North 7th Street #255
Brooklyn, NY 11249
Email: Info@kingstonimperial.com
www.kingstonimperial.com